DEAD MAN'S FIRE

OTHER BOOKS BY THOM REESE

THE DEMON BAQASH
CHASING KELVIN
13 BODIES

DEAD MAN'S FIRE

THOM REESE

SPEAKING VOLUMES, LLC

NAPLES, FLORIDA

2011

DEAD MAN'S FIRE

ISBN 978-1-61232-024-3

Acknowledgments

As always, I'd like to thank my wonderful wife Kathy. She's my inspiration and my strength, as well as being my most constant critic and supporter. You are the reason that I live and breathe. Trista, Amy, and Brittany, you continue to brighten my life. My favorite times are when I can simply sit back and watch the three of you together. It's magic! As well, I'd like to thank Jeff Granstrom for his feedback on this manuscript and his constant encouragement in writing and in life. You're a true friend. Thank you to Gaylon Kent, Cynthia Echterling, and Randall Dunn for your feedback on this project, and to Kurt Mueller at Speaking Volumes for believing in me. I'd also like to thank the talented actors who helped to bring the Marc Huntington Adventures audio dramas to life: Jeff Granstrom, Tanja Montez, Ken Chapman, Phil Smith, Rick Ginn, TJ Hampton, Troy Nelson, Allistair Baylardo, and Shannon Macintyre.

Chapter 1

Port Elizabeth, South Africa

Boarding the yacht wasn't the problem. Boarding without detection, sneaking below deck, stealing the priceless Cobra of Cyrus, then fleeing undetected, that was the problem. Recovery specialist, Marc Huntington – Hunt, to those who knew him well – rose quietly out of the cool, dark water and ascended three steps up the dive ladder located at the aft of the seventy-six foot motor yacht named The Lady of the Cape. Dana, his wife and partner, would remain in their rented, much smaller, craft unless needed. I.e., unless Hunt was discovered. Hunt was hoping Dana could stay off of the yacht for this particular operation.

"Do be careful," she'd said in that irresistible British lilt of hers. "I don't fancy a ruckus. We do have dinner reservations at ten."

Hunt had chuckled. "No ruckus. I promise. Heaven help me if I ruin our dinner plans."

"It's at De Kelder!" laughed Dana with mock indignation. "The waiting list is a week at best."

"I'm a Midwest boy. You sure we can't just catch a burger?"

"Oh, you are horrible," she'd laughed, smacking him lightly on the rump as he'd prepared to enter the water.

"I do what I can," smiled Hunt.

"Love you," she'd said with a peck to his cheek.

"Love you too," he'd said before finding her lips with his own.

Baruti and Abri Lekota, the owners of this floating Shangri-La, were attending a dinner engagement on another yacht docked roughly a quarter of a mile distant in another birth at the Algoa Bay Yacht Club. They were not due back for at least two hours. Unfortunately, this did not mean that the craft was unattended. Based on his research, Hunt knew that two guards were to be stationed, one fore and one aft. He also knew that they were rarely at their appointed stations. Often the two simply lounged on the forward deck, playing poker, and scoping out bikinis on neighboring vessels. Fortunately, this was the case as Hunt peered onto the bare deck, illuminated now only by the sliver of a moon. Even so, Hunt needed to act with care. The guards, seemingly lackluster or not, were former military and heavily armed. Being spotted could have deadly consequences.

Though the Lekota's were quite wealthy, and the yacht well stocked with fineries, until now, it had not housed a rare artifact worth millions. Hunt had been surprised that they'd not increased security since taking hold of the piece. Surprised, but not disappointed. From what Hunt had read Baruti Lekota was a man whose ego was so large as to dismiss any thought that someone could possibly have the gall to come aboard and take his property.

Hunt was fine with taking the man down a notch or two.

Besides, the cobra wasn't even his property. It had been stolen some six weeks prior from Sir Edmond Graham Foliar of Cheshire England. The authorities had been unsuccessful in locating the relic, and so Sir Foliar had offered a generous reward. Hunt wanted the reward money, and had subsequently tracked the cobra to this yacht. Nice and neat, the way he liked it. Now all he needed to do was secure the prize and slip off the boat without being detected.

The plan was for Dana to motor over to the yacht and chat up the guards with nonsense about being a tourist on holiday in Port Elizabeth. Her rather colorful east London accent and bubbly personality would likely entertain them while Hunt slipped aboard and made off with the treasure undetected.

That was the theory at least.

Dana considered the plan simplistic and droll. This, thought Hunt, was how Dana saw most of his plans. But, simplicity, he had learned, was a considerable weapon. An overly complicated plan made improvisation difficult when everything went deep south. And, in truth, that was where most plans went. Anyone with field experience knew that a plan was merely a starting point; ingenuity, decisiveness, and quick action brought you home alive.

It was mid-evening, eight pm local time, and Hunt's body clock had still not clicked over from Pacific Time U.S. But the water was cool, the breeze refreshing, and he was counting on an adrenaline kick to see him through. Truly, it wasn't so much the jetlag that got him as it was the idiot medication he took to stave the ferocious migraine headaches that had plagued him since the explosion on that final day in Iraq.

Hunt's gut tightened as he heard the single outboard engine approaching from the east, and then the subtle swish of water against fiberglass as Dana cut the engine and coasted lazily toward The Lady of the Cape. It was show time and that meant nearly anything could happen. "Hallo! Do either of you gentlemen speak English?" he heard Dana say. They both did. Hunt and Dana had done their research. Though, IsiXhosa was the most common language, English was used in international trade, and most of the wealthy – and their hired help – knew the language fairly well.

"I speak English," shouted one of the guards. It was the guard on the starboard side, the heavier and, most likely, less agile of the two.

"I'm a bit befuddled," said Dana. "Just in from out of town and all that." Hunt smiled. She was playing up her cockney accent, drawing on her east London roots in an attempt to entertain the two. Her colorful vernacular was a treat, and it was one of the things Hunt loved about her, but, having attended Cambridge University on scholarship and then going through intense language and speech training with MI6, Dana could turn it on and off at will, often times distancing herself from her working class upbringing with precise and delicate verbiage. Queen's English, she called it.

This was not one of those times.

"Blimey!" she said with ludicrous verve. "Do you blokes 'ave a zoo in Port Elizabeth? I just love a good zoo. An' fish 'n chips! All this water, you'd think there'd be bleedin' fish 'n chips on every corner."

Liza Doolittle, eat your heart out.

Suppressing a chuckle, Hunt crept up the ladder and onto the deck.

"Bugger this! The wind's kicking up," chimed Dana. "Does the wind always knock you about so?"

Five quick steps across the gently rolling deck and Hunt made the descending stairwell. Having memorized the floor plan and casually interviewed several close friends of the couple, Hunt knew exactly where to go. Once below, there was a small foyer-like area, followed by a hatch leading to the engine room. Hunt marched through this and to yet another hatch leading into the lush cabin, which could also be accessed from the forward side via a winding staircase. The room was spacious enough as far as cabins went: wood paneled walls, lush red carpeting, a Monet hanging above the headboard of the bed. But, like all offshore accommodations, it felt tight and ill-fitted to the unaccustomed. There was a queen sized bed directly before him now, a sink and a three sided closet to his right. Hunt made his way to the closet, opened it, and then knelt before the gunmetal gray safe on the floor.

Quickly, he removed a small leather case from his watertight backpack and, laying it on the carpeted floor, withdrew an E500XT electric lock pick, two picking needles, three tension tools, and a hex wrench. He could hear the two guards laughing at Dana from above – probably ogling her as well; the daughter of a British father and Vietnamese mother, her stunning Euro-Asian features, clear blue-violet eyes, silky black hair, and athletic physique, made her quite appealing to behold.

As a former Delta Force operative, Hunt had been a master lock pick, able to breach nearly any lock in under a minute, but his frequent headaches brought about by the bomb blast now made it difficult for him to concentrate on something so detailed. In truth, with his considerable combat experience, Hunt would likely have been the better choice for taking out the guards should there be the need, leaving the lock picking in Dana's expert hands, but he'd been bullheaded about it and so here he was.

Taking a long cleansing breath, Hunt narrowed his gaze, attempting to maintain focus. He nearly had it. Just a little twist and…

No.

Even with electronic equipment, he had trouble with the task. This wouldn't have happened before Iraq.

Virtually nothing was the same as before Iraq.

Hunt angled his head so that his right ear – his only functioning ear – was toward the hatch. He could still hear the voices from above and forward, but had he just heard something aft, a subtle thump perhaps? He paused, listened, waited another moment longer. No. Nothing. Not at the moment at least.

Returning his attention to the safe, he adjusted the E500XT, and then paused. There it was again. Someone was approaching from the engine room.

It was then that the figure appeared in the hatchway.

"Oh, bloody hell," whispered the man, who, like Hunt, was wearing a dripping wetsuit. "This is just brilliant."

No obvious weapon, casual stance, an easy grin, Hunt's gut told him this man was not an immediate threat. Still, he rose to meet the man face-to-face, legs spread wide, slightly crouched at the waist, ready to spring. Gut instinct or no, he had to be prepared for the unexpected.

"Who are you?" asked Hunt, whispering as well. "You're not on Lekota's staff." Still he scanned the man for sign of a weapon, while keeping a close watch on the intruder's hands and eyes, the two most obvious tells of an impending attack.

The intruder chuckled. "Great. A yank. Well, genius, it appears that I – like you – am here for the Cobra of Cyrus. Dated 500 BCE, or so I'm told. Worth more than a shilling or two as well."

Though tensed, and prepared for action, Hunt had to smile. "Perfect," he said. "A thief."

The man shrugged. "I prefer to think of myself as a liberator of fine property." His sharp devilish eyebrows furrowed just then. It seemed he'd just had his first good look at Hunt. "My God, man. What happened to your face?"

Hunt shrugged. "Suicide bomber. Iraq. Things could have gone better that day."

"Bloody well right they could have," said the man, who, unlike Hunt, had not the slightest hint of disfigurement. He was perhaps thirty-five, lean, not as muscular as Hunt, but firm none-the-less. He had deep-set chocolate brown eyes positioned below two expressive black brows. His still-wet hair was jet black. Not a silver streak to be found. His mouth was broad, and seemed to seek occasion to offer a perpetual grin. "So, how are we going to handle this?" he asked, inclining his head toward the safe. "Mind if I have a crack. Seems the lock's giving you a bit of a hitch."

Hunt smiled. "Not a chance, buddy. I'm here first."

"Well, yes, of course you were. But, you see, this isn't grammar school. You can't call dibs."

It was then that both men heard running footsteps from above. "Great! You alerted the guards," hissed Hunt.

"Me? I could hear you clattering about in here all the way from Wilshire."

"Sounds like they split up. One coming from the fore, the other aft."

"I'll deal with the fore," smiled the intruder. "As it seems you're the bigger aft!"

Hunt groaned. The man's humor was worse than his own. He might find he liked this guy. Without another word, Hunt moved to beside the engine room hatch. Yes, there was definitely someone coming. The guard had slowed some, apparently now deciding that stealth would serve him well. Hiding just within a small alcove adjacent the spiral stairs, the Brit had flattened himself against the wood paneled bulkhead, tensed and ready to spring. Hunt made eye contact. Both men nodded, grinned, and then it began.

Hunt had drawn the heavier of the guards – the one he'd assumed to be rather out of shape and less the threat for it. A quick roundhouse kick to the gut, an uppercut to the jaw, and the man dropped his weapon, a 9 mm Heckler & Koch MP5, a rather nasty weapon for routine security, thought Hunt. But, before Hunt could land another blow, two massive fists hammered down on the back of his neck. The man was much faster – much stronger – than anticipated.

Hunt fell to his knees, and continued directly into a roll, not allowing his opponent to land another blow. The weapon was only perhaps four feet distant, lying on the carpeting at the foot of the bed. But before Hunt could wrap his fingers about it, the guard's booted right foot connected squarely just below his left ribcage.

Hunt tumbled to his right, arms instinctively cradling his belly as his face struck a bedpost.

Just then, the other guard careened into Hunt's opponent, apparently tossed by the British thief. Impressive. It seemed the man had skills.

Still cradling his side with his right arm, Hunt rose unsteadily to his feet, ducked a rather vicious blow from the smaller guard, and was grabbed from behind by the larger man.

Hunt slammed an elbow into the man's gut, twisted, pulled, and flipped the burly man over his right shoulder, sending him somersaulting onto the corner of the bed, where he bounced once and then tumbled sideways onto the floor with a prolonged grunt. Before he could lift his head or gain his bearings, the man was zapped with a Taser. Hunt glanced quickly around for the second guard only to find that he was already down, apparently tased as well.

Grinning, Hunt nodded at his wife – who still held the Taser – just as the thief said, "Dana?"

Dana's eyes went wide. "Jonathan?"

"Wait," said Hunt. "You know her?"

"Of course, I know her," said the other. "Do you?"

"Yes!"

"Who are you?" asked both men simultaneously.

"I'm her husband," answered both.

Hunt's gaze slid from Dana to the thief and back again. "I think I'm missing something here."

"I'm her husband," repeated the man. "Who the bleeding hell are you?"

One of the guards quivered, jerked, and shuddered at Hunt's feet. He ignored the man. "Dana?"

"Well, Jonathan's an ex-husband, really," she said with a bit of a huff.

"No, not exactly," said the man called Jonathan as he gently ran his fingertips across a rather large lump developing on his left temple.

"Fine points," shrugged Dana.

"Okay, wait a minute," said Hunt as he stepped squarely between the two. "This guy…"

"Jonathan," said the man. "Jonathan Thorpe. Pleased to meet you." Thorpe extended his hand, a gesture Hunt ignored.

"Okay, Thorpe here. You're married to him?"

"Not any longer."

"Again," said Thorpe. "That's not entirely…"

"We're done, Jonathan. Bloody well deal with it," snapped Dana. Thorpe held up his hands in a sign of surrender and backed up a step as Hunt faced Dana directly.

"So are you divorced or aren't you?" asked Hunt.

"I'm legally married to you," was her rather evasive response.

7

Hunt glared at her, a piercing pain developing in his gut. "And, yet you felt no compulsion to tell me that you'd been married before, that you may or may not be divorced?"

"It's complicated."

"That's the best you can do – complicated?"

"Blimey, Hunt, what do you expect me to say?"

"Well, the truth comes to mind."

The larger of the two guards groaned, shifted a bit, and made a feeble move toward his Heckler & Koch. Annoyed, Hunt gave him a swift kick to the gut and tossed the gun onto the bed.

"It happened while I was with MI6," said Dana. "There are security issues, classified events and whatnot."

"Security issues about your marriage? Dana, I've rolled with your cloak and dagger MI6 baggage until now, but do you really expect me to believe that you were forbidden to tell me about a previous marriage?"

"Hunt, can we please…" But, Dana never finished the sentence, for it was then that her eyes went wide. The argument had lasted less than a minute, but that was all the distraction Thorpe had needed to open the safe and retrieve the prize. Now he stood, the guard's Heckler & Koch in his right hand, and the magnificent Cobra of Cyrus cradled under his left arm, its stunning ruby eyes glinting in the subtle artificial light and its silver coils seemingly wrapped around Thorpe's forearm.

"Really, Jonathan? A gun? We both know you won't shoot," said Dana with a rather dramatic roll of the eyes.

"Oh, no. You, my dearest, I would never harm. But my replacement… Well, sorry chap. You seem like a good enough sort, but all's fair and all that rot. Nothing personal."

"Oh, it's personal," groused Hunt. "It doesn't get much more personal."

"Hmph," shrugged Thorpe with a cheeky grin. "Well, yes, I suppose you're right. But, as for now, I bid you adieu. And as for Frankenstein here, really, she is out of your league, man. You've got to know that."

With that, he slowly crossed to the spiral staircase, being careful to keep the gun trained on Hunt even as he backed up the rounded stairs and out of sight.

When Hunt finally made the deck, he was just in time to see Thorpe pulling away in a dual engine speedboat. With a broad grin and an affable wave, the thief shouted, "Call me, dearest. We've loads of catching up."

Hunt kicked a nearby torpedo buoy as he stared grimly at the retreating boat. Jonathan Thorpe had stolen the Cobra of Cyrus right from before his eyes. If only that had been the worst event of the day.

Chapter 2

Las Vegas, Nevada

Dana sat on the fourteenth floor balcony overlooking the famous Las Vegas Strip. It was just past sunrise, there were no glaring lights; the street venders were not yet hawking their time shares, night clubs, and escort girls; the traffic was still sparse, the scene subdued, and she was absentmindedly surfing the web on her Dell laptop as she waited for Hunt to return to their high rise condominium after his morning run. It had been three months since Port Elizabeth and still Hunt was on a tear about Jonathan Thorpe. He'd settled some, of course, and clearly he planned to stay with her, but he was still angered at the deception. These weeks had been a frenzy of fights and forgiveness, of accusations and love making. It seemed she couldn't get a handle on her husband. One minute everything would seem fine – better than fine, really: cuddling, joking about, gifts of dinner dates and flowers – and moments later he'd be glaring at her, seething from the inside, seemingly ready to exploded with building fury.

She supposed this was to be expected. Hunt was an emotional man with a deep sense of moral certainty and intense loyalty. Part of it was his military background, she supposed. He had that fighting man's code of honor and commitment. In a man like that, there was no room for falsities, for gray areas or graduated levels of truth.

Unlike Hunt, who'd passed his days in the black and white world of a soldier, Dana had spent six years in the British intelligence agency, MI6, where nothing was defined, where every grin or nod, where even a "good morning" or "cheers" could have underlying meaning. He'd known this about her from the beginning, accepted it even - at least on the surface. But, now it seemed he had finally come to realize just what all of this meant.

She loved him dearly and hated keeping secrets from Hunt, but he was a complicated man, damaged by the events in Iraq and his subsequent dismissal from the elite Delta Force and discharge from the Army. Though much improved, Hunt still suffered from fragmented memory loss, severe headaches, and bouts of depression.

None-the-less, Hunt deserved the truth.

But much of Dana's life – including her brief marriage to Jonathan Thorpe – was connected to her time with and departure from MI6. By necessity, much of that time must remain shrouded. Even now, four years since her departure, there were things left undone, situations that could reach out from across the past and snatch her back into the world she'd left behind.

But, Hunt understood all of that. As a Delta Force operative, he'd partici-pated in classified operations. He knew the drill. It was Jonathan Thorpe that ate at him. It was the fact that she'd been married and not found it in herself to break that one secret, to share with him that one, all important, truth.

The fact that Thorpe was handsome and charming didn't help the cause. Hunt had never been a jaw-dropper, but he'd once had a certain rugged good looks. The explosion had robbed him of that. Though, his multiple surgeries had gone a long way toward granting him a more traditional appearance, he was still quite self-conscious of his face, and covered as much of it as possible with a neatly-trimmed beard, blond with flecks of reddish brown. Half of his left ear was missing and the entire left side of his face had been reconstructed. In theory, he had three surgeries remaining. Rebuilding the ear was to be the next. Hunt had always felt that Dana was out of his league, and, in his mind, Jonathan Thorpe had simply confirmed this conclusion. It didn't help that Thorpe had now taken to sending Dana the occasional flowers and cards.

What Hunt didn't get – at least not completely – was that he was her soul mate. Was Jonathan Thorpe good looking? More like gorgeous! Was he witty, charming? Yes! Sexy? My God! Did he still make her tingle? If she were to be honest with herself, yes. Even now, she shivered at the memories. The man was smooth, clever, sophisticated. His milk chocolate eyes could melt her to the core.

But, Jonathan Thorpe had another side as well. More specifically, he was a thief. Oh, he wouldn't use so crude a word, but it was a fact still. But, even in this, he had a certain flare, a vague code of conduct which, he felt, separated him from the common rabble. In his eyes, all laws were created by fallible men, most of whom were intellectually inferior to him. As such, why should he acquiesce to their insufficient laws and regulations? The items he stole, the fine pieces of art, the collectables, the bobbles of the sickeningly rich, none were necessities of life, none would alter the owner's lifestyle. Each was insured – often to a higher value than the true worth. In what way was Thorpe harming anyone? In fact, due to his movements within elite circles, he'd often had occasion to aid the side of good with bits of overheard information or hijacked hard drives and codes.

And hadn't this been how Dana had become involved with him in the first place? He'd been hitting many of Europe's richest moguls, infiltrating their circles in the guise of a wealthy investor. He'd made contact with several parties on MI6's watch list. Potential arms dealers, British and European citizens thought to be supplying Middle Eastern terrorists. A computer guru, Dana was sent undercover as a wealthy socialite turned hacker. She pretended to be bored with her family's repulsively rich lifestyle and to have taken to computer crime as a diversion. Coming from a similar background to Dana's legend, Thorpe had latched onto her – due as much to her exotic beauty as to her computer skills – and drawn her into what had, until then, been a one man operation. Through Thorpe's contacts, Dana was able to gain access to several otherwise unattainable computers, hacking in and installing monitoring software that gave the intelligence agency direct access to these hard drives.

The seduction had never been ordered, merely implied. But in a world of moral ambiguity, Dana had understood that likely this sacrifice would be expected of her. Grudgingly, at first, she'd allowed herself to fall sway to Thorpe's charms. This was for MI6, this was for England herself. What Dana hadn't counted on was that she might fall in love with the bloke.

Stranger still, it seemed that Thorpe saw Dana – who he knew by her alias, Martha Booth – as much more than a dalliance, and soon fell in love as well, sweeping her away to Morocco one weekend for a surprise proposal and subsequent – even more unforeseen – wedding, all before Dana could wrap her mind about the implications of it all.

Thorpe had been a mistake from the beginning. Dana knew this at her core, but her heart – that treacherous beast – had stepped squarely in the way. At first,

MI6 had tried to utilize this new complication to their best advantage. But soon they discovered – through Dana's own admission – that she could no longer be trusted to put the interests of her country above those of her husband. MI6 brought her in from the field, put her behind a desk, and tried to deny her access to Thorpe. But that was not so easy a thing. Though, by now disillusioned, Dana had still loved the man, and hoped to redirect him to a more honorable life.

Over the next several months, Dana would learn that this was an impossible task.

Shlickt!

What was that? A sound from behind?

Slipping quickly from her contemplation, Dana listened as the door opened. She heard footsteps marching across the living room and then heard the patio door slide open behind her. "I found a box of chocolates for you at the door," said Hunt by way of introduction. "I gave them to the porter. Told him to give them to his girlfriend. But, don't worry. I've got a spare Snickers bar if you're in the mood for something chocolaty." He offered a smile – forced, but a smile still – and gave her a peck atop her head.

Dana gazed up at her husband, her mind now fully in the present. "Jonathan's a scoundrel, Hunt. Don't let him get to you."

But, if he's such a scoundrel, why had she just spent the last several minutes mooning over his memory?

"Kind of pathetic, really," said Hunt with a lopsided grin. "Snappy looking guy like that panting at your heels and here you're married to Boris Karloff."

"Stop it!" giggled Dana as she gave him a quick squeeze. "You know you're the only one for me." She paused, cocked her head, and winked. "And yes, you can be a bit of a monster – just the way I like it."

Hunt bent to kiss her long and meaningful before straightening. He held a bottled water and two tiny white pills, which he then popped.

"That's the second time you've taken your meds in the past three hours," said Dana. "You don't want another incident like you had in Calcutta last week."

"I'm fine," he said. "Just my old buddy, the head-splitting migraine. We've got to get together once every couple of days. You know that."

He wasn't fine and they both knew it. She also knew it was next to useless to argue with him. "They're becoming more frequent. You really should consult Dr. Forrester."

Hunt leaned on the metal railing and stared across the street to the New York New York Casino's faux Statue of Liberty and colorful mock skyline. "I've had enough doctors to keep me for another decade," he said, now directing his gaze toward the cartoonish medieval-themed Excalibur, with its gaudy red and blue spires and inoperable drawbridge.

"I know that, Hunt. But this last surgery should have alleviated the majority of the pain."

"Well, I'll have to have a talk with my migraine about that." Hunt pulled the white terrycloth towel from around his neck and wiped sweat from his face. It was February, the temperature only a mild fifty-nine degrees, but he'd worked up a good sweat on his seven mile run up the strip and back. Stepping to behind Dana, he began massaging her shoulders with his strong muscular fingers. "So, gorgeous, you find anything on that missing Byzantine dagger yet?" Obviously, the subject of his health was closed.

"I just spoke with Greta Bachmeier at the Hall of Antiquities in Munich. Seems it may have changed hands again. And my black market contact heard that two diamonds are now missing from the hilt. I'm about ready to give up on the bugger. Mostly a nuisance, really."

Hunt grunted dismissively. "With diamonds missing, I doubt the finder's fee will hold. Anything else interesting out there? The Cobra of Cyrus comes to mind."

"I'll check if you make a doctor's appointment."

Hunt kissed her head again. "Really, hon. I need a break from the docs. Let's find something fun to keep my mind off the pain. The bedroom maybe?"

Dana giggled. "Hmmm. That holds promise. But, business first – otherwise, we'll never get anything done."

Hunt shrugged and grinned. "You don't know what you're missing."

"Oh, but I do. And that's why we'd better stay focused."

"Fine, fine," he mock grumbled. "About the snake?"

"No, the silver snake has yet to resurface, but I've found a thing or two." Dana tapped on her keyboard and brought up a photograph of a sleek silver and black car. "There's a stolen 1924 Rolls Royce Sliver Ghost in Haiti."

Hunt shrugged, not appearing overly interested. "Can't be many '24 Silver Ghosts tooling about Haiti. That has got to stand out. Wonder what kind of mileage it gets."

Dana bumped over to another website. "Here's another I was looking at. Milton Harding, the oil tycoon, has a twenty-two year-old daughter who's disappeared. Reading between the lines, it looks like she might have run off with a merchant seaman from Brooklyn. Harding's offering a million dollars for her safe return."

"The mil sounds like my kind of finder's fee," said Hunt. "But, the girl's not a minor. We can't forcibly bring her back to her father."

"Not legally," smiled Dana with an exaggerated wink.

"Keep that on the back burner," said Hunt. "I'd prefer to operate on the legal side of things. You know, avoid being arrested for kidnapping and all that nonsense. It can really dampen a day."

"Oh, you are a stick in the mud."

"To the core. I think that was one of your wedding vows, 'love, honor, and cherish the kill-joy.'"

"I've got one other," she said through a grin, her fingers once again dancing over the keyboard. "Paleontologist missing in South America," she said, reading directly from the report. "After contacting Chicago's Field Museum with a claim that he'd made a major discovery, Dr. Andrew Lindell was apparently kidnapped from his motel room in the village of Kutu, Brazil."

Hunt was suddenly agitated, leaning forward in order to read over Dana's shoulder. "Did you say Andrew Lindell?"

"Yes. Why? Do you know him?" Hunt looked nearly distraught, his eyes narrow, his jaw clenched.

Hunt stood straight, gazing absently out over the tourist wonderland. "That's Lucky's boy," he said. "Colonel Lucky Lindell. He was my commander when I first signed on with Delta Force. Eventually, he was promoted out of the unit and given a position at the Pentagon."

"I haven't heard you mention him. Do you still maintain contact?"

Hunt stiffened visibly, his face mask-like. "No. We lost track after…" Hunt trailed off, apparently unable or unwilling to complete the thought.

"After you were booted from Delta?" offered Dana.

Hunt nodded. "Yeah. That. The last time I saw Andy – the boy – he'd just gone off to college. Maybe nineteen years old at the time."

"Just so you know," said Dana. "There's no reward offered for his return. I'd thought of inquiring, but…"

"This one'll be a freebie, Dana." With that, Hunt turned and walked through the sliding glass door and into the luxury condominium.

Chapter 3

Hunt placed his purple Duncan yo-yo on the coffee table and stared at the cool black cell phone in his hand. He wanted to make the call. Needed to make the call. He knew he would make it. And yet he hesitated still. So many memories. So much baggage. So much that was still unknown. Hunt had been found at fault, true. But details from testimony were sketchy and the bomb had robbed him of many of the memories leading up to the event. He had fragments, yes. But only that. Nothing coherent. Nothing that made sense.

*****

The room is in chaos.

There is a burst of gunfire.

Racing forms.

Screaming children.

A roof collapsing.

Sanchez falling, blood spurting from between his fingers as he frantically tries to put pressure on his own jugular.

Jaffrey going down, a gaping hole where his intestines had been a moment before.

Shouts.

Accusations.

Confusion.

*****

Hunt squinted. The headache was nearly blinding. Colorful spots pulsated before his eyes. There had been testimonies against him, claims that he'd been drunk at the time of the operation, that he'd led his unit into a combat situation without direct orders from command and with incomplete intelligence, that he'd fired on a civilian – a child, a little girl only nine years-old.

Most of this made little sense. Incomplete intelligence, yes. No direct orders, quite possible. As NCO – non-commissioned officer – he had the authority to make the call. One couldn't always wait for ideal circumstances. But, drunk? Doubtful, and yet…

Possible.

Yes, Hunt could pound them back with the best of them. But, he'd learned his limitations during his college days. There'd been an incident. He'd been drunk. Things had gone poorly, but in the service, mostly nothing excessive. Like most fighting men, he needed that release, that opportunity to flush the brain of the bloodshed and loss. But Hunt hadn't been an alcoholic. At least, he'd never seen himself that way. And as to racing into a combat situation while inebriated…

Shooting a child!

He'd never do that. Couldn't see himself doing that.

And yet, apparently he had.

The reports were unclear, the testimonies vague. And yet, two men had died that night. Two of his men! Two men who he loved like brothers, whose lives were his responsibility. Two men who might still be alive today if Hunt had made better judgments during that critical hour.

Lucky Lindell hadn't been there that day. He'd already moved on to his stateside assignment. But, he'd known of the events, he'd followed the inquiry. He knew what Hunt had done.

And now Hunt planned to call and offer the man help in locating his missing son. Was he stupid or just plain dumb?

Hunt turned down his stereo. He'd been listening to Kiss – his favorite band since high school – the song, Black Diamond, had always lifted his mood. Retrieving his yo-yo, he marched over to the large picture window and gazed out over the glittering Las Vegas Strip. Even this early, tourists were marching the sidewalks. Homeless men sat on the elevated walkway between the MGM Grand and the New York New York selling bottled water to tourists. Cheerful couples posed for photographs in front of the brilliantly designed buildings. Cabs slipped from one lane to another, rushing gamblers to the next great table where they were sure to hit it big. Life. Everyday life in this tourist utopia.

Hunt's condo sat just a block back from the strip proper and was connected via enclosed walkway to the MGM. From his vantage, fourteen stories up, he could see it all: the brilliant lights at night, the fireworks on New Year's Eve, the bustle and excitement.

How senseless it all seemed just then.

How empty.

Hunt closed his eyes, took a long slow breath. He was going to make the call. Other than plain cowardly weakness, there was no reason to avoid it. Lucky was a friend. Andy was his boy. That was the bottom line. They could worry about emotional baggage and past crimes another time. Again, Hunt set the yo-yo on the coffee table. This time he dialed the phone.

It took nearly fifteen minutes before Hunt was finally connected to Lindell, and when he was, he nearly panicked and hung up like a teenage nerd calling the prom queen for a date.

"Colonel James Lindell," came the stern and uncharacteristically cautious voice.

"It's me, Colonel. Marc Huntington."

A pause, and then, "Hunt, it's been awhile."

Hunt turned and began pacing the room. He really wasn't sure exactly what it was he hoped to say. "Yeah, sorry about that. It didn't seem right to continue our friendship after what happened."

"After you were released from Delta and then discharged from the Army, you mean."

Typical Lucky. Straight to the point. "Yeah, that."

There was a pause, perhaps ten seconds or better. Hunt almost thought Lindell had hung up. And who could blame him? It had been Lindell who had promoted Hunt to sergeant major. It had been Lindell who had recommended that Hunt lead the team. It had been Lindell who had put Hunt in a position where he could endanger the lives of his men. Why would the man want to talk to Hunt? What could possibly be left to say?

"I'm only going to ask you this once," said Lindell. "What really happened that night?"

*****

A little girl: big brown eyes. Long hair. Trembling. Terrified.
Behind her, a man, an automatic weapon in his hand.
Flames.
Screams
Blackness.
Confusion.
Voices from behind...

*****

Hunt shook his head. "The truest answer I can give you, Lucky, is I don't know. I've got fragmented memories. And even those don't seem consistent from one day to the next. There was an explosion. C-4, I'm told. Must have rattled my brain. I'm sorry, colonel, I just don't have a concise answer for you."

Again, there was a pause on the line, and then a prolonged intake of breath. What Lindell said next nearly caused Hunt's knees to buckle. "I could have helped if you'd let me," he said in a quite, somber tone. "You killed a civilian, true. But, it was a combat situation. The testimonies against you were bad but not rock solid. There was no court-martial. Maybe there could have been a different outcome."

Hunt's eyes moistened. The colonel was on his side. He still believed in him. "Luck, you know, I didn't give much of an explanation there. Not sure how comfortable you could be defending me."

"I consider myself a good judge of character, sergeant. This thing's never quite added up. I stand by my decision to grant you that command. Now, why didn't you come to me sooner?"

Now, a tear escaped Hunt's eye and raced down his reconstructed cheek. Damn it, he was a fighting man. There was no place for tears. "I didn't want to involve you and risk your career over my mistakes," he said at last.

This time there was no pause. "True friends take risks for true friends, Hunt. You know that."

"Yeah. I guess I do."

"You still drinking?"

Ouch! Another arrow to the heart. "Aside from one horrible evening about three months ago, not a drop in six years."

"Let me guess. That woman you married, she's keeping you in line?"

Hunt allowed a brief chuckle. "Keeping me in line, yeah. Also the inspiration behind my one night binge."

"And your injuries? Have you recovered?"

Hunt's left hand rose almost unconsciously to his face. "Reconstructive surgery over the left side of my face. I lost most of my left ear." Hunt waited a beat, and then said, "I heard about Andy. Any word?"

"No. None." Lindell's voice went tight, emotionless, and yet, not entirely so.

"What's being done?" asked Hunt.

"The State Department's involved, but it's sticky. Andy's a U.S. citizen, but he was in Brazil on an expedition co-sponsored by a British university and a U.S. museum. There were American, British, French, Scottish, and German academics involved. You have us, the Brits, and the Brazilian government all trying to take lead on the thing, with the others clamoring in the background for their fair due. And while they're all squabbling over territory, not a damn thing's being done to find my boy."

"I want to help find Andy," said Hunt. This was why he had called. This was the heart of the matter. He hoped Lucky wouldn't shoot him down and lock him out of this thing.

There was a slight hesitation, not long, but noticeable. "You know you don't need to do that, Hunt."

"Colonel, do you know what I do for a living?"

And here, Lindell's tone changed to nearly bitter. "Yes. You use the military training and experience you gained under my command to recover stolen items and then charge the rightful owners substantial sums for their return."

Hunt squeezed the phone, nearly cracking the casing. How could Lindell get condescending at a time like this? "I don't charge anyone anything, Luck. I collect finder's fees, rewards that have already been offered before I ever get involved. I take risks, incur costs. There's nothing wrong with a guy making a living."

"A very good living, it seems. How much did that high rise condo on the Vegas strip set you back?"

Interesting. Lindell had obviously kept tabs on him through the years.

"I'm doing fine for myself – yes. It's called capitalism. It's one of the liberties you and I fought to preserve." Hunt paused, allowing a moment before switching gears. "Listen, Lucky. I find things: paintings, artifacts, even yachts. But, I also find missing people. This is what I do. I can find Andy. I can bring him back."

When Lindell next spoke it was with hopeful skepticism. "If multiple governments can't find him, how can you?"

Good. He'd come back around. Lindell had gotten his little dig out of his craw and was back in the game. "You said it yourself. They're bogged down in red tape. All the while, the trail is getting cold, and with every day that goes by, the chances of finding Andy alive get slimmer. I'm no longer a part of the U.S. military. I'm not restricted by their policies or diplomatic concerns."

Another long pause. A sigh.

"Lucky, I can bring him back. Just give me a chance."

Yet another pause, but Hunt sensed in this one that he'd broken through.

"I don't know who has him, Hunt. But, here's something that hasn't been released to the press: one of Andy's colleagues, a Dr. Daniel Cook, was found murdered the day before Andy disappeared. They're keeping this very tight. It seems the circumstances were rather unusual. This could be dangerous."

"True friends take risks for true friends, Lucky."

Lindell actually chuckled at this. "Touché," he said. "But, Hunt. I'm not in a position to pay the kind of money you're accustomed to receiving for your finder's fee."

"Okay, now that's just plain insulting. You can buy me a drink afterward – okay? And even then we'll be far short of even."

"I thought you'd quit…"

"A soft drink, Lucky. You can buy me a soft drink. Now, tell me everything you know about Andy's expedition. Who else was on it? What were they looking for? What did they find? Were there any rival groups – perhaps a bunch of thugs from Harvard – trying to muscle in on their territory? Had there been any indication that something might be amiss?"

Chapter 4

The Amazon Rainforest, Brazil

Hunt wiped the sweat from his brow with a red and white bandana and inhaled the thick moist air. Drank it, was more likely. The air in the rainforest was heavy, rife with oxygen, and nearly as humid as the Atlantic – the ocean itself, not the air above. Certainly the oxygen-rich environment contributed, but it was more than that which energized Hunt. He'd spent his life, a military man. He wasn't a scholar – well, he'd attended Indiana University for three semesters before enlisting, and had since learned several languages – but he wasn't one who studied the minutia. He couldn't name the dozens of different fauna visible from any one spot. He couldn't identify the various species of brightly colored birds that flitted about just below the leafy canopy some two hundred feet above. He couldn't classify the numerous reptiles or distinguish one primate call from another. To Hunt, it was all an amazing cacophony of life. There was such vibrancy, such an abundance of living things as to overwhelm. There were trees that could stand side-by-side in equal majesty to the towering buildings of New York or Chicago. There were fan-like leaves as wide as Hunt's entire arm span. Reptiles skittered about. Chattering monkeys leapt from branch to branch, peering down at the oddly pale couple motoring up the muddy road in their unfamiliar vehicle. Everything seemed to breathe, to move, to live. Hunt swore he had actually seen a plant grow before his eyes.

And despite the fact that the temperature above the treetops hovered somewhere over 100 degrees, only a meager ten percent of the sunlight penetrated the canopy, granting the forest's inhabitants a much kinder eighty degrees or so – seventy-nine, if he was to believe the merchant that had sold them their supplies. The man had claimed the rainforest maintained a consistent seventy-nine degrees Fahrenheit year round. Interesting.

Hunt and Dana were in a rented 1987 Jeep Wrangler moving slowly up the access road leading to the expedition site where Andrew Lindell had worked. The word "road" was a bit generous and often Hunt found that he was following something little more than an overgrown path. According to the GPS, they were less than two miles from the site. Judging by their slow progress and indirect route, Hunt surmised that it could still take them the better part of an hour to traverse the distance – this assuming the Jeep did not overheat for a third time. He wondered what drove the scientist to such a remote location, what it was they so desperately sought. The setting was amazing, of course, but access was difficult to say the least. Hunt couldn't imagine how the scientists could move anything large out of the place if such was the need. But, at least there was a road, he supposed. Without one they'd be on foot. There really was no way to move a vehicle through the thick vegetation. It would be futile and foolish.

"Well, I must hand it to you," said Dana as she swatted a red and yellow insect that had settled on her left thigh. "Two days ago when we were dining at the Jasmine in the Bellagio, I didn't think I'd end my weekend swatting at dragonflies in the Amazon."

Hunt laughed and pulled his iPod earphone from his right ear so he could talk, and pausing Kiss's unplugged version of A World Without Heroes mid-song. "I try to keep things interesting," he said, studying her exquisite face nearly as much as he did the road before them. Despite her complaints, Dana's blue-violet eyes seemed to dance with excitement and wonder. It seemed maybe this diversion was what they'd both needed. Too bad they were here on such urgent business. They might have turned this into a couples retreat.

Hunt slowed, maneuvering around a fallen tree, the diameter of which neared fifteen feet. Fortunately, it had only partially obscured the road. "Did you get things worked out with the Rescue Mission?" he asked.

Dana nodded. "Janice Marr is covering for me. I'll pick up one of her days when we get back. They're used to my ludicrous schedule."

"Well, you are a volunteer. It's not like they can fire you."

Dana scrunched her mouth into a Picasso twist. "No. But, it's worthwhile work. It needs to be done."

Hunt nodded. Dana had a good heart.

"I don't understand why we're not starting our investigation at the motel where Dr. Lindell was abducted," said Dana as she eyed a spider monkey lazily swinging above. "We passed right through the place on the way here."

Hunt shrugged. "And we'll pass through again on the way out. The local law enforcement – however minimal it is – has probably trampled all over that place by now. Any evidence will have been tainted or removed." Hunt paused while he slowly maneuvered the Jeep over a series of intertwined vines. The clutch was a bear, and the gearshift loose, but he managed to seduce the quarter of a century old vehicle into reluctant compliance. "I am hoping that the village government is at least minimally computerized," he continued. "Once we get there, you might be able to hack into the system and take a look at their findings."

"You must just love having a former MI6 computer geek as a wife."

Hunt smiled. "Whatever you are, you are not a geek. But, yeah, you come in handy from time to time."

Dana laughed and slapped him playfully on the arm. "You beast! Any other reason we're in this godforsaken jungle – other than your irrational desire to be eaten alive by every insect known to man?"

"Well, there's always revenge. You know, getting back at you for the Jonathan Thorpe fiasco."

"Hunt!" Again, she slapped his arm, this time with a bit of venom.

"Kidding. I'm kidding." He patted her left thigh. "Love you, dear."

"Oh, give it a rest."

Hunt nodded and withdrew his hand, returning it to the steering wheel. The terrain was becoming more difficult by the minute, the road less obvious. "As I see it," he said. "The crime took place in Kutu. But, whatever led to the crime happened at the expedition site. We need to talk to the people there if we want to learn the details concerning Andy's disappearance and the murder of his colleague."

The road took a sharp right turn and then angled upward, the grade nearing forty-five degrees. Hunt downshifted with difficulty and then proceeded slowly up the muddy way, hoping the temperamental transmission would hold. He wished they could have found a better vehicle, but the airport had been remote, and his options minimal. As it was, he'd had to leave a ridiculous deposit on this jalopy. The way was largely overgrown, and the couple was forced to crouch in order to avoid low hanging branches and vines. Hunt noted a spider monkey leaping from tree to tree, apparently following the jeep. Curious little fellow.

"Do you think Andrew was involved in the murder?" asked Dana as they made the top of the rise. "He did, after all, disappear right after the bloke was killed."

Hunt shrugged and then shifted gears, winding around another bend and then proceeding on a downward slope, the Jeep offering a loud *clank, clank, clank* in a not-so-subtle protest to the strain. He eyed the temperature gage, but there was little he could do to prevent its rising. "We don't have details yet. Too early to speculate, but Andy was never an aggressive kid. More of the bookish type. Murder seems a pretty big stretch."

"So, you think Andrew fled the expedition to escape the murderer?"

"That's my working theory, yeah. Andy may have feared that he was to be the next target."

"Supposedly, he'd made a significant find. That item could be the target."

"Exactly," nodded Hunt as he navigated around a partially decomposed tree trunk. The temperature gage was definitely on the rise again, but still, Hunt hoped he could nurse another mile and a half out of the beast. They'd already used three quarters of their water supply on the jeep and hoped to resupply at the excavation site.

"It'd be nice if we knew something about the artifact Andrew discovered," said Dana as she eyed the monkey, still tracking them from above.

"Agreed. That's one of the first things I hope to learn from Andy's colleagues."

Dana slapped a large pest from her arm and said, "I do wish you'd listened to reason and hired a guide, though."

"We don't know what we're dealing with yet. Not too sure I want to involve locals. Besides, we've got a military-grade map and a GPS."

Another rise and the jeep offered yet another objection, this time a clattering sound from beneath the hood. "Sounds like you might have dropped a lifter," offered Dana.

"Yeah," agreed Hunt. "I'm not too confident that this Jeep'll get us back out of here when the time comes."

"Hmmm," said Dana. "You see that? The monkey that's been following us. It just took off like a bullet from an Uzi."

It was then that the first shot was fired.

"Blimey!"

"What was that?"

"A gunshot, Marc. You may have heard some during your military career."

Another shot. There were chaotic sounds all about as the jungle's many nonhuman inhabitants scurried and screeched in response to the sharp reports.

"Yeah, yeah. I remember now," said Hunt as he turned the wheel sharply to the right. "Always hated it when they were aimed in my direction."

Another shot, this one striking the trunk of an adjacent tree about six feet above their heads.

Hunt jerked the wheel again, left, then right, surging around the bullet-pocked tree and aiming for a small clearing perhaps one hundred yards from the little road. It was then that the Jeep began to slip sideways. Inadvertently, Hunt had skirted along the edge of a steep and muddy ravine. In an effort to recover, he jammed the stick into first and turned the wheel a sharp left.

Another gunshot.

The wheels spun but gained no traction. Mud spewed from behind all four tires. The jeep shifted another two feet right, the left two wheels bobbling on the insubstantial ground.

"Hunt! She's going to tip!"

"Yeah. Picked up on that. So much foliage, I didn't even see the drop-off."

Hunt tried to finesse the pedal, hoping to gain the much needed traction, but the Jeep stuttered another four feet sideways.

"Dana, quick. She's gonna roll. Climb over me. Jump out my side!"

"What about our supplies?"

"Now, Dana! Or you'll be smashed when she tips"

Dana complied, quickly snatching her backpack from the rear seat, and scrambling over Hunt, knocking his arm, and causing him to shift the wheel slightly right. The Jeep rocked. Hunt pulled hard left.

"Hurry!" shouted Hunt. "She's going over any sec." Dana made the door and nearly tumbled over it and onto the leafy earth.

Another slide. Another surge from the engine.

Still maintaining control with his right hand and foot, Hunt opened the door and leapt just as the whining vehicle shifted one last time and then began its tumble down the chasm.

He hit the ground hard, and then, before he could gain a handhold, tumbled after the plummeting Jeep.

Chapter 5

Dana had only just managed to climb over the ridge when she heard the final whine of the Jeep. Turning, she saw Hunt make his desperate lunge. At first, it seemed that he might have landed just high enough up the grade to have attained nearly level ground. But, the slope was muddy and littered with loose stones, wood, and foliage. Hunt's steel blue eyes went wide as he grasped desperately for a hold but found only air.

Just as Dana made to make a frantic reach for Hunt's clasping fingers, another shot passed over her head. It wasn't even close, but still the distraction caused her to miss that final opportunity. She watched helplessly as he tumbled end over end down the heavily wooded slope to be swallowed by the dense foliage.

"Hunt!" she screamed. "Hunt! Are you injured? Hunt!"

No answer. Dana moved to find a passable way down, but another shot rang out. Damn the bugger! He wasn't going to allow her a rescue attempt. Hurriedly making note of Hunt's last known position, Dana crouched, and shuffled to behind a sprawling kapok tree. She needed to get to Hunt as quickly as possible. Who knew what injuries he might have sustained in the tumble, but necessity dictated that she deal first with the gunman.

Noting the bullet hole in the bark some three meters above her head, Dana deduced that the shots had come from the southeast. Judging by the angle, the shooter was somewhat elevated, perhaps twenty degrees compared to Dana. It was just past ten AM, and the sun peeked through the leafy canopy in golden streams of light. Almost tangible, the beams tended nearly to obscure as much as to illuminate. Dana inched forward, shading her eyes with her right hand, scanning a rise perhaps fifty meters distant. Something bothered her about the gunman – despite, the obvious fact that he'd been shooting at them – something just wasn't right. The caliber of the gun, for one thing. It was small caliber, puny even. Nothing a professional would use. But, it was more than that. Something else yanked at her brain.

Staying low, Dana inched out from behind the kapok, seeking a different vantage. There was a copse of low brush-like trees perhaps twenty paces to her right. She'd make for that, perhaps secure a better view.

Another shot.

Another miss.

Dana nearly dove to within the copse. That was it. That was what had been bothering her. The gunman kept missing. Not that this was a complaint, but these weren't near misses. These weren't shots a degree or two to the right or left. These shots, all of them, were far over her head. The assailant did not intend to kill, but merely to scare them away, or at the very least, delay them from reaching the excavation site.

Why?

What was this man's connection to the dig, and why was it so important that she and Hunt be kept away?

Dana considered brazenly walking out into the open to search for Hunt, but feared that the man might panic at her wanton behavior and retaliate with a well aimed shot. Just because killing was not the initial plan, didn't mean it wasn't an option.

Cautiously, she lifted her head, once again gazing to the southeast. With each moment she became more confident that she could get close to the gunman, maybe even overtake him. But, she simply did not have the time. Hunt could be bleeding to death, or have a severe concussion or broken limbs.

No. Her best option was to draw the gunman out, just a bit. Get a good look at him, maybe click off a photo on her cell phone, and then make haste in assisting Hunt. With luck, the assailant would remain at a distance and not interfere with her rescue attempt.

Moving deeper to within the heavy foliage, Dana crouched low, swinging further to her right. Three separate times, she took a stick in hand and tossed it back in the direction from which she'd come. The hope being that the assailant would wrongly assume that the swish of movement and sound was Dana, still lodged where he'd seen her last.

Three more steps, a scoot behind a deep green fan-like leaf. What was that she'd just touched?

Blimey! A snake.

Green and black, perhaps two meters in length and seven centimeters in diameter. The thing slithered away, more frightened of Dana than she was of it. She was not the type to scare easily. It wasn't of a poisonous variety, nor large enough to be a danger by way of constriction. Still, she wasn't entirely displeased as the thing disappeared within the grassy ground.

Peeking over the leafy cover, she squinted, trying to make out a form, or, at least movement, from where she assumed the assailant to be hiding. She had a pretty good idea as to where he must be. She'd heard the shots, seen the bullet-pocket trees. It wasn't hard to deduce the firing point.

Nothing.

Despite her skill, she'd lost the guy. Maybe he was more talented than she'd thought. Perhaps he'd played her for a dupe, feigning inexperience in order to draw her out.

Still crouching, she moved further to her right, bending low to avoid disturbing the foliage. There was plenty of cover. As long as she moved slowly and quietly, she would likely not be detected.

"I would like for you to remain perfectly still," came a male voice from behind. "I am, after all, training a gun on the back of your head."

*****

The monkey chattered incessantly. Hopping up and down on Hunt's back and slapping at his head with its tiny palms. How long it had been there, Hunt had no idea, but that it was annoying was a certainty. "Alright, alright. I'm awake," groused Hunt as he blinked, attempting to bring his eyes back into focus. Tenderly touching the back of his head, he felt a good sized lump. No blood though. That was a plus. The monkey leapt aside as Hunt rolled onto his back, being careful not to tumble down the subtly sloping ground. It seemed he'd come to rest on a slightly angled ledge of perhaps ten feet in depth before dropping sharply into leafy oblivion.

The monkey paced and stomped as Hunt readjusted. It was a cute little thing: black face, gray and white body, long flexible tail. Hunt thought it might be the one that had tracked them while they were in the Jeep. But, they all looked the same to him.

Cautiously, Hunt drew in and then extended each limb, assessing his injuries, noting each ache or pain, and cataloging the damage. Nothing serious, he determined. Plenty of cuts and scrapes; most likely some rather pronounced bruising. Nothing broken. Fair enough. He'd survived the ordeal. Adjusting into a sitting position, Hunt stared down the ravine, attempting to gain a view of the Jeep. The vehicle was obviously a loss – as were the supplies he'd carried in his backpack. But, the foliage was too dense, offering no hint to the Jeep's whereabouts. It could be resting an easy twenty feet below, or perhaps a couple thousand. Hunt really couldn't tell. This place was deceptive. There was simply too much greenery, too much sprawling life, to get a feel for the topography.

Okay. Hunt's supplies were gone. But the more pressing concern was Dana. Someone had shot at them. Had she been hit or perhaps captured? Was she alright? Reaching into his right front pant pocket, he withdrew his cell phone and pressed the green button. Nothing. No bars. No coverage. There was a recently installed cell tower in the village of Kutu, he knew, but apparently he'd tumbled to where the signal was obscured. He had no means to communicate. In his backpack, he'd had two field grade walky-talkies and his satellite phone, but those were of no use now. Why had it been his basic cell he'd carried on his person? Stupid, amateurish mistake. He simply hadn't thought there'd be a need. He could cry out for Dana, he supposed, holler her name, but that would likely alert the gunman. Better to make his way back up the grade and assess the situation than to draw undo attention.

Hunt glanced to his right. The monkey was gone. Strange little critter.

With a painful groan worthy an octogenarian, Hunt rose to his feet, and gazed up at the slope before him. He hoped he could make the climb before Dana had any serious trouble with the shooter.

*****

"Do not turn around," commanded the heavily-accented voice. "Keep your hands where I can see them."

Dana was unarmed and so remained still. She and Hunt were here in no official capacity and private citizens were not allowed to carry arms into the country. They'd had no opportunity to acquire local weaponry before entering the jungle. And in truth, they had hoped there would be no need. They were here to locate a missing person, not to do battle.

"I said, put your hands where I can see them," repeated the man, this time with a bit of a nervous edge to his voice. This was a dangerous one, surmised Dana as she complied with the command. He was obviously nervous, by the quiver in his tone, near panicked. Most likely he was involved in something he hadn't anticipated, something that threatened him. A man like this was prone to rash, illogical actions. She would need to be cautious.

"Who are you?" asked Dana. "Are you with the paleontological expedition?"

"I believe I'm the one who should be asking you to identify yourself," came the terse response. Judging by the vocal characteristics, he was standing back a ways, probably ten meters or better, definitely too far for Dana to disarm before he could click off a shot.

"We've come looking for Andrew Lindell," offered Dana, not so much to give information, but in order to gauge the man's response.

There was a pause, then the sound of the man shifting from one foot to another. She'd struck a nerve. He knew Andrew. Or, at the very least, knew of him. "I know no one by that name," lied the man.

"Well," quipped Dana. "The bloke's gone missing."

"I wouldn't know anything about that."

"We mean no harm. I'm unarmed. May I please turn around so that we can talk like civilized human beings?"

A pause. A shuffle. "No! Stay as you are."

Dana was at an impasse. Positioned as she was, there was no way to confidently disarm the man. And he was so nervous that she feared he might pull the trigger out of sheer panic. "Listen," she said after a moment. "I'd like to talk with you about the expedition. Can you tell me something about it? Perhaps what it is you hoped to find?"

"Quiet!"

Dana nodded, now not even willing to vocalize her assent for fear he'd blast off a shot. The man's voice had cracked. The least provocation and she'd learn what it felt like to acquire a bullet between the shoulder blades.

"Who are you?" he screamed. "Why are you here?" There was the sound of two angry steps forward. The man was losing control.

"My name's Dana," she answered in calm, even tone. "As I said, I'm looking for Andrew Lindell."

"Liar!" screamed the man. "You want the skull. It's all about the skull!"

Skull? That was curious.

"I'm sorry," she said. "I don't know about any skull. Care to enlighten me?"

"Stop lying to me!" screeched the man, his voice tight, nearly inhuman.

This was getting serious. Dana could almost sense his finger tightening on the trigger as he wrestled with whatever terror had placed that gun in his hand.

It was then that she heard a shout from her left.

"Hey! You! Buffalo breath! Over here!"

Hunt!

He was alive. Apparently uninjured. Or at least enough so to have hauled himself out of that ravine.

The gunman whirled shooting wildly toward the disembodied voice.

Seizing the opportunity, Dana dove to her right – away from Hunt's voice – landing behind a strangely contorted tree and scattering several sleek black lizards.

The gunman reacted to Dana's movement with two wild shots that went wide to her left.

"Missed me!" hollered Hunt, still from the same direction, but obviously closer than he'd been. "Marco!" he added, and then, "Oh, come on. You're supposed to say, 'Polo.'" A brief pause, and then, "Marco!" Hunt was playing the fool, attempting to unsettle the gunman, to disrupt his train of thought.

The gunman shuffled in place, and then, with a muttered curse, retreated into the brush. Dana considered taking chase. But she wasn't entirely sure how many shots he had left before reloading. She just hoped he didn't find his nerve, and come creeping back.

Dana waited nearly a minute, listening as the gunman fled into the distance, climbed into a vehicle, and sped off, apparently rejoining the road she and Hunt had just traveled. At this point, she shouted, "Hunt! The bloke's gone! I'm over here!"

"Yeah, yeah. Saw that," he said, his voice much closer now. The man was stealthy, she'd give him that. "You get a look at him?"

"No. The bugger snuck up behind me."

Hunt emerged from between several hanging vines. His military-cut blond hair was muddied, his bearded face bruised and scraped, and it seemed he might be moving with a slight limp. "Tsk, tsk, dear. Did MI6 give you any operational training at all?" Despite his disheveled appearance, he smiled that goofy grin of his.

Dana rolled her eyes. "And bleedin' Delta Force. Did they actually allow you to operate a motor vehicle? Drove right off the cliff, you did."

"Glad to see you too, dear."

"Likewise, oaf. You alright?"

A shrug. "Might need some TLC. Any takers?"

"TLC? For the man who dragged me into this Godforsaken jungle? I think not."

Grinning, Hunt put his arm around her and gave her a peck on the top of the head as they began walking toward the tiny dirt road. "I'm glad you're okay," he said, giving her a warm squeeze. He then went on to tell her of the Jeep's fate. They took a verbal inventory of what few supplies they had in her backpack. The terrain was not unbearable, and they determined that they could make the base camp in just over an hour. There they'd be able to ask for a lift back to the village of Kutu or, better still, to some larger bit of civilization where they could rent another vehicle and restock supplies. This, of course, after they'd spent some time interviewing the scientists on just what had happened to Andrew Lindell.

*****

About thirty minutes into their trek, Hunt stared forward with a peculiar expression and said, "Looks like we've got trouble."

At first Dana didn't realize what Hunt was saying and so thought he was referring to their assailant. "The gunman? No. He fled in a vehicle. The bloke was much too frightened to cause us any more trouble."

"Nah. Not him," said Hunt. "That."

And Dana gazed to where Hunt was pointing.

"Smoke."

"Yep," nodded Hunt. "Wanna take a guess where that's coming from?"

"Seems the general direction of the dig site."

"Right the first time."

Chapter 6

The Swiss Alps

The lodge was luxurious. Situated in the western Alps near the Swiss-Italian border and slightly shy of the summit of Monte Rosa, it rested at an elevation of some 14,000 feet or better. Hidden within a great evergreen wall off a gated road, the place was a winter utopia tucked away from all but the most trusted. Thorpe had been here once before when he'd delivered the valuable Cobra of Cyrus, and, like now, the place put him on edge. By all accounts, it should have had quite the opposite effect. The regal trees, standing majestic and ageless, the pristine snow, the doe and her babe grazing beside the large artificial lake. Everything about the place was serene, designed to relax, to invite.

That was, of course, except for the numerous guards, the electrified fence, and the retina scanners at the gatehouse. Each belied the retreat's true nature. Or, at the least, the true nature of the man within – i.e., the client.

Thorpe did not know the man's name. He'd heard rumors, done investigations, pulled in some favors, but what he'd received had been a conflicting hodgepodge of guesses, assumptions, and contradictory intelligence. In truth, Thorpe had the feeling that each tidbit had originated with the client himself, that the man had toyed with him, giving him the quite clear message that he was far superior to Thorpe in every significant way.

Well, that was bollocks.

Thorpe may not – yet – be a billionaire, but his skills were extraordinary, his intelligence exceptional, and his connections impressive by even the most scrupulous standards. Just the fact that this particular man desired his services attested to these facts.

But, the client paid quite well. And as Thorpe's particular expertise typically landed him beyond the small-minded laws of the small-minded governments, he had come to understand that he would be dealing with the likes of this man. Someone who also operated beyond the scope of established regulations.

Someone who would take exceptional precautions, who would desire secrecy and unquestioning loyalty.

Well, whatever.

The man paid well. He obviously had the means to play his little subterfuge games or whatever it was he did up here. Thorpe had his own agenda and it involved securing the greatest fee for each service rendered, but not so much so as to discourage a client from utilizing Thorpe's particular gifts on future projects.

This was the delicate balance. Appear too greedy and the man might go elsewhere. But provide a good reliable service, free of complications, at a substantial, yet not excessive price, and longstanding relationships could be established. It seemed he might just be on the verge of initiating just such a relationship with this man.

Thorpe was led into a broad chamber-like room. The angled ceiling with its dark rustic beams was perhaps thirty feet above his head. A roaring stone fireplace took up much of the western wall and radiated a musky heat even midway across the substantial space. The stucco walls were lined with large tapestries depicting weird scenes of battling beasts and strange multi-winged creatures torturing human subjects, of great and bloody battles between tall red-haired warriors and smaller, seemingly frail foes. The mahogany floor was peppered with broad, plush throw rugs, depicting similar scenes of carnage and destruction. One wall featured giant glass terrariums populated with various – mostly poisonous – reptiles. Crude statutes and vulgar idols were peppered throughout the space. Thorpe did his best to ignore the surroundings. His role was not to judge the man's bizarre and twisted tastes, but to help him to obtain the rare and elusive objects of his desire.

The client sat on a long U-shaped sofa looking out through a great picture window over his snow-covered property. A small reddish brown snake rested on his shoulder as he held a flute of buttermilk in his hand, sipping it only occasionally as he chatted with another man seated opposite him. Peculiar drink. Always buttermilk. Thorpe had never known another who drank the stuff. The client was tall, perhaps six foot four or better, lean, athletic. He had a pronounced brow which shaded his intense eyes, one blue, the other green. His skin was pale, yet healthy, his lips thin and humorless, the mouth a wide cut below an aquiline nose. His light red hair was trimmed slightly longer than a business cut, but not so much so as to draw attention. He wore a vanilla pullover sweater, sleek black slacks, and Prada loafers. He did not rise as Thorpe approached, but merely nodded toward the man opposite him on the couch. "Thorpe, Join us. May I introduce Mr. Graham."

Graham? The man's face seemed familiar. But, the name Graham didn't seem right. Where had he seen him? On television perhaps, on a news report? Well, it was nothing, supposed Thorpe. He probably just had a similar appearance to someone else. "Hello, Graham," said Thorpe. "A pleasure."

"Thorpe," nodded Graham.

"Have... Have a seat, Thorpe," said the client, not offering a drink, but merely indicating a space between he and Graham. His accent was American, east coast, perhaps Virginia or Maine. The stutter intrigued Thorpe. This man was supremely confident, proud, nearly tyrannical, so why the stutter? It wasn't pronounced, nor was it consistent. And yet it was present nearly always.

"Thank you, sir," said Thorpe as he lowered himself onto the plush leather sofa.

"You were, I suppose, sa... satisfied with our arrangement concerning your previous work?"

"Ah! The silver cobra? Yes, sir. Quite."

"Your compensation was adequate, I'm told."

"Well, yes. It was exactly as agreed upon." Why the devil was he bringing this up? Was there some problem with the artifact? It sat no more than eight meters to his left and looked to be in fine condition.

"I understand there was a mishap aboard the yacht, that you nearly bl... blundered the mission."

At this, Graham allowed a tight, poorly disguised grin.

"A mishap? No. In fact, quite the contrary," offered Thorpe. "Upon arrival, I discovered another party in the process of stealing the cobra. Despite this obstacle, I secured the piece and delivered it as promised."

"Yet, you were recognized," added Graham.

Ah! Now he understood. "That I was," agreed Thorpe. "Though, there was no means for the other party to connect me to you."

"You left them alive," said the client after a sip from his flute.

Alive? Of course he left them alive. He was a thief – an exceptional one – not some garden variety thug.

Thorpe smiled, leaning forward, forearms resting on his knees in a conversational manner. "With all due respect, my assignment was to obtain the cobra of Cyrus, and to deliver it in such a way as that there would be no connection to you or any of your staff. All of this was accomplished."

"W… Were you hesitant to use lethal force due to the presence of your ex-wife?"

Hmm, the man did have his connections. How he knew that bit, Thorpe had no idea. "I refrained from using lethal force," he said with a direct gaze. "Because I do not use lethal force. That is not a service which I offer."

Graham addressed the client. "As I told you. This one has his limitations." Ah, so Graham – or whoever he really was – knew a thing or two about Thorpe as well.

The client shrugged and enjoyed another sip. "Perhaps," he said. "Though, I find he has a certain skill." The man paused, gazing over the snowy expanse before them. After a moment, he asked, "Should I desire your services, do you have interest in further projects?"

"Most assuredly," said Thorpe. Rather stupid question, that.

"There's a certain piece. Very important to me. It… It's currently located in South America."

South America? Fascinating. "I could be interested," said Thorpe with a casual shrug. Already, his mind raced. Thus far, his dealings had been confined to Europe with only a smattering in the U.S. As such, he had no established connections on the South American continent. He could contact Miles Percy, he supposed. The man had a villa in Rio. Surely, he had a few ins about the place. And Thorpe had a thing or two on Percy. Yes. That would be a starting point, he was sure of it.

"Unlike your previous work for me," continued the client as he stroked the snake, "this project will not entail discrete inquiries at dinner parties, or hushed meetings in parliamentary chambers, but rather the ability t… to steal a much sought after item from one already in hiding."

Curious. "May I ask the nature of this item?" asked Thorpe.

The client smiled a thin mirthless smile. "Of course you may not," he said. "Not until I'm confident that we are to do further business."

"It might be worth noting," added Graham. "That this item is currently believed to be in the Amazon."

"The Amazon? The jungle, you mean? The rainforest?"

Graham nodded with oozing condescension.

Thorpe was intrigued. He worked primarily in a cultured environment, moving among the rich, learning of their holdings, acquiring that which was desired by another. Traipsing about the jungle, chasing down an object that was already sought, and assumedly on the move, may not be the best use of his particular attributes. "Curious," said Thorpe with a practiced grin. "Tell me more."

The client leveled his gaze at Thorpe. His queer eyes were bright, intelligent, and unrelenting. The snake had now slid down onto his lap where it then flicked its narrow tongue into the man's flute. "Simply put, I believe y… you might be more highly motivated than others where this particular venture is concerned."

"Well, that is interesting," said Thorpe. "What exactly is this extraordinary motivation?"

And here, the client smiled. "Dana Huntington," he said.

"Dana?"

"Yes," nodded the client. "Sh… She's in the Amazon with her current husband. They're purpose has nothing to do with the item in question, or so they think. But, I'm certain that if you were to fi… find them, they would eventually lead you to that which I desire." The man paused, lifted his glass as if to toast Thorpe, and said, "Interested?"

Of course Thorpe was interested.

Chapter 7

The Amazon Rainforest, Brazil

The smoke rose in great billows, seemingly becoming trapped beneath the vast green canopy of trees. Marc and Dana Huntington were still a ways off, but already they could taste the blackened air as it stung the backs of their throats. The wildlife was naturally agitated as well. Brightly colored birds fled the scene, vegetation shifted and shook as a result of frightened beasts, hoots and howls could be heard from all about as the forest's denizens rushed this way and that in panic. It seemed all of nature knew something was amiss.

On the plus side, the fire appeared to be fairly well contained, and even now, diminishing in intensity. There were no visible flames, only smoke, and even this was less dense than fifteen minutes prior. Still, the location did appear to be the excavation site and considering that the place was the location of a recent murder, it was unlikely that the blaze was an accident.

"I've been thinking of the gunman," said Dana as she skirted around a large tortoise-shaped stone and continued hiking toward the site of the disturbance. "He was far too nervous to be a professional. I didn't see his face, but he had a rather thick brogue. Several universities from the UK co-sponsored the project. He must have been from the expedition."

"Agreed," said Hunt. "The big question then becomes, why try to keep us away?"

Dana cocked her head. "I would think that obvious."

"Alright. I'll bite. Why?"

"Because he didn't want us to see whatever it was that he didn't want us to see."

"Ah!" laughed Hunt. "Now I'm so much more enlightened." Hunt stopped in his tracks, held up his right hand, signaling Dana to stop as well. "You hear that?" he asked in a near whisper.

Dana shook her head. "No. What?"

"A vehicle. Coming from behind." Signaling for Dana to follow, Hunt moved into a thickly-leafed grove aside the tiny dirt road. "Sounds pretty close," said Hunt. "And on that pitiful excuse for a road, he's not moving very fast. We should be able to get a good look at him."

Hunt watched as Dana shrugged off her backpack and retrieved a pair of field binoculars from within. Scooting to beside a rather mossy tree, she took position, gazing toward the coming vehicle through the powerful lenses.

It was less than a minute before the vehicle came into view. Hunt saw that it wasn't a Jeep, but a Hummer, bulky, forest green, and built like a tank. He wondered how much fuel the guy had to carry simply to keep the beast running. The things were guzzlers. And despite their off-road credentials, Hunt found these suburbanized versions highly impractical in the field. The man would have done much better with an actual Humvee – the military vehicle that inspired the domesticated Hummer.

"Looks like one occupant only," said Dana. "Black male aged somewhere between fifty-five and sixty. No visible weapon, but there could be something on the floorboard, or even the seat. I've no vantage for that."

"Judging by that soccer-mobile he's driving, I'm gonna guess he's a scholar, not a fighter. Let's find out."

Not giving Dana a chance to protest, Hunt stepped out into the path-like road just as the Hummer made the top of the rise. The vehicle had been progressing at no more than ten miles per hour, yet still, the man slammed his breaks, causing the beast to skid to a halt. Dana strolled up to beside Hunt as the man climbed from the vehicle. He wasn't excessively tall, perhaps five-eleven, but still managed a gangly appearance. His tan button-down shirt was sweat stained and half untucked. His dark chocolate face was long and lined, leathery in texture. The guy had spent a good deal of time out of doors. Most likely at dig sites, surmised Hunt.

"Hallo," said the man, as he stepped onto the dirt road and strode to the front of the Hummer to face Hunt and Dana. "Is there a problem of some sort?"

"Ah," smiled Dana. "I'm thinking he's from the expedition."

Hunt shrugged. "Agreed."

"British accent. Northern parts, most likely. Oxford is involved with the dig."

"Accent's a dead giveaway. A little more upper-brow than yours."

"Oh, you're charming."

"But, not as sweet as yours, dear."

"Who are you people?" asked the man, a bemused expression on his ageing features. As intended, the banter had apparently caused him to drop his guard.

"Oh, yeah," said Hunt, extending his hand. "I'm Marc Huntington. Friends call me Hunt."

"And I'm Dana Bell-Huntington," added Dana with a bit of a bow.

"My wife. Isn't she sweet? This guy isn't the shooter, is he, Dana?"

"No. Wrong accent. Besides, the gunman drove off in the opposite direction."

"That's what I thought." Hunt paused, grinning at the man. "In that case, can we hitch a ride?"

"I'm sorry," said the man, with an incredulous twist of the lips. "Names aside, who are you, and why are you here?"

"Yep. I do like his accent," said Hunt with a playful grin. "You really should spend some time with his type. You know, brush up on your hoity-toity."

"The man asked you a question," said Dana in mock exasperation.

"Yeah, yeah. What was that again?"

"Why we're here."

"Ah! Right. We're here to rescue Dr. Andrew Lindell. You didn't take him, did you?"

The wordplay worked. Hunt had switched gears so quickly that it took the man a moment to catch what he'd just been asked. His eyes widened, his jaw loosened just a notch, not a drop, but a bit of a gape.

"No," said the man after a moment. "I didn't take him. Andrew is my friend." Hunt saw neither anger nor obvious signs of deception in the man's response. If anything, there was indignation at the thought that he could be involved. None of this was conclusive, but, Hunt's gut feeling was that the man was being forthright. Of course, his gut had betrayed him in regard to Dana's secret past. Perhaps it wasn't quite so reliable as he'd once thought.

"Maybe you are his friend," said Hunt. "But, friends sometimes do some pretty lousy things. Take Dana for example. Until recently, I didn't know that…"

"Hunt! Stay on track."

"I'm just saying…"

"Sir," interjected Dana, with a fierce scowl in Hunt's direction. "Who are you; and what are you doing away from the dig?"

The man glanced from Dana to Hunt and then back again as if wondering what he'd just gotten into. Already, Hunt regretted broaching the subject of Dana's past, even in a joking manner. It just wasn't right of him. Idiot!

"I'm Dr. Gregory Milton, from Oxford," said the man. "I suppose that now, with Dr. Lindell missing and Dr. Cook deceased, I'm the default leader of the expedition."

"I know Andy Lindell," said Hunt. "I served with his father, who, by the way, is very concerned for his missing son. We're here to find him."

"Dr. Milton," said Dana. "Can you tell us of the circumstances surrounding Dr. Lindell's disappearance?"

It seemed the man took a moment to size them up, gazing from one to another, most likely assessing the legitimacy of their story. Finally, he nodded with a sigh. "I suppose it started about six months ago. A village lad found some bones. There had been a flood, much of the ground cover washed away. The boy saw a jaguar carrying a human femur."

"Human, you say?" asked Dana.

A Nod. "Yes. Fossilized."

"I'm guessing that caused quite a stir in the geek community," said Hunt.

A wry chuckle. "Absolutely. One thing led to another and our little band of *geeks* was assembled and given authority to excavate the area."

"And this Dr. Cook led the expedition?" asked Dana.

"Yes. Though, Andrew Lindell was his prodigy. They'd been working together since Andrew was an undergraduate student."

Interesting, thought Hunt. The two had a longstanding relationship. Now, one was missing, the other dead. "So, you guys start digging and find what?" he asked.

"Over time, we uncovered several bones, both human and animal, but no full skeletons. In a sense it was discouraging. We were hoping to find something of true significance."

"And what made you think this site had the potential for a major find?" asked Dana.

"The age of the bones," answered Milton, an obvious excitement creeping into his tone. Clearly this stuff jolted his juices. "They were quite early human specimens, brought to the surface through a long series of upheavals and erosion."

"I understand that Andy announced a major find," said Hunt. "What was it?"

Here, Milton's eyes came alive, his voice energized with sudden verve. "A skull. A complete human skull. In tact. Undamaged. Quite ancient, but, amazingly, contemporary in nature." Here he paused, perhaps contemplating whether or not to continue.

"And...?" prompted Hunt.

Milton nodded and sighed. "There were strange markings on the interior. Writings of some sort. Very unusual."

"Wait, wait, wait. Writings on the interior of the skull. Why would there be writing on the interior? How would someone even do that?"

"That, my boy, is a mystery yet unsolved."

At this point, Dana broke in. "Speaking of mysteries. I fear we've allowed you to delay us from a rather pressing matter. There's a fire to the west. We fear it might originate at your dig site, Doctor."

Not surprisingly, Milton's eyes went wide, his jaw dropped. "My, God," he said. "No."

Chapter 8

The blaze was primarily contained to within the camp. A broad river wrapped around the eastern and southern borders of the site, while the sheer rocky base of jagged cliffs occupied the northern boundary. Only to the west was there the opportunity for spread, and yet, this had not occurred. By the time the trio arrived, the blaze had all but burned itself out.

But the devastation to the camp was complete. Horrible. Ghastly.

"I don't get it," said Hunt as he pulled Dana aside to speak privately. "The burn pattern doesn't make sense."

"Tell me what you're thinking," said Dana as she kicked about some of the scattered debris looking for clues as to the origin of the blaze.

"To begin with, no survivors. According to Milton, there were twelve people at the camp. We've got twelve bodies."

*****

Fragmented memories from Iraq
An explosion.
Close quarters – indoors.
Screams.
Charred remains.

*****

"Someone should have survived," said Hunt after a prolonged pause. "Someone." Taking a deep breath to help steady his treacherous emotions, he took a couple of steps from Dana and pointed at the perimeter. "Look at this. Water. That river's what, ten, fifteen feet across? Probably no more than six feet deep at the center? You wanna tell me why no one thought to jump in the water when the whole place went up in flames?"

"They didn't have the time."

"Exactly. But, why?"

"The fire moved too quickly."

"It would have had to be awfully fast, Dana. This was broad daylight. They weren't caught in their cots. The total devastation hints at something catastrophic. Normally, I'd say an explosion, except…"

"There's no evidence to support the conclusion. No detonation point. No shrapnel. The damage all points to heat, but no blast."

"Right. I've been over this site three times now. I find nothing indicating explosives or incendiary devices."

"Flamethrower?"

"Nah. No spray patterns. And I find it hard to believe that no one would escape if it was just some nut-job with a flamethrower. He couldn't be at all points simultaneously."

"This all speaks to an accelerant, but we've found no residue."

"Not yet. But, we don't have proper testing equipment." Hunt paused, gazing across the camp. "But, yeah, I'm with you. I think an accelerant was used. Something that would burn very hot, very quickly, and then burn out before the blaze could spread beyond the camp. I'm betting that if we had a means of testing the soil that's exactly what we'd find."

"And here sits Milton," said Dana. "Uninjured."

Hunt glanced to the man. He sat on a large stone at the foot of the jutting cliff, his head buried in his hands, his body convulsing with sobs. The man had barely spoken since discovering the carnage. "I'm not willing to go on record that he's innocent," said Hunt, still gazing at Milton. "But, for now I'm buying his grief. He seemed genuinely shocked by it all and his Hummer was filled with supplies from Kutu."

"Which supports his story."

"Right. Makes sense that he could have been on a supply run when this happened. No evidence to the contrary."

"We can't rule him out," said Dana, her voice firm, but not without compassion.

"No. Not yet. But, if I was to guess, I'd say he didn't start this fire. Call it my gut."

Dana knelt, staring at a body, a peculiar twist to her lips.

"What are you thinking?" asked Hunt.

"I'm not sure. Something's dodgy. But I can't quite put a finger on it."

Hunt nodded and then stepped away to survey the wreckage. "Well, let me know if it comes to you." The place was littered with blackened blobs of matter, the remains of equipment and chairs and footlockers and of all the day-to-day items connected to a rainforest expedition. And of course there were bodies, ghastly ruined bodies, young and old, male and female, though, in many cases, none could dare guess which was which. They were scattered about the ground, some curled into fetal positions, others with outstretched arms as if pleading for salvation. Two lay embraced, as if each was attempting to comfort the other even through intense personal agony.

The smell of burnt flesh assailed Hunt's nostrils, and so he breathed through his mouth, but still the stench permeated the air. It would get worse, he knew. It always got worse. He was an ex-military man. He'd seen bodies – more than his share – he was accustomed to scenes of carnage and devastation. But, even when he steeled his heart, when he wore the stern mask of a Delta Force operative, he'd never been able to completely detach himself from the human tragedy of it all. Some might call him weak for this, perhaps claiming that it could cause him to be ineffective. In truth, he'd sometimes thought these same thoughts. But, at his core, he knew that this shock, this horror at the madness of senseless violence was what kept him whole – or at least an approximation of whole. He would not allow himself to consider these deeds inevitable or somehow acceptable. Maybe this made him a lesser man from a military standpoint. But in the end, it was the only way he could face his reflection each morning.

And now this.

This was not connected to any grand political move. This wasn't sanctioned by nations. This wasn't done out of any high-minded principle. Hunt had no idea as to the motivation behind this, but he was certain that these deaths were both deliberate and unnecessary.

Vicious, calculated tragedy, plain and simple.

One human being extinguishing the lives of others of his own kind.

No. Not of his kind.

True human beings don't do this.

There was plenty of ugliness in the world, but the vast majority of people could never fall to such sickness, such evil. At least Hunt liked to think that they wouldn't, that we all don't harbor such blatant cruelty, such inhumanity. The ability to kill? Yes. In self defense or even adrenaline-fueled anger, yes, but not this coldhearted, calculated, indiscriminate execution of fellow persons. This took a special kind of monster.

The waste. The terrible waste.

Lowering his head, Hunt turned so that neither Dana nor Milton could see his face. With clenched jaw, he wiped the subtle moisture from his eyes and stared coldly ahead. Every fiber in him screamed to flee this place, to escape the memories it aroused. He didn't need this. He was out of the force. He was supposed to be free of this insanity.

But, Andy was missing.

Andy was somehow caught up in this.

Hunt still remembered him as a young teen, awkward and nervous as he left for a date, excited about a scholarship, distraught at the death of the family dog. Hunt was only perhaps ten years older than Andy, but the kid had always called him Uncle Marc. Though Hunt's primary relationship had been with Andy's father, Hunt had many strong memories of the son. There was no way that Hunt could leave him to whoever had committed this horrid act.

"Hunt, are you alright?"

It was Dana, approaching from behind. Hunt swallowed, blinked, attempted to appear unmoved. He would need to deal with these emotions – both new and lingering – but not now. Not while Andy was still missing.

"We need to talk with Milton," he said through a constricted throat. "We need to find out what he knows."

With that, Hunt turned, and marched toward the weeping man. He heard Dana sigh and follow close behind. She knew him well enough. She could read his state of mind.

"Milton, we need to talk," said Hunt as he stepped to before the man.

Milton looked up, his deep brown eyes moist and red. "They're all dead," was what he said.

Something got through to Hunt. He'd been ready to interrogate the man – forcefully interrogate him – anything to find Andy, anything to vent the anger he felt within. But as their eyes met, Hunt read the pain within, understood some of what the man was feeling. Milton knew these people, lived with them, laughed, argued, perhaps even loved some of them. What was Hunt's anger compared to this man's personal agony? "Listen, um, Dr. Milton."

"It's Gregory." His voice was soft, listless.

"Gregory, listen, I know my timing sucks. But, we're going to need your help. Andy Lindell's missing and I promised his father I'd bring him back alive. Right now, you're my only lead."

Dana stepped forward, and then knelt to face Milton at eye level as she placed one sympathetic hand on his shoulder. "Hunt's right, Dr. Milton. It's important that we know what happened the night Dr. Cook was killed. We need to know every detail leading to Andrew's disappearance."

Milton stared at her and then up at Hunt, and then returned his gaze to Dana. He nodded. "Give me a moment to compose," he said.

"Certainly," nodded Dana. She was much better at this than was Hunt. The female touch, he assumed. Or maybe the human touch. Maybe Hunt had lost more of his soul back in Iraq than he'd thought. Maybe his soul was already shattered, only shrapnel remaining. Maybe he was as broken down as his father's old seventy-nine Pinto.

"Alright," said Milton with some effort. "Let me see if I can make some sense of this."

"Go on," said Hunt.

Milton closed his eyes and then nodded almost imperceptibly. "We'd been here just over five months," he began. "There had been a number of minor finds, but nothing of true significance. It was toward the end of the day, what was that? Last Tuesday? Yes. Tuesday. It was at the end of the day when Andrew rushed through the camp toward Daniel Cook's tent. I'd tried to dissuade the lad. Daniel had been on the telephone, and it seemed our primary backer had threatened to rescind our funding."

"Was there some issue?" asked Dana. "Some reason for the backer's reticence?"

Milton nearly snorted. "Backers are not scientists. They expect immediate results and stay with a project only so long as something more exciting doesn't appear on the horizon. Our dig, it seemed, had lost its shine."

"But, then Andy found something," offered Hunt.

"Yes, yes. He'd found the skull. It didn't seem consistent with the bulk of our discoveries, but Andrew was convinced it would date within the same range as the rest. Cook saw it differently. He felt the find would date much later. The two argued over fossilization, color, texture, erosion. Andrew charged that Cook had allowed his personal bias to cloud his judgment. He was convinced that he'd found something that could very well rewrite the entirety of natural human history."

"Okay. They fought," said Hunt. "Are we talking about screaming, shouting, fists? What level of confrontation?"

"Nothing so dramatic," said Milton. "All theoretical."

"Okay, so, geek mumbo-jumbo. Anything else?" Hunt saw Dana roll her eyes at this. Undoubtedly, she thought him tactless. She was probably right.

"Well," said Milton. "Daniel denied Andrew's assumptions as to the date of the skull, but he did find it a rather curious specimen."

"The writing on the interior," said Dana. "That seems quite strange."

Milton nodded. "Well, it's unheard of, really. I wish I'd had the opportunity to examine it."

"Dr. Milton," said Dana. "Why was Dr. Cook so adamant that this was not a legitimate find?"

"It was the date Andrew assigned to it that irked Daniel. About two-point-five million BCE. This was a contemporary human skull, Mrs. Huntington."

"What do you mean by contemporary?" asked Hunt.

"Not Cro-Magnon, not Homohabilis, not Australopithecus."

Dana nodded. "And, at this site, what had Dr. Cook expected to find?"

"Well, he hoped to find Australopithecus. Another Lucy. Certainly not a modern human skull that would muck up all of our evolutionary assumptions."

"But, Andrew believed that the skull dated back to about two-point-five million BCE, like the other fossils found at this site?"

"Exactly."

Interesting, thought Hunt, but nothing that should have led to murder or kidnapping. "I need something else, Greg. Think. Was there anything else said? Anything that sticks out as unusual?"

Milton seemed to hesitate for a moment. There was something. Hunt could sense it in the sudden tightness to the man's jaw, in the eyes no longer making direct contact.

"Come on, Greg. Give me something to work with. I can tell you've got something rattling around your head."

"The Amazon skull."

"Okay. I'm lost."

A sigh. "According to Andrew, Daniel believed this might have been the Amazon skull."

"Okay," said Hunt. "We're in the Amazon. I'd think any skull found here would be an Amazon skull."

Milton shook his head and then raked his fingers across his salt and pepper hair. "No, no. He spoke of a specific skull. Nothing scientific. It's just a bit of local lore about an ancient skull endued with the great mystic power to awaken the dead. A bunch of rot, really. I don't know why Daniel mentioned it at all. In fact, he tried to retract it, to deny any knowledge of the lore. I sincerely hope none of that nonsense gets out. Reputations could be ruined."

Hunt was more concerned with Andy's life than with a deceased scientist's reputation. But he held his tongue for the moment. No need to alienate the man now that he was giving them something.

"Tell me about Dr. Cook's murder and Andrew's disappearance," said Dana.

With this, Milton rose. He seemed agitated, possibly unsure as to what to share and what to withhold.

"Greg, people are dead. People you knew and worked with."

"Do you think I don't know this?" shot Milton. And then, after a brief pause. "I'm sorry, Mr. Huntington. I understand the need. I'm simply overwhelmed. These people were like family to me. I have no wish for their memories to be soiled."

Hunt stepped closer to the man, made direct eye contact. "Listen, Greg, I understand your concern, but we're not here to destroy any reputations. My only goal is to find Andy Lindell and get him home safely. The rest of this is all peripheral. Now, help me find Andy."

Milton nodded, while beginning to pace. He kept his gaze to the ground, avoiding the ghastly sights surrounding them. "Andrew was upset. He stormed about the camp for most of the evening, afraid that Daniel would dismiss the find and never have the skull carbon dated."

"Did Andrew tell anyone else of the find?" asked Dana.

"Everyone. He spent the evening complaining about Daniel's cavalier response. A very inappropriate attitude, really. Such things are best dealt with between colleagues and not made public."

"And how did Cook respond to this?" asked Hunt.

"Furious, of course. He called Andrew to his tent. They argued. Finally, Andrew stormed out, claiming that he was leaving the expedition."

"And then?"

Milton hesitated, working his jaw.

"Come on, Greg. Out with it."

"Daniel was found dead the next morning. His entire body burned terribly."

"Let me get this straight," said Hunt. "The tent was intact, not burned? The damage to the man himself was the only sign of fire."

Milton nodded. "Yes. That would be correct."

"And Andrew? How did he respond to this event?" asked Dana.

"Utterly panicked. In fear for his own life. He packed and left within the hour."

"And the skull?"

"It seems likely he made off with it. No one realized this at the time, of course. We were all focused on the murder."

"And no one considered that maybe the skull was the motive of the murder?" asked Hunt.

"Or that, perhaps, Andrew could have been involved?" added Dana.

Milton shook his head and threw up his arms in frustration. "We're scientists! We're not accustomed to thinking in terms of motive and murder."

Dana stepped forward, addressing Milton face-to-face. "Dr. Milton, the authorities, I assume, considered Andrew a suspect, especially once the skull was discovered missing."

At this, Milton offered a bitter snort and resumed pacing. "Dear, lady, you must use the term authorities loosely when discussing remote areas of the Amazon. Daniel was an outsider. As far as the locals were concerned, we could deal with our own problems. Besides, they're a superstitious lot. When they heard about the skull, they became fearful and left us to our own devices."

Hunt stepped forward, stopping Milton mid pace. "Okay. So the locals stayed away. My understanding is that Andy went to Kutu. That's about twenty-five miles from here."

"Correct. It's where we go for supplies. It's about as civilized a place as you'll find for nearly two hundred miles. But, by civilized, you must understand, I'm comparing it to primitive tribal villages."

"Understood. And it was from there that Andy disappeared."

"That's what I've been told, Mr. Huntington. Obviously, I was not present to know the details."

Chapter 9

Somewhere over Central America

Jonathan Thorpe grinned at the pretty young flight attendant, sipped long on his rum and Coke, and then, setting his glass on the tray of the empty seat beside him, returned his attention to his laptop computer where he'd just downloaded some additional files on Marc Huntington. Pathetic really. He told himself that he was researching the man because he'd likely encounter him during this assignment, but he knew it was jealously at the core. He'd been investigating the former Delta Force operative since he'd learned that Dana had gone and married the bloke. Interesting material on Huntington, though. Some mysteries to be unraveled – maybe exploited.

Thorpe took another sip, closed the Huntington file, and opened another. This assignment troubled him. None of it was as he would have planned. Traipsing about the jungle was hardly his forte. Thorpe was in the business of acquiring fine works of art. Some of these were ancient and could be classified as artifacts, but many were of a more contemporary nature. But, at the core, these all had a similarity: they were each quite valuable pieces, sought by the filthy rich to enhance their private collections, and, more importantly, to stroke their egos.

Having painstakingly established an alternate persona as one of their own, Thorpe moved among these elite circles, nodding and grinning, discussing latest acquisitions, and generally ingratiating himself to the people he would soon burgle. None realized this was the very thief they had once hired to acquire their masterpieces. He felt at home in mansions and galleries. He knew how to schmooze information out of wait staff and disenfranchised teenaged sons and daughters. He was adept at bribing personal assistants and even embittered spouses. He knew how to work the system.

But, this was not art.

This was not stealthily breaking into a gallery or a home. This was chasing a fossil through the Amazon jungle on the heals of murder and theft. This was dealing in an unfamiliar country in an uncomfortable environ, chasing after something of which he knew nothing.

Thorpe shook his head, sipped at his drink. He was nearly due for another. Clicking onto yet another web page, he sighed. The information on the Amazon skull was sketchy. Most of it superstitious nonsense and speculation. Until this past week it had been considered nothing but legend. Thorpe was still not convinced to the contrary.

How could his client know that this particular find was, in fact, the Amazon skull? There were reports of writing on the interior of the cranium. That, he had to admit, was bizarre, though it did fit with the myth surrounding the skull. And how had the client learned of the find so quickly? Thorpe had scoured news releases concerning the events both at the excavation site and in the small village of Kutu. He'd read about the two scientists, one missing, one dead. There was mention of a major find, but details concerning the fossilized human skull were not so easily found. Thorpe had contacted informants who had then contacted their own informants in order to learn even the most insignificant details concerning the find. It was as if a cloak of secrecy had descended upon the thing.

What was so special about this skull?

There were the legends, of course. The purported powers of the skull, its supposed ability to raise the dead. But, that was superstitious rot. Certainly the client, obviously a wealthy and learned man, believed none of this.

In truth, it probably came down to the man's unusual tastes. All of his art and artifacts were supernatural or occultic in theme. Some seemed outright satanic: an ancient Byzantine sculpture of a multi-winged demon, a sixth dynasty Egyptian tablet depicting a serpent devouring three human heads, a 1509 Hieronymus Bosch painting of tortured souls amidst savage flames. A mythical human skull would probably be a centerpiece to such a collection of the bizarre and disgusting.

Thorpe had attempted to do more research on the client as well, but had learned very little. The man, it seemed, was a ghost. His property in the Swiss Alps was owned by a corporation, which was owned by another corporation, which was owned by a Venezuelan non-for-profit charity, which was loosely connected to a Texas-based corporation. Every lead led to multiple disconnections, all designed to hide the man. Thorpe had been unable to learn anything from the client's employees, nor from vehicle registrations, mail deliveries, or covert surveillance equipment. As to accessing computer files, the security procedures would cause MI6 to murmur jealous praise.

Thorpe didn't like operating in a cloud. It was his practice to maintain the upper hand, to always have some delicious nugget about a client stashed away, some tender piece of meat to pull out on the off chance that the man might one day seek to purge his conscience by ratting Thorpe out to the authorities.

But, Thorpe had nothing on this strange bloke.

Well, he supposed, nothing was a bit of an overstatement. There was the photograph. He'd come across it quite by accident, really. But, he had it none-the-less. It had been in Newsweek Magazine, of all places, just right out there in the open. Surely, the client, who shielded his identity with such rigid ferocity, had been unaware of this monumental breech in his security. But, there it was on page fifty-two of the July 14 issue. The photograph was not of the client, not specifically, but rather of the United States Speaker of the House. But there, just behind and to the left, apparently talking with the Secretary of State, was the client. Unmistakable. The man was tall, with light red hair swept back, a severe angled face, and broad brooding brow. He wore an impeccable black Prada tuxedo and held a tumbler of what appeared to be his perpetual favorite, buttermilk. Oh, yes, that had been the client.

Yet, still, Thorpe had been unable to put a name to the face. No one admitted to knowing the man – or to even seeing him at the function. Even the photographer who snapped the shot had no recollection of him having been in the frame.

Thorpe sighed and sipped at his drink. There were more pressing problems at hand than the identity of his anonymous employer. One being that he did not travel alone. The client had sent two security persons along to help with the more "unpleasant" aspects of the quest. I.e., if there was trouble, these two, one male and one female, were adept at the killing arts.

Bloody brilliant.

Thorpe felt so much better knowing that trained killers watched his every move.

And watch him they did.

True, their stated assignment was to aid Thorpe in locating and retrieving the skull, but, in truth, Thorpe felt they were to spy on him as well, to make sure that he didn't learn too much, either about the skull, or, more importantly, about the client.

The male was a thug, plain and simple. An Aussie who had fought in Iraq, he rarely spoke, but rather stared silently ahead, simply nodding when addressed. This aside, Thorpe was keenly aware that the man had some level of intellect. He might appear a brute, but he was a voracious observer. Never once since boarding some ten hours prior, had Thorpe managed to avoid his gaze. The man hadn't so much as gone to the lavatory for five bleeding minutes! Not only did he eye Thorpe, but he scanned the cabin, noting the flight attendants and other crew members who might take a stroll through the first class compartment. He tapped on his laptop computer, not enjoying social networking such as Facebook or Twitter, playing games, or watching videos, but reviewing diagrams or schematics of some sort. Even so, he was keenly aware of everything within his vicinity.

The female, though, thirtyish, fit, with the rail-thin form of a thirteen year-old boy, had at least engaged Thorpe in conversation, mostly probing, but still, her clear amber eyes and subtle grin had provided a provocative diversion. She was a Yank – southern, judging by her accent - a light skinned African American with alluring lips and a sharp tongue and a quick wit. He could not trust her, he knew, and was certain that she would readily slay him should the order come through. But at least she would converse. And this, to Thorpe, was a means of cracking the mystery which was the client. Thorpe was expert at manipulating conversation, at drawing information from a source. This woman, he felt, he could exploit.

Glancing across the aisle to his right and offering his lady-killer grin, he said, "This skull, why do you suppose our employer is willing to expend such resources on it?"

The woman, Tina Collins, by name, glanced up from her word search puzzle, grinned a saucy grin, and said, "The way I figure, he must want it pretty bad."

Well, that was bleeding unhelpful!

"Yes, well, obviously," said Thorpe. "What I was wondering is, why, perchance, do you suppose he wants it so ardently?"

Her large beautiful eyes focused on him but revealed no emotion. "Our employer desires quite a few things, Mr. Thorpe. He's hired us not to question his motives, but to accomplish his goals."

"Yes, well…" began Thorpe, but the woman cut him off.

"Darlin', don't go thinking that you can wriggle information from me simply because I engage in a little small talk. That would be a serious mistake." With this, she intensified her gaze, her nearly translucent eyes peering into his with a fierce determination that caused him to look down and away.

What had just happened there?

He was almost never intimidated by mere wordplay.

"Johnny," she said with a smirk. "You seem confused. Is there a problem?"

Bloody hell!

"No. That is… You, my dear, are a charming and beautiful young woman. I was struck by the combination of your quick agile mind and your stunning allure."

"Bull," she snapped. "You hoped to manipulate me. And when I saw through it, your overdeveloped ego lost its bearings. I've read your file, darlin'. That British charm and obnoxious schmooze won't work on me."

"Apparently not," muttered Thorpe.

"Listen," said Collins. "I'm not all too sure why the boss likes you so much, but he's obviously found a use for you. Fine by me. As long as he keeps paying me, I'll jump through his little hoops all day long. But hear me, Mister British upper crust snob; if he gets tired of you, or if you do something to screw with my money ticket, well, I know sixteen different ways to kill you right where you sit. Comprende?"

Thorpe held her gaze for several long seconds before speaking. "And I know ten that will cause you such misery that you'd wish I had done you the favor of a quick death."

Tina Collins smiled a warm and luscious smile. "Then we understand each other."

"Perfectly," nodded Thorpe.

Chapter 10

Kutu Brazil

The constable was a short round man, deep brown, with little hair upon his unevenly shaped scalp. His hazelnut eyes were wary, and his demeanor guarded. He was not a lawman first and foremost. Dana could tell this from the onset. In a village the size of Kutu, there was likely little need for a fulltime law enforcement presence. The man had not wanted to speak with Marc and Dana, but had essentially allowed himself to be cornered into the conversation. Hunt could be annoyingly persistent when the need arose.

"So, who exactly did see Andy Lindell?" asked Hunt as he placed his palms on the man's desk and leaned forward to within two feet of his face.

"The motel clerk," replied the constable in heavily accented English.

"No one else?"

The man shook his head and looked down toward his folded hands.

"Excuse me," said Dana. "Perhaps I could ask a question or two." Hunt nodded and stepped away. He knew well enough that Dana could sometimes coax better information out of a subject than could he. Hunt tended to allow adrenaline to lead the way. And while this might serve him well in a life and death battle, it was not quite so effective in areas of diplomacy.

"Sir," said Dana as she half seated herself on the front right corner of the desk. "I understand that we are here in no official capacity. But, we're not interested in the murder, nor in the stolen artifact. Our sole purpose is to locate the missing Andrew Lindell. His father has hired us to find him."

"I do not know where he is," said the man.

"I understand. My question is who within the village did see him and did any of them interact with him?"

"He is not here."

Dana glanced up at Hunt who looked like he was dangerously near to saying something entirely inappropriate. "Yes," she said, speaking before Hunt had the opportunity. "Let's try it this way, when was the last time he was seen and by whom?"

The man shrugged.

"Do you know where he was last seen?"

"The motel."

Dana nodded. That was consistent at least with previous reports.

"Did he have anything with him?" asked Hunt, now stepping forward. "I'm thinking maybe a human skull."

"Hunt," said Dana. "I highly doubt he carried that out in the open."

"Yeah. But, show him the picture. Maybe that'll jog his memory."

Gregory Milton had forwarded a digital photograph of the skull to Dana via email. Slipping her smart phone from her pocket, she pulled up the image and then showed it to the constable.

He did not respond well.

*****

The constable had panicked, nearly screaming at the sight of the skull, he'd hurriedly rushed Hunt and Dana from the room, locking the door behind them. Hunt had grumbled and groused, stomped about some, and then, giving up on the man, had marched up the uneven dirt road toward the motel where Andy Lindell had last been seen. He flipped his ever-present yo-yo about – a tension relieving device, he claimed – and inserted an iPod earphone in his right ear, probably listening to his favorite band, Kiss. Men, she had concluded long ago, were simply little boys with whiskers and hormones.

Dana understood Hunt's frustration, but in truth had not expected much from the constable. They were outsiders, poking about in an already tense situation. The man was now dealing with twelve deaths from the fire, another burning death, that of Daniel Cook, and the missing Andrew Lindell, who, despite Hunt's view that Andrew was obviously innocent beyond all reasonable doubt, seemed to be at the heart of the whole mess. Add to this the local superstitions surrounding the skull, and it became a very volatile situation. They would need to be delicate in their search for the missing scientist. Probe too deeply into a culture's superstitions and the locals could behave violently.

Moments later, Dana watched as Hunt fumbled with the lock to the motel room where Andy had last been seen. The desk clerk had been absent, and, in truth, it was probably better that they searched the crime scene unencumbered by the prying eyes of a local. The village most likely had less than fifty residents, and served mostly as a stopping point between the airfield some thirty-five miles southwest and a larger village five hours to the north. Tourists, she knew, passed through here occasionally as a supply stop before venturing further into the jungle on their adventure holidays. As well, there was a cell tower on the outskirts of town, which would require occasional maintenance. Beyond these few and infrequent connections to the outside world, the village was fairly well isolated.

The motel was situated on the main road, well, the only road, really, and was at the northernmost point of the community. No locals were currently visible and the motel apparently had no current occupants. This, of course, could change at any moment, but for the time being it seemed they were unobserved.

"Would you like me to pick the lock for you, dear?" asked Dana. She knew that his difficulty with the task originated with his migraines and resulting lack of focus rather than with any lack of skill. Hunt simply could not concentrate on fine details while his head felt as if it'd just been bludgeoned by the entire Buckingham Palace guard.

Hunt continued to fumble with the picks. His squinted eyes and pained grimace revealed to her the truth of it all. "No, Dana. I've got it. Just give me a sec."

"Hunt, you've got one of your headaches. Please, let me…"

"Nah, nah. We're good," said Hunt with a quick grin. "Just, keep an eye out will you? I don't want anyone to see us breaking into this room." Hunt inserted the pick once again, his hand shaking as he did. "Ever wonder why Andy fled here to Kutu?" he asked.

"The nearest civilized village, I suppose."

"True. But, if Andy was trying to steal this Amazon skull thing, wouldn't he hightail it out of the country? He had a vehicle, why not drive to the airstrip? It took us what? Three hours from landing till we were in Kutu? Why park his butt here overnight?"

"Alright," said Dana. "Granted. So, what is it you're thinking?"

"Maybe Andy wasn't so much fleeing as he was seeking."

"Seeking what?"

"Not sure. Something to do with the skull, I guess." Hunt paused, twisted his wrist ever so slowly. "Oh, come on!" he whispered in flimsily-disguised frustration.

Silently, Dana knelt to beside Hunt, kissed his cheek, and took the picks from his hand. Three twists and a jiggle and the door opened.

"Great. So much for my fragile male ego," groused Hunt. Though, he said it through a grin.

"You're still my alpha male, dear."

"Grrr. Me Hunt, you... Ho boy."

Hunt had stopped mid sentence, his form becoming taut, his eyes narrow. The smell was strong, but not yet overpowering. Dana peeked past his shoulder and through the doorway following his line of sight. "Blimey," she said.

"Yeah. Kinda crispy."

They entered the small, sparsely furnished room, each scanning the scene. Hunt marched to the back of the space, peering around the corner to the toilet area. "Clear," he said.

The body was horrid. It lay face up on the bed, a male, the skin badly burned, the features contorted. The eyes were brown, still open, staring sightlessly at the ceiling. The fingers were curled like claws and the legs drawn up and seemingly frozen in a position halfway between fetal and extended. Dana made a point to breathe through her mouth in an attempt to minimize the effect of the ghastly odor.

"Nothing else in the room is burned," said Hunt as he approached the bed. "It's almost as if he deep fried from the inside out. Look at the skin, the way it's blistered and popped."

"That's it," she said with sudden realization. "Yes. That's what nettled me so." She'd had trouble pinpointing exactly what had so bothered her before, but the cadavers at the excavation site, and now this one, were peculiar in many aspects. The skin was not charred as one might expect from exposure to flames, but rather, it seemed as if the blood had literally boiled, rupturing vessels and causing them to burst through the epidermis. "Judging by what's left of the clothing, I'd say he's a local," she added.

"Yeah. Seems that way."

"Could be the motel clerk, I suppose."

"Or, yet another party after that skull," offered Hunt as he leaned closer to the body. "The flesh is burned at the breach points," he said. "See this? The skin over here is nearly unaffected, but where the break is, it's charred nearly to black. There seem to be burst points like this all over the body."

"Like a sausage left boiling too long, the skin begins to burst," added Dana, once again remembering the bodies at the dig site. Why hadn't she picked up on this before? Perhaps too much input, she supposed. So many bodies, so many questions, she hadn't taken the time to truly examine any one corpse. There had been no need. The cause of death had seemed obvious.

Not so much, now.

Dana pondered this. What would cause such a thing? Presumably, none of the charred bodies had been literally boiled. Though, the more she thought about it, the more she realized that no external source had done this. Something had happened internally. "I think we'd best be going," she said suddenly.

Hunt shook his head. "Nah. Not yet. There might be evidence on the body, and…"

"Don't touch that body!" shot Dana.

Hunt turned to face her, the question in his eyes. "What are thinking?" he asked.

"That, yes, this man was burned, but no, this does not appear to be the result of exposure to flame. This has nettled me since we saw the bodies at the dig. Something very peculiar about the corpses. And now it comes to me. I'm worried that there might be some sort of contaminant."

Hunt back off a step. "Such as?"

Dana shook her head. "I'm unsure. But, now that I look at this man, and as I think back to the other victims, I must conclude that whatever the source of heat, it was internal."

Hunt nodded. "Do me a favor, click off a few shots of this place – both body and the room itself – and then we'll get out of here."

*****

They strolled back down the dusty road tossing about theories, swatting at insects, and generally attempting to set a course of action. It was late afternoon and Milton had agreed to meet them around five pm. He'd had several urgent calls to make concerning the twelve deaths and had planned to spend the day at the small ramshackle building serving as the village hall, general store, and all around gathering place. There was a decade old Hewlett Packard computer with internet service – however spotty – as well as clear cell reception. Milton had hoped to achieve contact with his university and receive direction as to how to conduct things from this end.

The residents of Kutu made no effort to hide their apprehension as Hunt and Dana passed by. Most would whisper and point, some would shout at them, making shooing gestures with their hands. A young mother gathered her two small children and pulled them forcibly into their tiny shack. An elderly man, sitting on a rusty green barrel, pointed at them with a long and gnarled finger, chanting ominous words in an unknown tongue. In talking with one young man, apparently less taken aback by these meddling outsiders than the majority of the villagers, they had learned that the Amazon skull, or Deus Esqueleto (god skull) as they called it, was the centerpiece of local lore. It was thought to be the severed head of a great warrior cut down while defending his people. His spirit had remained with the skull to watch over the land and protect it from invaders. It was believed that in times of great need, the skull could raise an army of the dead to defend the territory. That this mythical – truly religious – item had not only been uncovered, but had apparently been stolen by an foreigner, after which a plague of fiery death had descended upon the dig site, acted as proof to these people that the strangers were evil and could not be trusted.

No wonder the villagers whispered and cursed as they walked by. There sacred totem had been defiled – stolen – and fiery death was the result.

Standing beside the town well, Dana stared across the way to the old wrinkled man on the barrel. Still, he pointed in their direction, chanting and hissing. He wore contemporary clothing: a peach-colored polo shirt, cutoff blue jean shorts, and red Converse All-Stars, but she wondered if he might be some sort of shaman hurling curses in their direction. "Creepy one, that," said Dana after sipping from her just-refilled canteen. "I hope he's the village loony and not the mayor, or whatever authority it is they have down here."

"Yeah. I'm with you there," said Hunt, now absentmindedly playing with his yo-yo.

After a moment, Hunt added, "I've been thinking about the skull."

"Deus Esqueleto," offered Dana.

"Yeah. God-skull. If Andy made his way into town, unknowingly lugging around their most sacred object, an item of legend, never before seen by human eyes."

"At least not for several millennia."

"Right. Who knows what they might have done to him."

"And," offered Dana. "Anyone caught giving us information might be shunned or worse."

"Exactly," nodded Hunt. "I'm amazed we got that kid to talk with us, much less anyone in the know. Still, we've got to find a way to..." Here, Hunt paused mid sentence. "You see that?" he asked.

Dana nodded. "Milton."

"Yeah. Driving into the brush. Strange. Can't imagine why he'd go deeper into the forest. According to the map, there's nothing down that way."

"There must be a path or small road of some sort. His vehicle couldn't traverse virgin jungle. I don't suppose you have any ideas as to where he's going?"

"Not a clue, Dana. But, we're gonna find out. That, I promise you."

Chapter 11

The Amazon Rainforest, Brazil

"Hunt, are you sure we're still on the right track? It's getting dark and I can't tell if we're even on the path anymore," said Dana as she shielded her eyes from the rain. The downpour had been sudden, but not unexpected. The place was called a rainforest for a reason.

Hunt grinned. Dana was amazing. Her computer skills could make Bill Gates blush, her clandestine experience was second to none, but she'd done very little field work outside of urban areas. For such an experienced operative, it seemed a glaring gap in her résumé. "We're good, Hon," he said, pushing aside a coarse pale green vine. "We're on the trail and I can still make out the Hummer's tracks."

"Well, hoo-rah for all of those carrots you eat. I can't see a bloody thing between the dusk and the downpour."

And neither would Hunt if they didn't find Milton before it got much darker. Most of their equipment had been lost with the Jeep, among it, night vision goggles and a military grade lantern. Dana carried a small flashlight in her pack, but as the darkness grew, one thin beam would hardly illuminate the landscape.

They'd been following Milton's trail for nearly three hours, and were far too deep into the forest to consider turning back toward Kutu. Darkness descended quickly in the Amazon. Better to continue forward and hope that Milton had stopped in a place of relative safety rather than to try to retrace their steps such a distance in near utter darkness.

There were curious sounds from all sides. The rainforest, with its abundant life, was never quiet. But, now the night creatures were stirring. A new shift was coming on duty and Hunt could nearly feel dozens of reptilian and mammalian eyes upon him. So far, they'd had no real confrontations with wildlife. But, it would soon be pitch dark. They were entirely out of their element. It would be easy – likely even – for one of them to step on a creature or otherwise disturb the jungle inhabitants.

And what of Milton? Unless Hunt had entirely misjudged the man, he couldn't see the academic setting up camp alone in this setting. It didn't fit. Obviously, he had a specific destination in mind. True, the man was traveling in an off-road vehicle and Hunt on foot, but the foliage was dense, the path overgrown and muddy, even in a vehicle Milton could not have gained much time on them. The going was simply too slow. In truth, the terrain was better suited for pedestrian travel rather than motorized. Case in point, several times during the past hours, they'd actually been close enough to hear the Hummer's engine ahead, even spotting it once.

But, the sound was deceptive as well. Twice recently, Hunt could have sworn he'd heard the vehicle sounds from behind, not ahead. Obviously the engine noise reverberated and echoed, bouncing off the hard wood of the numerous trees. Still, this sense of duality troubled him and so he remained on alert.

The pulsating flash of lightening illuminated the way as the couple made their way over a gradual rise. The path then turned sharply right and descended at a steep angle. Hunt knelt, squinting raindrops from his eyes as he ran his palm across the muddied ground. Yeah. He could still feel the indentations left by the Hummer's heavily ribbed tires. They hadn't been washed away entirely - not yet at least. Dana brought out the light, and they cautiously proceeded down the mud-slick grade.

There was now a sound from the left, footfall, not human, but that of a quadruped. Hunt lifted a finger to his lips indicating for Dana to remain silent. He paused, scanned the darkness. Even as Dana shone the light upon the brush, he could see no more than four or five feet before him, definitely not into the surrounding wall of plant life.

Whatever the creature was, it paused, perhaps sniffing the air, assessing these intruders to its domain. After maybe thirty seconds, Hunt heard it move away through the undergrowth, most likely in search of more interesting fare. He let out a breath he hadn't realized he'd been holding.

"A creepy crawler, that?" smiled Dana.

Hunt nodded. "Yeah. If you say so." With that, he turned to continue the trek and nearly walked directly into the stationary Hummer.

"So much for carrots," laughed Dana.

"Guess so," said Hunt as he made his way around the vehicle. "No sign of Milton. He must have continued on foot."

Dana nodded, though he could barely see her now. Very little moonlight managed to sneak through the gently shifting canopy above. "He doesn't seem all that fit," she said. "It could be slow going for him."

"Agreed. I'm guessing we're pretty close to his destination. Can't imagine him straying too far from his SUV – especially at night in a thunderstorm."

Hunt moved to the driver side of the vehicle and knelt. Taking the flashlight from Dana, he used it to scan the ground, methodically searching the muddy grassy surface. "Okay. Got it," he said after several moments. "Footprints leading off to the left." He rose, moving in the afore mentioned direction. None of this made sense. "Why would Milton come all the way out here?" he asked.

"I've been pondering that myself," said Dana as she moved to beside her husband. "He was obviously distraught at the deaths of his colleagues, quiet but not secretive on the ride to Kutu. I sensed no deceit at the time."

"Yeah, and then he ditched us to take a joyride through the rainforest. What changed?"

"We don't have enough information to answer that."

"Nope. Not yet. But I'm going to be looking at Milton in a different light when we find him."

"That might be sooner then we thought," said Dana. "Look forward. Ten o'clock."

Hunt shone the flashlight beam as indicated. "Ah. Now, who's been eating carrots?"

There was a small cave opening perhaps ten feet before them, barely discernable through the thick brush. The entrance itself was no more than three feet high and four wide. It was partially obscured by tangled brush, and was made up of jagged stone. One would need to be careful upon entering.

"Yep. He came through here," said Hunt after examining the ground leading to the cave entrance. "See how the brush is disturbed."

"You're going to make me crawl in there, aren't you?" quipped Dana with a brave, yet, slightly nervous grin.

"Well, not alone, if that's what you mean."

"Oh, now I feel so much better."

"Oh, quit grumbling. At least we'll be out of the rain."

*****

Unlike the muddy ground of the rainforest, the cave floor was solid, made of a rough gray stone. Though level in spots, it sloped gently downward. The two were forced to crawl for the first ten minutes or so as the cave ceiling varied from three to five feet in height. The thin beam of the flashlight waved erratically as they crawled, illuminating uneven walls of mostly smooth, nearly glassy purple stone. The ceiling pitched and dipped like an inverted ocean scene frozen in time.

Eventually the space expanded to nearly six feet in height, though the walls had narrowed to barely over five feet from one side to the other. From this point forward, Hunt, at five foot nine, was able to proceed in an upright manner. The air was cool and damp, perhaps twenty-five degrees below that of the exterior rainforest. Hunt could feel goose bumps rise all along his bare arms and fought back outright shivers. Having been surrounded by the constant onslaught of sound in the rainforest, the cave's near complete silence brought with it an eerie dread. Hunt heard nothing save their footfall, no squeaking bats, no trickling water, nothing. Hunt had never experienced anything even approaching claustrophobia, but here, in this narrow, uneven tube of a place, he had to mentally reject the first clamoring of panic from scampering into his brain.

"I can see my breath," he whispered as the passage finally widened to the point where the two could walk side by side, albeit, quite snuggly.

Dana nodded. "It seems to drop another four or more degrees for every five hundred meters. The wet clothing isn't much of a help."

"I'd give you my top shirt, but it's just as wet as yours," said Hunt as he wrapped an arm around her. He was wearing an unbuttoned olive drab shirt over a black Kiss concert T-shirt.

"I'm losing a bit of bearings," said Dana. "Not all too clear on how deep we've gone."

Hunt understood completely. The place was constantly veering off one way or another, making it near impossible to orient. Pulling a field compass from his Velcro thigh pocket, he said, "Heading northeast right now, but that changes every few yards. I've no idea where this leads." And then, after a pause, he added, "The grade is getting steeper. Careful. The stone's kinda slippery."

"Damp," agreed Dana.

"Yeah. Must be a water source somewhere along here, but I haven't heard or seen any indication of it. No sign of the rain seeping in. I'm missing our night vision gear about now."

Nearly five minutes later, they came to a spiraling grade, almost corkscrew-like in configuration. Very strange for a natural formation, thought Hunt. But there was no obvious evidence of human design or tampering. Unless they wanted to retrace their steps back to the cave entrance, there really was no other option but to continue forward down the winding way. The passageway was small and tight. Hunt's broad shoulders made for a cramped fit. Down it went, the grade becoming almost vertical in some places. Often, the couple found the need to press their palms against the cool stone walls in order to slow their descent. As such, Hunt lodged the flashlight under his right armpit in an effort to free his hands.

"I can't imagine Milton coming this way," said Dana after a near slip that just about sent her tumbling down the pitch black slope.

"I'm with you, hon. But, I haven't seen any other outlets. He's down here somewhere."

"Well he had better lead us to Lindell; otherwise I might not speak with you for a week. Foolishness, this is."

"Promises. Promises. Hey, look ahead here." Hunt directed the flashlight beam to a spot some fifteen feet forward of them. "Does that look like an offshoot to the right?"

But, before Dana could reply, something cool and slimy slithered between their feet. Both started, lost their footing, and tumbled forward down the grade. The flashlight bounced once, twice, and then went black as it skittered across the rocky surface. Hunt felt Dana slam into him repeatedly, once atop him and then below, and then atop again. Frantically, he tried to straighten his body, hoping to press against the narrow walls like the emergency breaks to an elevator, but he was continually bludgeoned both by Dana and by jutting stones and uneven folds in the walls. Worst of all, he had no idea what lay at the bottom of the grade. For all he knew, they were tumbling toward a five hundred foot drop.

The back of Hunt's head slammed against a jutting stone. Instinctively he reached out as he tumbled past, grasping the thing momentarily, but unable to secure a grip. Still, it slowed him some. With each similar contact, he willed himself to do the same, to make those blind stabs, to grab, clutch, anything that would slow the decent.

At some point he realized that Dana was no longer tumbling along with him. Had she sped ahead of him or had she somehow staved her progress and was now above him? Still plummeting, barely coherent, he had no answer to this.

And then he connected with something large and very solid. The force of the impact tossed him to the right where his left temple slammed against the cave wall.

Another tumble.

Another smack.

And then nothing.

Chapter 12

Turkey Run State Park, Central Indiana
19 years ago

Hunt raced through the woods, well off the trail, past the fallen oak he'd noted as a landmark, and down the gentle slope toward a partial clearing. Sugar Creek glistened far below and off to the right, the water frozen and snow covered. The frigid Indiana air bit at his exposed cheeks. Gusty wind cut through his down jacket. He was just a boy. Well, almost a man. Seventeen was old enough to go to war in some countries. He was old enough to drive and had even almost had his first girl.

Well, maybe not quite almost. But, Jennifer Peters had said maybe… Someday. And then she'd giggled, pecked him on the cheek, and exited Hunt's beat up Ford Escort before he could fumble out a response. Even now, he wasn't sure if he was more excited or disappointed at the encounter. He'd never had the nerve to ask her out again. Not after asking her *that* question and receiving such an ambiguous response. He knew he shouldn't have done it – asked her, that is. It was just that… What? That all the other guys were bragging – whether truthfully or not – about their many conquests? Or was it that he really felt that Jennifer should be that special first one? They'd dated for almost three weeks and he found that he couldn't go more than a few seconds at a shot without thinking of her. But, then he'd blurted out that life-altering question. And where once they had shared a comfortable closeness, a near tangible energy between them, now there was only space. Lots and lots of space. Empty and emotionless. Cold as the cosmos and likely just as endless.

Hunt hated space. Or, at least, he would learn that he hated space. That vacuum in a relationship. That emptiness that should be brimming with… Well, he wasn't exactly sure what it should be brimming with, but he was pretty certain that whatever it was, it was no longer something he and Jennifer would ever share. He'd blown that one. There was no going back.

But, that wasn't now. That wasn't today. Today, he was racing through Turkey Run State Park, down in central Indiana, a good hundred miles south of his own little corner of the state. "The Calumet Region," they called it, where he was from. Northwest Indiana – "Da Region." Less than an hour outside of Chicago, it was still part of the suburban sprawl, and yet kept one foot in the ever-diminishing rural world as well. Occasional cornfields still dotted the landscape, rusted out pick-up trucks zipped along Ridge Road, and kids grew up in roughly equal numbers to work the fields, the steel mills, or college textbooks.

As for Hunt, he was a high school senior. His hockey team – Hunt played right wing – had had a game down in Lafayette, and the coach had scheduled an afternoon at the state park as a treat for the boys on the way back north.

They were playing capture the flag, and had marked off a large wooded area of probably three quarters of a mile square or better for the boundaries. Hunt had the opposing team's flag – white, terrycloth, and rust stained – clutched tightly in his right hand as he bound over a fallen maple, turned right, and sprinted down a brush covered embankment leading to his own team's goal line. Toby Weinberg was on his heals and gaining. Only Hunt's quick pivots and his ability to leap and redirect like a pro running back had allowed him to make it this far. Weinberg was fast. So was Hunt, but Weinberg had longer legs. Still, Hunt was clearly the more athletic of the two. He had perhaps another hundred and fifty yards to the goal, and he'd just heard Weinberg curse as he'd nearly stumbled over the fallen tree trunk.

Hunt smiled, clutched his prize, and pressed just a little harder into his final sprint down the gently sloping way.

Hunt didn't know if he heard the words first, or felt the impact. In likelihood, the two were simultaneous. "Yeah, Moose! Yeah!" cried Weinberg as Jimmy "Moose" Mulligan slammed into Hunt from the left. Hunt hadn't seen him coming, had had no idea that he was in Moose's sites. The blow was hard, knocking Hunt from his feet, sending him tumbling down the grade, the prized flag still clutched tightly in his fist.

Moose came by his name honestly. At five ten, he weighed in at nearly two fifty. It wasn't all muscle, but it certainly wasn't all fat either. The guy was solid. Notable around the school for his ability to hurl a softball nearly the entire length of the football field, he was the hockey team's goalie. Moose had wanted an offensive position, but his sheer mass had made it difficult for him to make the quick cuts and turns necessary. Still, despite his size, he'd somehow turned out to be a skilled goalie. Not only was he solid, but he was surprisingly quick and agile for a guy his size.

Hunt felt the ankle snap somewhere amidst the second roll; it was almost a surreal feeling, painful to be sure, but the twirling horizon and constant bumps and smacks of the fall distracted him from the severity of the injury – at least until he made the bottom of the grade. At that point, it would all come screaming home like an angry tornado on a trailer park. Moose was tumbling with him as well, his bulk smacking against Hunt's shoulder, then belly, then shins. Still, though, Hunt refused to give up the flag.

When finally they reached the bottom of the grade, Hunt lay on his back, his teeth clenched, his ankle screaming. He didn't know it then, but the injury would end his promising hockey career. At the time, though, all Hunt knew was pain.

Near blinding pain.

That was, until he saw Moose.

The hulking brute lay maybe ten feet to Hunt's right. He was on the ice. Right out there in the middle of the creek, his square head turned at an awkward angle, his legs and arms splayed, a dark blue stain creeping across the crotch of his blue jeans.

How had he managed to roll all the way out onto the ice? His bulk, Hunt supposed. Inertia. There was just no stopping a rolling Moose.

"Moose?" said Hunt, though the pain made it difficult to speak. "Hey, Moose! You okay?"

Moose didn't answer.

Toby Weinberg had made the scene by then, cautiously sidestepping his way down the embankment in uneven skips and hops. His first order of business had been to snatch the prized flag from Hunt's outstretched hand, but then he caught sight of Moose Mulligan and the thing dropped with a lifeless flutter to the ground.

"Oh, crap," he said, in a barely audible tremble. "Crap, crap, crap."

It was then that they heard the first crack.

Loud. Sharp. Crunchy.

They saw Moose's midsection sag for perhaps five or ten seconds, and then the ice gave way altogether with a loud *CEEEEERRRRRAAAAACCCK*!!!

Moose's eyes opened at the last, wide with terror just as he slipped to beneath the water. Sugar Creek is not terribly deep, in some places one can stand in it and not get a wallet wet. But, Moose Mulligan had found one of those prime spots where only an NBA player could stand with head above water, and Moose was not blessed with NBA stature.

"Crap, crap, crap," said Weinberg again, just in case Hunt hadn't heard him the first time.

Hunt rolled over in an effort to better see the creek. Each movement caused new shots of pain to slice through his leg, and he could barely contain the scream that pounded at the back of his teeth. "Come on, Moose!" he said, more to himself than not. "Get your big lunky head above water!"

Weinberg was beside him, dancing about as if he had to pee. "Aw, crap, crap, crap. He ain't coming up."

But, then Moose did surface. His broad face was redder than a boiled lobster, his brown eyes were wide with panic, he heaved for breath as both of his arms plopped onto the ice, his frantic fingers grasping for some sort of hold and finding none.

"Crap, Hunt, we gotta do something," stammered Weinberg. "He ain't gonna stay up."

No, he wasn't. Already Moose was slipping below. Weinberg pranced uselessly back and forth like a dog that saw a cat just beyond the screen door. Thus far, none of the other kids, or the two coaches, had discovered the incident. Hunt thought he could still hear the shouts and whoops of play far in the distance, but his mind didn't really register this. He was busy trying to figure out just how to get Moose out of the water alive.

Moose bobbed again, going under for nearly thirty seconds before reappearing. Weinberg, the good Jewish boy, muttered, "Oh crap, oh crap, Mary mother of God, oh crap, oh crap." Another prance, another twirl. "We gotta do some-thing, Hunt. What are we gonna do?"

How was Hunt supposed to know what to do? He was just a kid, just like Weinberg. But, the kid was looking to him for direction, looking to him for some sort of leadership. Hunt was the team captain. He'd been told by coaches and teachers alike that he was a natural leader. But, didn't a leader have to have some sort of a clue? Didn't he have to know where he was going before he could lead someone else there?

But, there was no time for that now. No time to ponder his role, or whether he was capable of making life and death decisions. Right now, he simply needed to act. He could figure out if he'd acted appropriately later. "We've got to get to him," said Hunt.

"But, the ice is too thin. We'll fall in."

Weinberg was right. Of course, he was right. But what other option did they have? They couldn't just leave the guy to drown.

"Find a long stick," said Hunt. "Something we can use to reach out to him."

"He's gotta be ten feet out there. We ain't gonna reach him with no stick."

"Just find one!" shot Hunt. "What's your plan, to stand there peeing your pants and watch him drown?"

"Shut your face, Huntington! I ain't peeing my pants."

Well, that was productive.

"Okay, fine. What do you think we should do?"

Weinberg paused for a minute. His eyes looked up and to the left as he searched his brain for the elusive solution. His lower lip curled under his teeth and his hands balled into tight fists. "We've gotta go out there," he said at last. "We've gotta get a long stick and crawl out on the ice, and… Oh crap, crap, crap."

Good, thought Hunt. Weinberg was back in the game. He wasn't a bad kid, probably not a coward, just scattered, prone to panic.

Moose bobbed again, sucking in what sounded like ten gallons of air, before dipping under again, his arms swatting violently at water and ice. Hunt didn't think he had much longer.

"I think my ankle's broken," said Hunt, knowing this with near certainty. "I can't move too well, but I can still crawl. You find the longest stick you can. And while you're doing that, scream for help. I'll start crawling out onto the ice."

"How will I get the stick to you?"

"Just throw it, I guess. Now, get going. And yell for help."

Weinberg did as instructed, pacing back and forth, picking up sticks and branches and then discarding them almost immediately. All the while he screamed for help, his voice taking on a warbling almost falsetto-like tone.

Hunt inched out onto the ice. Even through his leather gloves, the cold seeped into his fingers, and even more so through his blue jeans, numbing his legs near instantaneously. The ankle screamed at him, useless and throbbing, and his arms protested at being called upon to drag the entire body with so little help from the legs. "Hang on, Moose," he cried when the boy's head bobbed above the green and white surface. "I'm coming for you."

But then Moose was gone again, nothing but bubbles and froth to mark his presence.

At first, the ice seemed solid enough. Hunt didn't notice any cracking or popping, no give or flux as he inched closer and closer to the frantic Moose Mulligan. He could still hear Weinberg hollering somewhere off in the far distance. And were those other voices? One of them might even be Coach Haller.

Weinberg had not returned with a branch for Hunt to use, but by now, Hunt was nearly close enough to reach out and grab Moose's hand the next time the boy surfaced. The problem was that Hunt was beginning to hear subtle pops and crackles from beneath him. If he was to get hold of the guy, Hunt was pretty sure the ice would not support them both as he hauled Moose out of the creek.

But what alternative did he have but to try? He couldn't exactly sit by and watch the kid drown. Damn! Where was Weinberg with that branch? And Haller! The coach should be here. This was his responsibility. He was the one who was supposed to be there for the team.

And then, Moose was above water.

Hunt reached forward, stretching as far as he could. "Moose! Take my hand! Fast. Before you go under again."

But he was already gone. Hunt had still been just a couple of feet too distant to make the grab. Cautiously, slowly, but with an urgency he'd never before known, Hunt moved closer, closer.

The ice protested his weight. Hunt saw a crack slither out to his right with a series of *pop, pop, pops*. Still, it hadn't actually given way. He inched closer yet. Almost there, only inches more.

Pop, pop, pop.

The ice shifted. It didn't break through, not yet, but oh did it want to.

Moose was up again, his breath shallow, arms flaying. His eyes were closed. He had no idea that Hunt was even there.

A frantic grab.

A miss.

Moose went under.

Hunt propelled himself forward, stabbed his hand into the frigid water where he found a handful of Moose's wavy blond hair.

He pulled, but Moose was too heavy.

The ice shifted. Hunt was now angled down, water lapping onto his chest.

He pulled again.

This time Moose's arms came up, grabbing Hunt at the bicep, nearly pulling him in.

No. Not nearly. He was sliding forward as the ice crumpled beneath him. The frosty water slapped him in the face, invaded his nostrils, threatened to fill his mouth. He was in to his waist now, still clutching Moose by the hair.

And he was going to die! He knew it. Right here. Right now. These were the last few moments of his life.

Frantically, he tried to angle up, to find air, to find life, but he couldn't do it. Not while holding Moose. And even if he released his grip, still the hulking goalie would cling to his arm, unwilling to release his one lifeline.

Hunt's vision became dark. His lungs were already near bursting.

And then there was pain in the ankle. The left one. The broken one. Not that same pain he'd been feeling since the injury, but something else. Something sharper. Almost as if someone had grabbed hold and began to tug.

The pain was too much. Hunt screamed. Water rushed into his open mouth.

And then...

And then...

Chapter 13

Amazon Rainforest, Brazil
Present Day

Hunt blinked.

Chasing away the jumbled images of his adolescence, of Coach Haller yanking him out of the water, slapping his face, of Moose Mulligan's gasps and chokes as he was pulled free of the frigid creek, shivering and retching.

Hunt blinked again.

Attempting to see.

He was dry. Not in the creek. Not in Indiana.

Another blink.

Nothing. Still, he saw nothing.

A blackness, nearly tangible in its intensity closed in about him, surrounded him – penetrated him. Was it possible for darkness to literally penetrate a person?

Hunt had been a military man. He'd witnessed horrible things, participated in numerous missions. He'd commanded a unit, led men into combat, even watched some of them die. But, despite the entirety of his life, the utter completeness of the darkness brought with it a terror that seemed nearly tangible as it crept through his limbs and into his bloodstream to race through his veins, to infect his form and his mind with its paralyzing poison. And the very fact that he was so alarmed frightened him all the more. For he was not accustomed to this level of fear. This was alien to him, a foul stranger invading his being, and he wanted none of it.

Above all else, Hunt needed to regain control of his own mind. He was unfocused, confused, the memories of his present situation only now becoming tangible. He closed his eyes. Breathed. Attempted to remain calm, to chase the fuzz from his brain and reorient himself to his circumstance. The cave. He was in the cave. That, at least, he now remembered. And, Dana. Where was Dana?

She had fallen too. They'd been together, tumbling one over the other – like he and Moose back in high school.

And then not.

She'd been there and then gone.

Where was she? Had she been injured? Or worse? Hunt tried to adjust himself, turning his head, calling her name. He attempted to sit upright, but he was in a peculiar position, perhaps three quarters inverted, his left foot – the one once broken during high school – caught in something that prevented him from tumbling further down the grade. He wasn't quite sure what the obstruction might be. Perhaps two closely spaced rock formations or a narrow crevasse.

His torso was crammed amidst dull rounded protrusions, uneven and painful. But, not jagged. At least they weren't jagged. He contracted his gut and pulled himself up as if doing crunches on an inverted plane. Fumbling in the dark, he felt about his left foot in a frantic effort to release it. After perhaps two minutes, he fell back onto the stony bed, his belly cramped and pained from the task. It seemed the foot was caught in a warped formation, more or less shaped like the double helix of DNA, but without the rungs connecting the two twisting columns. Based on what he'd felt with his fingers, it seemed the spiraling stone widened just above the foot. Hunt was fairly certain that if he could slide his foot up perhaps twelve inches, that he could free it with little difficulty. The problem was that the whole of his weight was pulling down and away, disallowing him the leverage needed for the maneuver.

What he really needed was a sledgehammer, something big and mean, with enough weight to smash the restraining stone and free his foot. Obviously, this was not at hand, but he was lying on a bed of stones. If he could pry one free, perhaps he could strike the helix stone with enough force to break it away.

Hunt twisted to his right, feeling around with both hands, pushing and tugging at each stone within reach, attempting to determine if any were loose or less secure. One pulled free almost immediately, but this was so unexpected that Hunt allowed the thing to bobble in his grip before losing it entirely. As with the earlier stone, it tumbled down the grade. This presented another problem. If Hunt did break free, it was likely he'd plummet down the way. He had no means of determining how deep this went, but judging by the bouncing stones, it was quite a way down.

Had Dana fallen all that way?

Dear God, he hoped not.

Hunt now twisted to his left in an attempt to reach some of the stones not yet tested. This caused additional pain in his trapped ankle, but it was bearable. With therapy, the old high school injury had eventually healed near completely, and the current predicament caused scraping and pressure, but he didn't sense that any bones were broken.

After several attempts, Hunt finally identified a stone, oblong in shape, perhaps resembling a three foot long Cheeto. It took quite an effort to free it, but once he had, he felt he had something usable. The thing's balance was all wrong, and as such, it was clumsy, likely to tumble from his hands. But it had a good weight to it, not quite a sledgehammer, but it might get the job done.

Once again, bending at the waist, Hunt reached toward his foot with his left hand, while holding his newfound tool in his right. About six inches above his trapped ankle, Hunt discovered a narrowing in the stone. It was still at least four inches in diameter, but that was better than the six or better elsewhere. It was to the left of his foot. Hunt would have preferred the right – that would have given him a much better angle on the thing – but still, it seemed the weakest point.

Holding his curved stone like a left-handed slugger, Hunt whacked at the helix-shaped formation. The vibrations sent tremors up his leg, but with each strike he heard tiny pieces of stone break away to skitter down the incline.

Encouraged, he swung: once, twice, three times. Still the helix stone held firm. He struck it again, and then again. And then, just as he was about to lean back for another breath, the thing broke free and Hunt tumbled once again into the darkness.

Chapter 14

Dana landed some twenty feet below Hunt, though she had no way of knowing this. Hunt was unconscious, his brain trudging through adolescent memories in its long journey back to consciousness. Though Dana called his name repeatedly, there was no response. By the time Hunt came to, Dana would be beyond earshot and miss his calls.

Amazingly, Dana was relatively uninjured. She'd come to rest on a somewhat level area, and felt fairly well banged and bruised. Still, aside from a few scrapes here and about, she'd fared quite well.

She hoped Hunt could say as much.

The utter darkness was disorienting and made her next decision difficult. Her instinct was to retrace her steps up the grade, hopefully coming across Hunt in the process. Dana was in fine shape. She was agile, athletic, trained in three separate martial art disciplines, but she was not a skilled rock climber, and, attempting to do so while blind would require a rare mix of lunacy and optimism that she just didn't claim as her own.

The better choice would be to proceed slowly downward, feeling her way along the cave wall, and calling for Hunt as she went. She knew that under these circumstances she could conceivably walk right past her husband and never know he'd been near. Only if he was conscious and capable of responding to her call, could they reconnect. Clearly, she would need to feel about as she went, probing the adjacent areas with her feet in search of her potentially unconscious and injured husband.

Her other nagging fear was that she'd blithely stroll off of a cliff. As such, she decided to hug the wall to her right and inch slowly down the grade. With each step, she would extend her left foot, ensuring that there was solid ground beneath before scooting forward. All the while, she continued calling Hunt's name, praying that somehow he would respond.

Bleeding fantasy, she knew. But she thought it none-the-less.

As with Hunt, the darkness seemed all encompassing, seemingly wrapping itself about her, clawing at her, pressing at her. Dana had to fight off the panic which continually threatened to overcome her. She knew that if she let this happen the result could very well be fatal, that acting irrationally in this environment would likely result in her tumbling off some tremendous drop or colliding with a sharp and deadly formation.

She decided that her best course of action was to occupy her mind with the mystery at hand, while still remaining cautious and slow in her forward progress. In this way, she could avert panic and maybe even work a bit of this bugger through.

As such, she inched forward, slowly, so very slowly, and thought back upon the past several hours.

Gregory Milton was the first conundrum. Both she and Hunt had felt the man to be genuine. They'd spent quite some time with him as he'd driven them to Kutu. He'd explained much about the expedition, its goals, successes, and failures. He'd clarified the relationship between the late Daniel Cook and the missing Andrew Lindell. They had been very close. But the argument had been heated. Dana knew through experience, that even between the dearest of friends, nearly anything could happen under such circumstances. Righteous anger, adrenaline, and desperation could be a deadly cocktail.

Now, Cook was dead, and despite Hunt's protestations of young Lindell's unquestionable innocence, Dana couldn't help but think that the lad was involved. The claim was that Lindell had been kidnapped in Kutu, but that story reeked of rubbish. How an experienced and intelligent person like Hunt could fall for that rot was simply a testament to his loyalty as a friend and not to impartiality. Cook was found dead, Lindell had disappeared with the skull. Logic would dictate that the lad had killed his former mentor and then fled the scene, apparently faking his subsequent kidnapping in Kutu. And not faking it all too well. An anonymous tip that someone had seen Lindell dragged from the room? Please! Lindell most likely called the tip in personally.

But then, where had he gone? The skull was only valuable as a scientific anomaly. Hiding it away indefinitely would accomplish nothing. In fact, it seemed to Dana, that the longer the skull was unaccounted for, the less genuine its value. Too many opportunities for it to be altered or even substituted. Chain of evidence, they called it in law enforcement; she was certain the same rule would apply with scientific finds. Logically, Lindell had no clear motive for hiding the skull. Even if he had killed Cook, he would still want to get the fossil into the proper hands in order that it be authenticated.

So, again, where was Lindell?

And this all brought her back to Milton.

What did he have to do with any of this? Yes, at first he had seemed genuine, but then he'd raced off into the forest and into this black hell of a cave – not that they'd found any evidence of the man! But, the more she thought about it, the more she became convinced that Milton was somehow connected to Andrew's disappearance, or, to the murders, perhaps both. He seemed a gentle soul, but even gentle souls could harbor evil well below the surface and out of public scrutiny.

And what of the gunman they'd encountered prior to meeting Milton? Though she had not actually seen the sniper, she was certain that it had not been Milton. The accent was all wrong, and even the timbre of the voice was younger. And though accents could be altered or outright faked, she failed to see what purpose Milton would have had in attempting to warn them off with gunfire only to return a short time later to offer them a ride.

No. That made no bloody sense. There was another player involved. Lindell, she supposed, could have been the gunman, but then, why the false accent? Lindell was a yank, the accent was Scottish. He could have been trying to disguise his voice. But still, that didn't feel right. Lindell had fled the area. That was the only logical determination. Whether it was a voluntary exit or not could be argued, but she saw no scenario where Lindell would be creeping about the jungle with a bleeding rifle.

No. Someone else was involved, and once they determined who that was, then they could make some real progress toward finding the Lindell lad.

That was, if they ever made their way out of this bloody cave!

A sudden right angle in the cave wall brought Dana fully back into the present. A wall directly before her. The surface was hard and smooth, but with gentle undulating waves of stone. There was little use in standing about pondering the scenario, and so she simply followed the wall around to the left. By this time she'd begun to regret her decision to continue deeper into the unyielding darkness. Despite calling out, despite constantly feeling about the unseen floor, she'd still found no sign of Hunt. And now she was much further down – and thus all the more trapped – for her efforts. She could easily imagine herself moving deeper and deeper into this black abyss, never to return.

Panic swept over her, creeping up her arms, clawing at her bowels, tickling her throat. Would she ever see light again? Was she trapped here forever? What about Hunt? Had he even survived the fall? Had she, by continuing deeper, left him injured or dead, only a few meters from where she'd begun? She wasn't sure how much more of this she could take. It seemed the inky darkness continued into some black and unforgiving eternity.

And then, just as she thought she could withstand it no longer, just as she was ready to scream in fits of fear and frustration, to give up and simply slide down against the unforgiving wall and wait to die, she saw the dim and wavering light in the distance.

Chapter 15

Hunt tumbled down onto the same level space Dana had occupied some forty minutes earlier. By this time, she was much further down the way, just about to come across the cavern, and the mysteries held within. But, Hunt was flat on his back in the utter darkness. Shaking his head, he rose to a sitting position.

There was an egg-shaped knot at the crown. But it wasn't sticky. No blood. Probably nothing serious. That was good at least. He'd feared the injury might have been much worse. The pain sure made it seem so. As it was, he doubted he'd sustained so much as a mild concussion. What more could a guy ask out of a day?

Hunt cocked his head, took a deep breath, and smiled an involuntary smile.

That smell.

That lingering fragrance.

Perfume. Dana's perfume. Musky, a bit heavy, but not overpowering. She had been here. And not only had she been here, more importantly, she was no longer here. That meant that she had moved on, which in turn meant that she was not injured so badly as to be incapacitated. Dana was presumably alive and mobile. Now, all he had to do was follow his nose.

*****

Hunt made the chamber thirty-two minutes later. The place was an anomaly in its own right. Truly cavernous, the chamber had a domed ceiling littered with stalactites. The walls were rounded with gentle ebbs and indents, the stones, varied in color and texture. But the true curiosity to the cave itself was that many of the stones had a natural luminescence, bathing the chamber in a weird wavering light; cool blue and pink in hue, it was nearly hypnotic.

Dana was toward the center of the area, apparently examining something situated on one of numerous stone slabs that filled the majority of the space. "Hey," he called. "Any chance a guy could get a cup of hot cocoa? It's freezing."

"Hunt!" shrieked Dana as she rushed to him, squeezing tight, and reminding him of every bump and scrap he'd acquired in the last hours. "Easy, easy, easy," he said. "Damaged goods here."

Dana immediately pulled back. "Oh, I'm sorry. Are you injured badly? I was worried you might have been killed."

"I'm okay, hon. Just took some hits in the tumble. What about you? Seems you're as vivacious as ever."

She cocked her head with a grin. "Vivacious, I doubt. But, relatively fit, yes."

Hunt nodded. "Good, good. I was worried about you."

She paused, examining him. "You look rather deathly."

"Migraine. I took a blow or two to the head. Feels like my brain's spilling out my ears, but my meds are back in the Jeep."

"Well, not all of them," smiled Dana as she reached to within her left hip pocket and withdrew a zip-lock bag. "I always carry spares for an emergency."

Thank God. He'd thought his head might finally explode. "Emergency? When do those ever happen?" he asked in an effort to downplay the extent of his need.

"Oh, with you, my dear, never."

"Gimmie those pills before I fight you for them."

She smiled and tossed the bag to him. Hunt pulled two free and swallowed them dry. Thank God. He truly hadn't known how much longer he could have gone on like that.

After a moment's pause, Dana said, "Hunt, this cave, it's a bit of a mystery."

"Yeah, the phosphorescent stone. Very cool."

"That, yes – looks to me like a mix between agate and manganoan calcite. Both are florescent. Peculiar combination, I suppose. Captivating, though."

"How do you know this stuff?"

"Education, dear. It's a wonderful thing. But listen, there's more of a mystery than glowing stones. I'm not quite sure how to explain it."

"I'm listening."

To this, Dana took his hand and led him down a gentle slope and into the main section of the chamber. It took only a moment for Hunt to understand exactly what Dana had meant. Bodies. Dozens of them, laid out on stone slabs in neat rows of six, filling the majority of the considerable space.

"Notice the clothing?" asked Dana as Hunt moved cautiously forward.

"Yeah, yeah. It's all ancient, but representing different cultures and eras. Based on the armor and sword, this guy looks like maybe from the iron age, that one's a bushman. That looks like some early form of Viking." Hunt turned and indicated another form. "He might be a samurai."

"Notice anything else?" asked Dana as she stepped to beside Hunt.

"No decomposition."

"Yes. It's almost as if they could be sleeping."

"Well, if so, that's one freaky slumber party, all lined up in rows, arms folded across their chests. I'm sticking with dead."

This was incredible. Hunt had never seen anything of its kind. What possibly could be the purpose of this? And, how could they be so perfectly preserved? No decay. No odor. Even the skin tone lacked the deathly pallor. He supposed it could have something to do with the dry cool atmosphere of the cave. Maybe something to do with the air? And what of the clothing. Hunt was by no means an expert, but these did not look like costumes, but rather authentic dress from various places and historical periods. They were too worn, too random to be costuming. Some garments had apparently even decayed with time, only the thinnest threads remaining. There were rips and bloodstains, fabric worn thin at the knees or patched imperfectly. There were little trinket's and variances that a costumer would simply never consider.

Hunt stared down at a burly man of about thirty years in age. He wore leather armor and thatched footwear. A scabbard held a sword of iron. On his right cheek was a scar stitched shut by what appeared to be sheep gut. The stitches were a rich yellow/brown, thick and uneven, the wound only partially closed. This was in no way the result of modern medical procedure. And the man's teeth. Some were missing; the ones remaining were yellowed and uneven. Several were chipped or cracked. The man had never seen a dentist – quite possibly, he'd never held a toothbrush. Again, not of this century.

Hunt moved to another corpse, a woman. Her hair had been long and brown, her lips narrow. She wore the coarse loose fitting garb of an ancient peasant or slave.

How bizarre.

It was difficult to believe that these people were really of the eras and locales indicated by their dress, and yet Hunt's brain screamed that they couldn't be anything but. This whole thing had taken a weird turn into the Twilight Zone and Hunt had no idea where to go with it. "Any sign of Milton?" he asked in a halfhearted attempt to refocus.

"None," said Dana. "But, I will admit to a certain level of distraction."

Hunt grunted his agreement. "Well, he came into the cave. No doubt he's close by."

"I'm amazed at the variety of people here," said Dana. "Look at this one in ancient Egyptian garb." She indicated a young woman with jet black hair, high striking cheek bones, and dark luscious skin.

Hunt nodded. "If these people really are from the periods and locals indicated by their clothing – and I'm not ready to concede that point – how did they get here? It's not like Cleopatra there could hop on a 747 and book a flight to the Amazon."

Dana had moved to perhaps two rows over and was closely examining a young Asian boy. "Oh my God," she whispered after several moments.

"Yeah?" said Hunt wondering what else Dana could possibly have found.

"This body," she said. "It's warm."

"Warm?"

"Yes. Warm. As in alive." Dana laid her palm upon the cheek of the boy and then slid down to his wrist, squeezing it gently. "There's a pulse," she said, and then moved to the next body to repeat the process. "This one as well. Warm to the touch with a faint trace of pulse."

Hunt could not accept this. It just made no sense – not that anything here resembled sanity, but still. "Dana, they're not breathing. Look at them. Well preserved, yeah. Incredible, even. But, these people are dead."

Dana released an exasperated sigh. "At first I thought the same. But, if you look closely, if you touch them, you'll understand. Maybe they're in some sort of deep coma or drug induced hibernation, but they are alive."

Grudgingly, Hunt clasped the wrist of the young Egyptian woman. Yes, it was warm to the touch, and the skin was subtle, not rigid. Rigger mortis had not yet made a visit. But no, he did not feel a pulse. There was no rhythmic throb, no ebbing and flowing of pressure, not a thing to indicate…

And then he felt it.

Weak, nearly indiscernible, but yes, Dana was right, there was a pulse. Hunt leaned over the young woman and put his ear to within two inches of the girl's mouth. Nothing. At least nothing that he could feel. Still, if this woman was living then she had to be breathing, however minimally.

Hunt moved to the next body, and then the next. In each case, he found the exact same state. "I'm not a doctor, Dana, but I don't get this. How are these people alive? If they're breathing, I can't see it. Obviously, there's a pulse. But, what about food and water? How long could someone survive, even in a comatose state, without sustenance?"

"I don't have answers, dear. Only questions. But, I am certain these people are living. Perhaps it's something akin to hibernation."

Hunt nodded. As crazy as it all seemed, he couldn't find grounds to disagree. Raking his fingers across his head in frustration, he gazed over the numerous rows wondering what this could all mean, what insanity could have brought this about, and more directly, was Andy Lindell somehow involved? It was at this point that Hunt's gaze landed on a dark lean figure laid out on a slab in one of the back rows. "Milton?"

"What did you say?" asked Dana.

"Milton. Over there, laid out on one of the slabs."

"Oh dear, this is not good."

"Well, not if you're Milton."

The two moved through the many rows toward the inert figure. Milton was the sole occupant of this row of slabs, and Hunt felt a chill run through him as he realized that these empty spaces were meant for newcomers to the party.

Milton's eyes were closed, his mouth hanging three quarters open, and his dark skin so dry as to be nearly brittle. His large hands were crossed at the chest, and, like his inert companions, he was fully dressed.

"He's still breathing," said Dana. "Visibly, I mean. Not like the others. His chest is rising and falling."

Hunt nodded. He'd noticed this as well. Apparently, Milton was still in the early stages of the process. Maybe he wasn't completely gone. Hunt patted him on the cheek. "Wake up, sleeping beauty. Siesta's over. Time to join us living folk." Hunt slapped his cheek a little harder, and then gave him a gentle shake at the shoulders. "Come on, Greg. You've gotta wake up and tell us about all this craziness."

Nothing. Not the slightest response. The eyes remained closed, the lips gently parted. There was no indication of impending consciousness whatsoever.

"Greg. Dr. Milton. You need to wake up, and I mean now." Hunt shook him harder this time.

"Hunt, you'll hurt him."

"As compared to what? You think he'll be better off if I let him slip into the big sleep?" Another shake. "Milton! Wake up. If you don't want this date on your death certificate, then bring it back around." Hunt shook him again, and then patted his cheek. "I'm not getting anything, Dana."

"Yes you are, Hunt. Look at his eyes. I think they fluttered."

Hunt patted the cheek again. Yes, there was something. Subtle, barely discernable, but there none-the-less. "That's it, Greg. That's it. Come back around for me." Another shake. Milton released a dry cough. Another few moments and the rheumy brown eyes fluttered open. "Good Man, Greg. Good man."

"Dr. Milton, can you hear me? It's Dana Huntington."

Another cough and a rumbling growl.

"He's coming round," said Hunt. "Pull out your canteen."

Dana nodded, slipping the metal cylinder from her belt as Hunt lifted Milton gently, using his right hand and forearm to move him into a semi reclined position. Unscrewing the cap, Dana attempted to give Milton a sip of water, but it just dribbled onto his chin and then down onto his shirt. Dana was about to try again when the scientist shook his head slowly from side to side. "No water," he said in a husky cough. "Not yet."

"Good job, Greg," said Hunt. "You had us scared."

Milton nodded slowly. "Lay down," he said weakly. "Lay me down."

Hunt nodded, gently lowering Milton to his previous position. "What's happening here? It seems like a scene from a George Romero film."

Milton's eyes fluttered, almost, it seemed, uncontrollably, but then they settled into a more moderate blink. "Skull," moaned Milton with some considerable effort. "Skull."

"What about the skull?" asked Hunt. "Who are all of these people? What caused this?"

"The... skull... is the... key."

"Still not much help, Greg."

"Dr. Milton," said Dana. "We need more information if we're to assist you."

"Find... skull... or we all die."

"Great. Now I understand perfectly," quipped Hunt.

Milton's eyes fluttered again. He wheezed, before expelling a thick clear drool onto his cheek.

"Hunt, I've been monitoring his pulse. It's getting weaker. I fear he's slipping back under."

Hunt nodded. He'd feared that possibility. Milton was still deep in the danger zone. "You got your med kit in the backpack?" he asked.

"Being married to you? Always."

"Good. We need a stimulant. Something to get his pulse racing. You know, an intravenous Red Bull drip, something like that. We can't let Milton slip into full coma mode like his friends here."

Dana nodded, slipped her pack from her back, and unzipped it.

"Greg," said Hunt in an effort to keep Milton conscious while Dana prepared her magic. "Can you tell us anything? What made you come here? Did someone inject you with something that caused this?"

Milton's eyes fluttered again, this time independently of one another.

Creepy.

Dana was once again beside Hunt, now holding a hypodermic needle at the ready. Part of her MI6 training had been in emergency medical procedures. While she was far from a doctor, her natural intelligence and real-life experience probably made her more knowledgeable than many emergency medical technicians. "I'm going to give him an epinephrine pick-me-up," she said. "Otherwise known as adrenaline. We don't know what caused this state, so I'm a bit leery. It's never good to randomly mix medications, and there's likely something unknown in his system. I'll give him a small dose."

Hunt stepped aside as Dana, with three sharp tugs, slid Milton's khaki shorts to midway up his leg and then injected him in the outer thigh. Again, the eyes fluttered, but now in sync. Hunt allowed a subtle sigh. That, at least, seemed natural.

"We'll need to watch him closely. Keep an eye out for obvious allergic reactions and whatnot," said Dana as she withdrew the hypodermic.

Hunt nodded, once again moving to beside the scientist. "How's that, Greg? Any better?"

It seemed Milton heard the question. His eyes squinted, his jaw clenched. He may have been attempting speech, but all he managed was a guttural moan.

"Come on, Greg. Articulate. You sound like Dana at five AM." Hunt jostled him gently. "You with me, doc? Anything you want to say? You know, like what's with the zombie zoo?"

Milton's jaw clenched. His eyes came open, wide and seemingly sightless. Hunt saw no recognition in those orbs, no movement either vertically or horizontally. The pupils were fixed and dilated, the stare eerily unmoving. Yet, still, the man spoke. The voice was dry, painful sounding, yet intelligible. "There's... some sort of... agent inside... skull. Causes... problems."

Problems. Well, that was an understatement.

"Where is the skull now?" asked Dana.

Milton gasped twice, long and rattling. "Andrew... took for analysis."

"Good, good," said Hunt, though he found it difficult to gaze into the bulging sightless eyes. "Tell me about Andy. Where is he?"

Milton's teeth clattered together like those of a toy Halloween skull, making it very difficult to understand his words. "Coo... Coo... He... doesn't want the... skull exposed."

"Who doesn't want it exposed?" asked Dana. "Are you speaking of Andrew Lindell?"

"No... Not Andrew." The words were becoming softer, more indistinct, while, simultaneously, the teeth clattering increased.

"If not Andrew, then who?" pressed Dana.

"Cccc... Ccoo." He stammered, but was unable to form the word.

It was then that Hunt heard movement from behind and to the right, the direction from which he'd entered the cavern. He turned, seeing a small Caucasian man of perhaps forty kneeling near the narrow entranceway to the chamber. Upon realizing that he'd been seen, the man's pale eyes darted right and then left, his narrow mouth twitched beneath a thin nutmeg mustache, and he rose to face Hunt. "Eh, hello," said the little man in a thick Scottish brogue. "I believe he was referring to me."

"Hunt," whispered Dana. "That voice. He was the shooter. The gunman that fired upon us in the Jeep."

Ah! Well, here was one piece of the puzzle coming together at last.

"Who are you?" shouted Hunt as he took a step toward the intruder, sincerely wishing he had a gun at this moment.

"Well, I suppose you could say, I'm the leader of this expedition," said the man almost apologetically as he took a step back. Hunt had a bad feeling. This man was timid, cowardly even. On the surface this might seem an advantage for Hunt, but he knew that cowards were often the most dangerous of opponents. They rarely thought things through rationally, but were prone to rash and often deadly decisions. One never wanted to confront a man driven primarily by fear.

"Daniel Cook?" said Dana. "He led the expedition. That's Cook, I'm nearly certain of it."

"That right?" called Hunt. "Are you Cook?"

The man nodded. His mustache twitched. Why was this guy so ridiculously nervous? Something was very wrong here.

"Interesting," said Hunt. "Dr. Cook, hot rumor is - you're dead."

Cook shrugged a little boy's embarrassed shrug. "Yes, um, that is what everyone believed, and so I, um, allowed them to continue in that line of reasoning." His eyes darted again, right, left. His right hand fumbled for something in a pants pocket. "But, as you can see, I'm quite well." He paused, glanced nervously at a small object, now held in his hand, and then continued. "Eh, as for you and the young lady, well, um, I do apologize, but I simply can't allow the scientific community to learn of the skull. It's… complicated. It could ruin everything." Here, he started walking backwards, toward the only exit to the chamber, eyes locked keenly on Hunt. "And so, as unfortunate as it may be, I cannot allow you to leave this cave – ever. Um, I do apologize."

Cook turned and ran. Hunt was already in pursuit, but was clear across the chamber. He'd only closed about half the distance at the time of the explosion.

Chapter 16

Gravel was still trickling down about Dana in clattering waves as she lifted her eyes searching through dust and smoke for sign of her husband. The sound had reverberated about the chamber and her ears felt as if she had cotton stuffed within. "Hunt! Are you alright? Hunt!" Her own voice sounded distant and muffled. Something trickled into her left eye.

Blood.

What a bloody nuisance!

Tapping about her forehead, she determined that she had a short jagged cut of about two centimeters in length nearly dead center. Not deep. Nothing earth shattering. Though, the thought of a scar did flit across her mind. Vanity, she supposed. If there was a scar, there was a scar. It wasn't as if there was anything she could do about it – at least not at the moment.

"Hunt!" she called again. "Hunt!"

"Yeah, yeah," came a dry voice from about eleven o'clock. "I'm here."

Dana was to her feet now. A bit wobbly, true. It seemed the room pitched about like a Tilt-o-Whirl. But then she righted herself, managing a cautious walk in the direction of Hunt's voice with all of the poise and grace of a drunken orangutan. Balance, she knew, was centered in the inner ear. The blast had been a shock to these. Most likely, this would all even out after a short time. Unless, of course, there was any permanent damage. Presently, her major concern was Hunt. Another head injury would not bode well considering the man's already tenuous condition.

She found him leaning against the base of one of the stone slabs blinking dust from his eyes.

"You okay, Hon?" he asked as she approached.

Dana nodded. "I'm fine. A bit dusty, a modest scratch to the noggin. Nothing to worry about. Seems you were lucky," she said.

Hunt grunted. "I wasn't that close and it wasn't an impressive charge. Probably some explosives Cook grabbed from the dig site. Big enough, though, to seal us in." Hunt spanked some dust from his clothing and then asked, "Have you checked on Milton? Is he injured?"

Dana had not. In truth, she hadn't given the man a thought. Her first concern had been Hunt.

Milton was still conscious as they moved to beside him, though clearly distressed, eyes bulging, lips curled in a tight grimace, his fists opening and closing, Adam's apple bobbing in syncopated triplets. It seemed to Dana that a man in his condition should be sweating profusely, but Milton's skin was dry, almost parchment-like.

"Hey, Greg. You okay there?" asked Hunt.

Milton attempted an unsuccessful grin. "Alive. I suppose... that should suffice."

Dana stroked his head, and patted dust from his taut face. "Just relax, Dr. Milton. We'll get you free of this room. I'm certain Hunt encountered situations such as this during his military career."

Hunt eyed her curiously. "Let me think, sealed in a cave with no food, sparse air, and a few dozen zombies. Nope. Nothing comes to mind." He then turned to make his way toward the now nonexistent exit. "Get what you can from Milton. I'll see what I can do about freeing us."

Dana nodded and returned her attention to Milton. "Are you able to answer some questions?"

Milton nodded, but Dana was not entirely convinced that he was capable of in-depth conversation. "I have several questions," she began. "For one, there was a charred body in Andrew Lindell's motel room. Any thoughts on that?"

Milton shook his head. Slow. Weak. The man's skin was so taut Dana imagined she could nearly hear his neck creak with each movement. She felt terrible pressing him for answers when he was in such a state, but knew there was really no other option. "How about this cave," she said. "Peopled by comatose bodies dressed in historical garb. Care to clarify that bit?"

Milton swallowed, an action which caused obvious pain. His eyes blinked, but as with earlier, his gaze was dreamy, far away, seemingly focused on another place. "Apparently, there's an agent," he began. "Coating... the interior... of the skull."

"An agent?"

He nodded in a near spasmodic jerk. "Yes... Unsure what it... might be."

"So the skull was here. What of Andrew Lindell?"

"I... had discovered... cave... previously. As had Andrew. We had heard... rumors. Local lore. This... was not part of... sanctioned dig site... due to... local superstition. Kept it secret. Cook, Andrew, myself. Only ones who knew. I thought... perhaps he had... returned here with... skull."

"So, you knew that Andrew might be here. Why didn't you tell us?"

To this, Milton remained silent, offering no response.

After a moment, Dana tried another approach. "What happened when you found Andrew here in the cave?"

"He had... skull. We talked... Argued..."

"And?" prodded Dana as Milton trailed off.

"I asked to... see skull. To touch. There is writing... within. I touched."

Dana nodded, understanding. "And whatever was in the skull, this agent, as you call it, infected you, slowing your vital signs, leaving you near comatose."

Milton swallowed in a harsh rasp. "Or... worse," he nearly croaked. "Dear lady, look at those about us.... Have they been lying here... for hours? Decades? Or maybe centuries?"

Dana heard the shifting of stones from behind. Hunt hollered, "Hey, I think I might have found an opening here."

Milton drew a long and noisy breath. "After I became... disabled," he continued, "Andrew panicked... Fled with skull." He gasped once again. It sounded raw and quite weak. "Cook will... try to stop... him from revealing... the find."

Dana heard more shifting stones and rubble as Hunt said, "Yeah. Here we go. Just a little bit further."

"You must... find skull," said Milton. "Cure contained within."

"Within the skull?" asked Dana. How bizarre. It seemed like something out of a fantasy novel.

"The... writing. Translate... the writing."

It was then that Hunt pulled loose the final restraining stone sending a cascade of rock spilling about the place in clattering splendor. The charge must not have been placed correctly; otherwise the resulting blast would have been far more troublesome.

Hopping down from his perch atop the rubble, Hunt made his way back toward Dana and Milton. "That Cook guy's a creep, but fortunately he's not a demolition expert. There was a lot of displaced rock, but no actual cave in. It'll be a tight squeeze over the rocks, but I think we can wriggle through." Hunt strolled to beside Dana. "Hey, Greg, you still breathing?" He paused for just a moment. "Listen, I heard some of the conversation. Can you give us anything concrete? Something that will help us find Andy?"

A gasp and a rattle. "Mr. Huntington… Breathing… slowing a bit. I believe the injection your… lovely wife gave me is… wearing off."

"Dana, you want to hit him with another dose?"

Dana paused for a moment before answering. Despite her training, she was far from a being a physician. And the agent or virus – whatever it was that ailed this man – was an unknown. She simply could not anticipate the outcome of another injection. "I'm afraid another dose could prove lethal. Even in the best circumstances… There are just too many unknowns."

Hunt nodded, accepting her explanation.

"Mr… Mrs… Huntington… A word, please."

It was Milton, his breath becoming shallower still, his eyes glazing to dusty amber. It seemed he was not long for consciousness. Struggling to will his lips into compliance, he stuttered, "Cam… Camer…" and then trailed off.

"Did you catch that, Dana?"

"Yes. I'm fairly certain he was attempting to say camera. He wants us to take his camera."

"Photo… skull…" gasped the fading man.

"Right, right. There are pictures of the skull in his camera. He already sent you one earlier."

Dana nodded. "Perhaps there are photographs of the writing on the interior as well."

Hunt nodded. "Yeah, okay. Greg, is that it? You said something about the skull having the cure, something like that, right? The writing on the skull might detail a cure?"

Milton did not answer, but instead, expelled a long hiss of air. His eyes fluttered shut, his limbs twitched feebly, and his lips drew together in a deathly grimace. Milton had succumbed with hardly a sound. A check of his vitals would confirm that he did, indeed, still have a pulse, however weak. But, like his silent companions, his breathing was so minimal as to be indiscernible.

Milton's camera was in a hip pouch along with several personal items: a nail file, aspirin, his passport, nothing else of use to the Huntingtons. Upon retrieving the camera, Dana slowly scanned through the images. Yes, there were several of the skull. At first glance it looked like any other human skull. And this, Dana knew, was part of Cook's complaint. He'd expected a more prehistoric version, early man, something to confirm his suppositions, and when this anomaly had been found amongst other ancient bones, it caused him to fear that the scientific community would challenge established evolutionary assumptions. Dana understood his trepidation, but was irked none-the-less. Scientists were supposed to seek truth – even if it didn't fit a prized hypothesis. Dana wondered if perhaps Cook's concern lie more with some other facet of the skull – perhaps the writing – rather than the age of the find, but this was only a feeling, nothing concrete.

"Ah! Here's one of the skull's interior," said Dana, holding the camera where both she and Hunt could view the tiny screen.

"Hmmm, yeah. Not a great picture, but I can see the writing."

"Let me see if there's a better example."

Dana flicked through until she found a shot that clearly displayed the writing. Milton had obviously added additional lighting in order to better reveal the text, perhaps shining a flashlight onto the thing.

"Interesting," said Dana. "I'm not a linguist, but that resembles no alphabet I've ever seen."

"I bet that text is even older than Pig Latin," offered Hunt with a grin.

Dana sighed. Sometimes Hunt didn't know when to avoid bad humor. "Curious," said Dana as she squinted in an attempt to better view the script. It was very precise. Even though the characters were unfamiliar, Dana could recognize that the penmanship was delicate and exact, stylish even. Perhaps the ancient world's version of calligraphy.

"Is that some sort of ink?" asked Hunt. "Or is that carved into the bone?"

"Neither. Look at the borders of the characters. I believe this may have been burned into the surface."

"How does someone even do that? That script is tiny. In today's terms, probably no bigger than an eight font."

"I have no answer for that."

And Dana didn't. This was a true anomaly. The whys and hows continued to tally and there were no clear answers to be found.

It was then that they heard another sound, the clatter of shifting stones. Both turned just in time to see two legs disappearing over the mound of stone at the exit. "Someone was in here," said Hunt as he raced across the room. "Hey! Hey you! Get back here!"

Almost diving onto the stones, Hunt scrambled up the shifting pile and then inched over the narrow opening at the crest, disappearing from view. Dana followed closely, but by the time she'd begun to creep through, she heard Hunt's voice in the darkness beyond.

"No go, hon. I heard him race off to the right. But its pitch black out here. No way I can chase him. We're going to need a light source when we leave this place."

Dana nodded, retreating back down the shifting slope. "We could use some of the phosphorescent stones," she suggested.

Hunt scrambled back through. It was a very tight fit, nearly too tight. "I have no idea who that was," he said as he reached level ground. "Not Cook, definitely. But, someone was in here watching us."

"No. Not Cook," agreed Dana. "He wouldn't have sealed himself in with us. We'll need to be very alert. This thing is getting a bit dodgy."

Hunt smiled. "Yeah. Dodgy. I guess you could say that." He paused, glancing in the direction of Milton and then back to Dana. "Okay. Let's hang onto the camera. I'm sure those pictures will come in handy. But for now, we need to get back on task." He turned, gazing toward the pile of rubble. "Everything ties to that skull," he added. "And Andy Lindell's still missing – and presumably in possession of the skull. In my book, that means he's still in danger."

"Missing, yes. But, not kidnapped as we'd been led to believe. Doctor Milton saw Andrew here in this cave. Apparently the lad fled, leaving Milton behind and slipping into coma."

"Yeah, Not the best etiquette. My concern is Cook. He's very afraid of something having to do with the skull and doesn't want word of it to get out. It appears he burned his entire base camp and nearly everyone in it in order to keep this find a secret. There's no doubt he's hot on Andy's trail." Hunt paused, gazing at the tight space they would need to crawl through in order to escape, and then back at the inert Milton. "There's Cook and then whoever just slipped out of here. It's imperative that we're the first to find Andy. We've got to get moving."

"And Milton?" asked Dana though she was fairly well certain she knew the response.

"I'm afraid he's going to have to stay put for now. There's no way we can drag him through that jagged gap without doing him serious damage or safely carry him through the darkness and up the winding grade. Here, at least, he's relatively safe. I'll contact Lucky Lindell and ask him to task a team to get him out."

Dana nodded. She abhorred the idea of leaving the man behind, but what option did she have? And what of the others? There were dozens of living people in this chamber. She and Hunt had no means to aid any of them. This whole thing had turned horrible and she was certain it would get much worse before long.

She had no idea how right she was.

Chapter 17

Jonathan Thorpe and his two companions crouched hidden behind a row of tall spindly trees, drenched and cold from the recent rain, as the Huntingtons exited the cave, weary and bedraggled. The question at hand: should they continue to trail the two adventurers or investigate the cave for themselves?

Thorpe's objective had nothing to do with the Huntingtons, per se. None, beyond the fact that Dana and her husband sought the man believed to have taken the skull. As such, they could potentially lead him directly to his goal. But, Thorpe didn't relish relying on Dana and her simian husband to do his investigative work. His own skills were rather astounding and he had difficulty believing that these two could be as efficient as he. Still, Dana was a talented individual and the Amazon rainforest was more than slightly askew of his customary haunts. If there was something to learn in that cave, likely she would have uncovered it. Enhancing his investigation by observing theirs was not the worst option.

As such, he'd slashed the Hummer's tires, ensuring that the two would be on foot and thus easily trailed. The vehicle had belonged to the scientist, Milton, he knew, but rightly assumed that the Huntingtons would attempt to utilize it. Strange that Milton was not present, though. That, in itself, might warrant investigating the cave. Milton was likely connected to Lindell and thus the skull.

"I don't see the skull," whispered Tina Collins, the female "bodyguard" as-signed to him by the client. Simon Haas, the male, stood behind them, silent and brooding. The lumbering Aussie made Thorpe feel uncomfortable. He simply couldn't get a true read on Haas. And in his experience, this more often than not led to unpleasant surprises.

"No, my dear," said Thorpe in reply to Collins' statement. "I'd be amazed if they'd found it that easily. Dana's carrying the same backpack as when they entered the cave and otherwise they've added nothing."

"Well, darlin', it could be in the backpack."

Thorpe shrugged. This woman wasn't thinking things through. A common aliment to those of common stock, he supposed. "Ah, well, you see, that's where you fail to consider the situation. No one with half a fraction of an IQ would cram a priceless artifact into an already brimming backpack."

Collins snorted. "A simple, 'No. I don't think so,' would have done the trick." And then she added with a sly smile, "You really do have quite a high opinion of yourself, don't you, Johnny?"

Oh, this was going to be a long and terribly miserable experience.

"My, apologies, dear lady. No offense intended. And why must you insist on referring to me as Johnny?"

"Why, darlin'," she smiled that luscious smile. "Because it irks you so."

Thorpe sighed and then watched as Dana and Hunt made their way to the Jeep, discovered the flattened tires, chatted a bit, and then moved to beyond their view. "Now," he said. "I suggest we follow the Huntingtons. We can use our equipment to listen to their conversations from a distance and, with luck, determine what they've learned. If need be, we'll return to the cave once we've determined the Huntington's next move."

"I'll inspect the cave now," said Haas in a rare font of verbiage.

"Ah! Well, you see, I've been put in charge of this little holiday, and I believe the best option is to eavesdrop on their conversation in order to learn a thing or two. After which, we can determine the value in returning to the cave."

Hass simply stared at Thorpe, the barest hint of a grin on his broad thin lips, a subtle air of contempt in his dark eyes.

What was Haas thinking? The client had clearly placed Thorpe at the head of the expedition. Haas and Collins were merely the muscle behind him.

Or were they?

There was something about the Aussie, something that had nettled Thorpe from the beginning. The silent brooding had led Thorpe to believe the man a dullard, but perhaps he'd been a tad quick with his assessment. Haas was the client's man. Much more so than was Thorpe, who was merely contracted on a per assignment basis. Could it be that these two had a second agenda, one not known to Thorpe? Did the client have a purpose here beyond locating an old bone for his bizarre collection? Suddenly, it seemed this was more than a possibility, but a likelihood. Thorpe was being used. For what, he couldn't be sure. But he was of an intelligent sort. He'd figure it out. Perhaps, if he played this just so, he'd finally have something on the mysterious client, some piece of leverage to be brought out at an appropriate time. Thorpe did not like being played for a dupe, but, oh, he did love turning the tables.

"Listen," he said after a moment's pause. "Thanks to Mr. Hass's brilliant insight, a new plan has come to mind. Tina, you reconnoiter the couple – I'm assuming they won't travel too far distant at night without so much as a flash-light – while Haas and I investigate the cave. I believe our needs will be best served in this manner."

Thorpe didn't really like the idea of leaving the woman alone in the forest, but there was something about Haas. Thorpe in no way desired to leave the man unattended for any length of time, especially in a place where true clues might be found. Collins was a cocky little southern belle soldier girl. She'd be fine.

*****

Unlike the Huntingtons, who had lost most of their supplies when their Jeep tumbled off a cliff, Thorpe and his companion were much better equipped, and thus, much more able to navigate the ink black cave with little difficulty. Thorpe had been using night vision gear for several years now, and often wondered how thieves of the past had gotten on so well without it. They hadn't, he supposed. Many had been caught simply because some nosy neighbor had noticed a flashlight beam flitting about someone's supposedly-empty home.

They made the chamber in just under twenty minutes. It was a difficult entry at best. Hunt had cleared out enough stone for an adult sized figure to wriggle over, but many of the stones were jagged and the cave ceiling was hard and uncompromising. It was impossible to squeeze through the space without some manner of rip, tear, or scrape and Thorpe almost decided against the venture, thinking that perhaps the Huntingtons had been deterred at this same spot, but there was that eerie glow coming from within, and this simply begged investiga-tion. Besides, Haas, though silent, showed no inclination toward aborting the effort and Thorpe wasn't about to allow him to investigate the cave alone. Keeping an eye on the one who was keeping an eye on him, he mused. Peculiar world, this.

Removing his night vision goggles upon entering the cavern, Thorpe stood in awe. The shimmering phosphorescent stones were nearly hypnotizing with the various shades of pink and green. Beautiful, really.

And then, of course, there were the bodies.

As with the Huntingtons, Thorpe's first impression was that they were dead. It was Haas's actions which brought him to the realization that something was particularly unnatural here – beyond the obvious, that is.

The large Aussie surveyed the room and nodded approvingly with an overt smile. It was almost as if he'd expected this scene. Marching to the nearest body, he retrieved a penlight from his breast pocket and pulled an eyelid open, flashing the light onto and then away from the eye. He repeated the process with the opposite eye.

"The pupils will be non-responsive," said Thorpe. "These people are obviously dead."

Haas moved to the next slab saying, "Your job is to locate the skull. I'll tend to this."

"May I remind you that…"

"Zip it, mate. You've got your orders. I've got mine. Now, run along and find your little skull."

Well, so much for subterfuge. Haas had just vocalized that which Thorpe had suspected. There was more than one mission, and Thorpe had been kept in the dark. This nettled at him, but he suppressed the urge to scowl. Instead, he asked, "Who are these people? How did they come to be here? And why are you treating them as if they're alive."

"Need to know, mate. And you don't need to know."

"Well, that's…"

"That's all you're getting." He made a quarter turn, staring into Thorpe with those crisp dark eyes. "Listen, I have no issue with you. So, let me do what I've come to do."

Thorpe nodded. "Right, right. My apologies."

Well, well, well, what an interesting turn of events. Thorpe could act contrite, but he was not one to be sidelined. Already he was thinking through alternatives and options. He and Haas would have it out, he was certain of that.

But he need be careful. This client, this very peculiar client, paid quite handsomely. And so, yes, Thorpe might need to endure some nonsense, but it wasn't worth aggravating the situation. And so, he began scanning the area in search of clues to the skull's whereabouts. He felt an eerie chill creep up his back as he made his way through the rows and rows of slabs. Blank, deathly faces all about him, mouths slightly agape, arms crossed at the chest, each dressed in clothing from another place and time. He wondered how they'd come to be here, what this all meant, and what connection the client might have to it all.

And then he discovered Milton.

The two had never met, but Thorpe had seen him from a distance. He'd followed the Huntingtons as the Huntingtons followed Milton. And now here he was, laid out like the rest. His dark chocolate features relaxed and still, his large mouth opened only slightly, his eyes closed, head cocked ever so slightly to the left.

Dead?

It appeared so.

But now he was beginning to wonder.

Thorpe had been keeping a surreptitious eye on Haas and found that the man had been taking both blood and tissue samples, as well as collecting hair fibers and fingernail clippings. Something very peculiar was at hand, and yet, for the moment at least, Thorpe felt powerless to pursue the enigma.

Well, enough, he supposed. Thorpe was a patient man. In time, he would learn what needed to be learned. Haas might not be the dullard he'd first assumed, but he was no Jonathan Thorpe either.

As to Milton, Thorpe had the queer feeling that the man yet lived. There was no overt sign, but he just seemed... not dead.

Eventually, Thorpe did feel for, and then discover, the pulse, but this did not detour him from searching the man's pockets. Surely, there was a clue somewhere here to be found.

It took a few minutes, and Thorpe was nearly ready to relinquish the attempt, but then he came across a small piece of yellow paper shoved to within a pocket within a pocket in the man's pants. Unfolding it quickly, he read it over twice. And it was only then that his lips curled into a broad and joyful grin.

Chapter 18

The Huntingtons spent the remainder of the night beneath the canopy created by a copse of squat and leafy trees. Fortunately, the thunderstorm had passed. There were still occasional spurts of precipitation, but for the most part they were able to remain fairly dry. Hunt took the first watch and Dana the second. But, Hunt was by nature an earlier riser and accomplished little more than two hours sleep. Aside from insects, they had no direct encounters with wildlife, though they could hear nearly continuous movement about them. The place was teeming with life: various reptiles and primates, each unique in its own fashion, colorful birds floating effortlessly just below the treetops some two hundred feet above. Amazing. A person could spend a lifetime here and not see all the variations there were to see. Hunt made a mental note to return one day when he could appreciate the place simply for the experience.

It was only now just after five AM and Hunt had already contacted Lucky Lindell, updating him on the search for Andy and requesting that a team be sent to investigate the mysterious cave and its even more peculiar occupants. Even this close to the cell tower at Kutu, it had been difficult to get reception, but Hunt had found that once he'd climbed to the top of the nearest rise, he was able to accomplish the task. Lucky had sounded disheartened that Hunt had not yet found his boy, but Hunt had renewed his pledge to find Andy and bring him home safely. Andy might be caught up in some serious matters, but by all indications, he was still alive, and that, felt Hunt, was the primary concern.

Hunt scrutinized the green expanse before him. Ever since exiting the cave, he'd had that familiar yet peculiar feeling that they were being watched. Yet, he'd found no evidence to support the feeling. Wildlife, maybe. In a place such as this, he doubted there had been a single moment when one creature or another hadn't been spying on them.

Hunt contemplated for a moment, and then once again slipped his phone from his pocket.

"Who are you calling now?" asked Dana who had followed him up the rise and now, seated beside him, was taking an inventory of their remaining supplies.

"Eldon Troxel, the archeologist. Remember that ancient document we recovered for him awhile back? I'm thinking he might be some help."

Dana offered an "Oh, God. Not him," expression. She and Eldon were not fans of one another. "Wasn't he booted out or some such rot?"

Hunt rolled his eyes. "He... left archeology under dubious circumstances, yeah. But, he still has his brain, Dana. Might be a help with this skull thing."

Dana snorted, but offered no further objection as Hunt punched in the number. It took three attempts, but eventually Hunt managed to raise a strong enough signal to get through. Suddenly Eldon's voice was in his ear with a hearty, "Go Cubbies!"

"You answer your phone, 'Go Cubbies?'"

Hunt saw Dana roll her eyes as she muttered, "The man has about as much class as a rodent at a Buckingham Palace ball."

"It's my phone," chimed Eldon. "I'll answer it how I please. Though, I guess, this time of year, I should be plugging The Bulls. Who's calling me at the crack of dawn?"

Eldon was a unique individual. He had multiple degrees, at least two of which were doctorates of one kind or another, but he talked like a working class bleacher bum. A stranger would never know the brilliant mind hidden behind the unshaven face and cocked back baseball cap. Dana had once quipped that he was about as couth as a cockroach in a diamond. Hunt wouldn't go that far, but Eldon definitely had his own special way. "It's me, El. Marc Huntington. And yeah, it's early here too." Hunt paused for only a second. "Now that I think about it, we might even be in the same time zone. But, I'm half a world south of you."

"Hunt!" quipped Eldon with some enthusiasm. "You still with that British broad? She don't like me."

Hunt grinned and said, "Eldon says, 'hi,' hon."

"He probably called me 'that British broad.' Tell him cheers and all that."

"Dana misses you too, El. You got a moment?"

"It's what? Five, six, in the morning? You startle me outta blissful slumber. I'm awake now. Sure, I got a moment for you, Hunt. What you need?"

Dana rose, hefted her pack, and indicated that she wanted to scout the perimeter. Hunt nodded and returned his attention to Eldon. "We're in the Amazon, El. Tracking a missing paleontologist."

"The Amazon, huh? I get it. You decided to pick up a gig south of the equator where its summer. Me, I'm wearing two sweatshirts and still have my thermostat set on blast furnace."

"I wish it was voluntary, El. The son of an old friend of mine is missing. I'm trying to find the guy before he gets himself killed."

"Okay. Fair enough. Bring me up to speed and tell me how I can help."

Hunt gathered his thoughts for only a moment and then continued. "There'd been a significant find. A fossilized skull. There was debate over the age of the thing. Big ruckus. Seems these science geeks take their stuff way too seriously because people started dying and going missing."

"Got it. So, the PHDs were arguing over the dating of the find."

"Yeah, one guy said it couldn't date very old because it was the wrong kind of skull for the strata, the other said, blah, blah, blah. Now people are dead."

"Well," said Eldon. "What ya gotta understand is science ain't always exactly so scientific. Ya got all these PHDs standing around trying ta stay funded and make a name for themselves. To do that, they've gotta discover something significant. So, they find a skull, or a femur, maybe a medieval Rolls Royce. You'd think they'd just send it off to a lab, have it dated and that would be that."

"I'm guessing it's not."

"Nah! These guys, they know what date they want, so they find a lab that'll give them that date. It' kinda like the mortgage industry leading up to the recession. They knew how much they'd want a house to go for, so they'd find an appraiser that'd give them that number. Now, they're not all that way, but even under ideal circumstances, dating's a dicey deal. A lot of it's subjective, left to interpretation and assumption."

Hunt nodded, though Eldon couldn't see this. "One of the paleontologists was afraid that if the skull was dated the wrong way, it would screw up all of their evolutionary assumptions."

"Well, hey. There's your motive for murder. But, listen. You're talking paleontology, here. I'm an archeologist. Not sure how much help I can offer."

"There's ancient writing on the inside of the skull."

"'Scuse me?"

"Writing on the inner cranium. And get this, a couple of guys who've had contact with the skull have died, apparently incinerated from the inside out. Another has slipped into... I don't know what to call it. A kind of suspended animation. There's dozens of others like this, all lined up in a cavern on slabs. And each is dressed as if from another place and time throughout world history. Very weird."

"Hunt, you did not wake me up just for some wacko practical joke, did ya?"

"Telling no lies, El. I've got digital photos of the writing from the inside of the skull. Care to take a stab at the translation?"

"Translate ancient writing from the inside of a prehistoric skull? How could I pass on an opportunity like that?"

"Good, El. And thanks. My phone's got email capabilities. I'll pop the pics off to you. Obviously, the sooner you can get back to me, the better. Supposedly, the writing contains some kind of cure for the comatose crew. Aside from that, I'm not sure exactly how this is going to help me find my guy, but the more I know about this crazy skull, the better idea I'll have of what he might be thinking. At least that's the hot theory."

The two said heir goodbyes. Hunt immediately sent the entire folder taken from Milton's camera. He'd just pressed "send" when he heard Dana's screams.

Chapter 19

Dana made her way down the gentle slope and away from Hunt. She wanted to scout the area in the daylight, perhaps take a look at the cave entrance, investigate the contents of Milton's Hummer. With luck there would be some sort of clue in the glove box, or perhaps taped under a seat – some such cloak and dagger nonsense. According to Milton, Andrew Lindell had been at the cave. Were there footprints or tire tracks that could be followed? She wanted to investigate these as well. That is, assuming these had not been washed away by the rain. And who had slashed the Hummer's tires? Lindell? Perhaps. Maybe he had been trying to stop Milton from giving chase. But if that was the case, why slash the tires? Milton was immobilized. He could have simply taken the car keys from him. But, the keys had still been in Milton's pocket. She and Hunt had confiscated them for their own use.

And what of Cook?

He would be an obvious choice for a culprit. Slashing the tires could have been an attempt to slow pursuit. That, she supposed, made the best sense.

But, the man himself. He'd been thought dead. Obviously, this wasn't the case, so whose body had been mistakenly identified as Cook's? Another scientist, she supposed. And what of the body in Andrew Lindell's motel room; like those at the expedition, burned as if from the inside out? Dana's guess was that this was the motel manager, simply an innocent victim to whatever insanity was on a rage.

And what was the insanity? What exactly was happening? The expedition site burned at excessive but short-lived temperatures, all occupants dead. Couple that with the dozens of people lying in some queer suspended animation within a cavern. There had to be some logical – some scientific – explanation for it all.

Making her way to the Hummer, she first inspected the tires. All four slashed. The incisions were perhaps four inches in length and punctured clear through. Not jagged as if someone had struggled with the task. The blade used would have had to have been quite sharp to penetrate so cleanly and the arm wielding it strong enough to slice in one uninterrupted slash.

Not the slight and nervous Cook, she thought. No. Definitely not Cook.

But, then who? The mysterious third party from the cave? The man who had slipped out while she and Hunt were with Milton? Quite possibly.

Dana checked the glove box. Empty. Not even registration or insurance documents. Peculiar, that. She inspected under the seats and in the back of the cab. Nothing of note. Aside from the missing registration information, the vehicle was just as it had been when Dana and Hunt had ridden with Milton to Kutu. There were two canvass sacks containing gear from the dig site, as well as the supplies Milton had purchased during his previous trip only hours before. All was in order, nothing out of the ordinary.

Dana slowly made her way around the Hummer in an attempt to make out footprints on the leafy ground. There were broken stems, a partial print here and there in the few spots where dirt was visible. But, the spot was so overgrown with vegetation that it was difficult for Dana to determine if six people had walked around the vehicle or only one. Maybe Hunt could make sense of it all. That was more his line of expertise than hers.

Dana hesitated.

Had she just heard something?

Well, yes, of course she'd heard something. The rainforest was awash with the constant chirps and chatters of wildlife. But, this was something different. Something human. A sneeze. Dana knew full well that animals sneezed as well. But, her instinct told her that this was not a beast. She couldn't have given an explanation as to why she thought this, but it settled firmly in her mind none-the-less. And, there. A rustle. Still distant. Now, a large blue and red bird rose from the direction of the sound and fluttered away. The bird could have caused the sound, she supposed, but no. That sneeze had not originated with any bleeding parrot.

Pretending not to have noticed, she continued her inspection, now moving toward the cave entrance. She didn't venture within – she still had no flashlight, and the cave would be as dark during daylight hours as at night – but instead studied the ground about the entrance. Despite the recent rainfall, she could still identify several sets off footprints. But they were all atop one another and she could determine nothing other than that there had been recent foot traffic. Very recent, if she were to think about it. Because she did not see the prints she and Hunt had made when entering the cave, only those made on their retreat. The others had been washed away by the rain.

Ah, this was peculiar.

Dana was able to identify her own footprints, smaller than the rest, as she was a female. But a few feet off, not directly in front of the cave, and set amidst the confused mix of prints, was another such set. Smaller than the rest by several sizes. But, the imprint was different than the one given by Dana's boot, the tread having a block pattern where Dana's was zigzag. Another female had been here. And recently – since the rainfall. Who might that have been and what was her connection? Dana had to assume this woman was connected to the man who had been hiding in the cavern. But then, she had no notion as to who that might be either.

Ah! There again.

A sound.

A different sound. Separate from nature, or so it seemed.

Was that a voice she'd heard?

Pretending to continue her inspection, Dana turned slowly right, acting as though she was studying the ground, while in fact, she was scanning the scene to her west. She took a step, then another, and another, scrutinizing the ground, and eying the area perhaps thirty meters forward. At first she saw nothing. It seemed all was as it should be. But then there was a flurry of movement as several birds took flight simultaneously. There was a rustle of brush.

And then they were there.

Several men baring weapons. Villagers by the look of them. Yes, villagers. There was the constable they'd met the day before. And beside him, that little weasel Cook.

Now in the open, all need for subterfuge evaporated, and the group bolted forward as one. Dana turned, fleeing toward where she and Hunt had spent the night. "Hunt!" she hollered, hoping to give him forewarning. "Hunt! Men with guns! It seems we're not welcome here!"

Dana leapt over a low row of thorny brush and angled right, now sprinting full on, fan-like leaves smacking her face and hands. She nearly tripped, but righted herself. A small dark animal, perhaps a young boar, scurried out of her path. There was shouting from behind, mostly in Portuguese. The voices sounded much too close.

Allowing a quick glance back, she found that three of the men – seven in total, she now counted – had managed to separate from the pack, and were closing in on her.

"Hunt! We're under attack!" she shouted again, and then cut left down a slope leading to a tiny stream. The ground was an uneven mixture of leaves and mud, and Dana essentially hopped down the way, angling slightly to the left, for risk of falling into a tumbling roll.

The lead man was close now, only a few meters behind. He seemed more capable in this terrain than she. No surprise, that. This was home territory for the bloke.

Now, she cut right, left, right, zigzagging in an effort to confuse the man.

It didn't work. He was only seconds from reaching her when Hunt appeared as from nowhere, tackling the villager with a flying leap that sent both men tumbling the few meters to the bottom of the grade and into the puddle-deep stream. The man's gun went off with a booming report, scattering wildlife and causing everyone to pause momentarily, most, inspecting themselves for injury. Everyone had been within firing range.

The pause was momentary at best. Dana ducked and swirled, right leg extended, sweeping counterclockwise and sending the nearest assailant face down into the brush. Nearly leaping backwards, she elbow jabbed another, and then managed a roundhouse kick to the next villager. But, she was off balance, the kick feeble, and he was able to snatch her foot, pulling sharply upward, sending her clumsily to the ground.

The last thing Dana saw before being pulled roughly to her feet and held at gunpoint was Hunt's inert form lying face down in the trickling stream.

Chapter 20

Bloomington Indiana
17 years ago

Hunt wasn't a frat boy but Moose Mulligan was. And so, Hunt usually managed to weasel his way into most of the frat parties. Hunt and Moose had become close friends after the incident in Turkey Run State Park. Coach Haller had declared that if not for Hunt, Mulligan would have surely died. Something about a life and death experience creates an impenetrable bond that no one can severe, and so the boys found themselves almost immediately inseparable. After high school, the two went off to Indiana University together and were roommates their freshman year. The following semester, Moose joined the Acacia fraternity. Hunt wasn't a fan of the Greek system and remained a "dorm rat," as Moose called him. But it was all in fun. Mulligan would never have allowed one of his frat brothers to call Hunt by this same name.

Moose no longer fit his nickname. In the months following the near drowning, he had lost over sixty pounds. The connection was that Moose determined to learn to swim, and soon thereafter began working out with the local age group swim team. He was a senior, and it was too late for him to join the high school team and compete, but on the age group team he was able to start off with some of the younger swimmers and work his way up. He actually had a knack for it and, given another year or so, might have become quite good. Soon he was swimming better than three thousand yards per day and could finish the 100 yard freestyle in fifty-seven seconds. Far from record breaking status, but very solid for a guy who couldn't stay above water a few months prior. Add to this his growing spurt, and the formerly chunky Moose became tall, nearly lean, and very fit. He was athletic, had a good sense of humor, but, largely due to his former weight issues, remained uncomfortable with girls.

For his part, due to his ankle injury, Hunt had been forced to sit out on athletics for the remainder of high school, but continued to pump iron throughout his recovery. As soon as his ankle was healed sufficiently, he began running the local bike route. It was a twelve mile loop, snaking through the town, and Hunt started with a three mile stretch, and soon worked his way up to a daily six. Twice a month he would run the entire twelve mile loop. The ankle still gave him some pain, mostly when he tried to ice skate. It seemed balancing on a thin blade put a bit too much stress on the joint, but otherwise, Hunt was as good as new. He hadn't played football competitively since his freshman year in high school, but since hockey was no longer an option, he tried out for the football team as a college freshman and somehow eked onto the team where his position was running back.

It was a Friday night, mid October, Hunt's sophomore year, and he'd made a couple of significant plays in this week's game. Coach Duncan had said that if he kept it up, he might get a chance at a starting position as a junior. Hunt was feeling good. And Moose was at his side. It was a typical Friday night at the frat house. Most of the guys were drunk or nearly so, there were about fifty percent less girls than guys present, and nearly every guy was looking to get lucky – the vast majority would not succeed.

Hunt and Moose were fairly far gone. Hunt found a particular freedom in alcohol and enjoyed "getting loose" as he called it. Moose was telling a joke about a chicken farmer. After detailing how the guy had purchased the farm, the chickens, and the feed, yet still had no success with the chickens, Moose concluded with the farmer telling his wife, "I can't figure out if I planted them too deep or too close together." There were groans and laughs. Moose was always a big hit at the parties. Too bad he froze up around women. They obviously liked him.

Moose was launching into another joke, this one about a traveling salesman, a nun, and a hound dog, when Hunt caught Tricia Lyons' eye. They had Sociology 210 together and had fallen into a low level, but mutual, ongoing flirtation. Hunt left Moose to his jokes and made his way to where Tricia stood chatting with two friends. She was slender, with long brown hair combed straight and cut with bangs. She had wire rimmed glasses and the cutest smile he could imagine. "Hey," said Hunt as he approached the group of girls.

"Hi," said Tricia with a giggle and smile. "I didn't know you were a frat boy."

Hunt shrugged. "I'm not. A good friend of mine is, though."

"You were good in the game tonight."

"You saw me? I was only on the field for three plays."

She cocked her head. "I saw you."

Both fell into an awkward silence. After a moment Hunt said, "Want some fresh air?"

She did, and they retreated outside, Hunt grabbing another Budweiser on the way. They sat on the front steps of the house and talked mostly about nothing: football, Sociology class, annoying siblings and even more annoying professors. The air was cool and fresh, the leaves a golden carpet on the gently sloping lawn. The moon was nearly full, the sky cloudless. And Tricia somehow became more beautiful by the minute.

At some point, Hunt wrapped his arm around her, and soon they were kissing – her initiative, not his. They held the kiss long, neither wanting to break the spell. Her tongue darted into his mouth. He responded in kind, tentatively at first, but soon with building enthusiasm. Hunt was fairly well buzzed, yet still had the sense to be nervous. Was this the beginning of a relationship, a one night stand, or simply necking on the front porch? What should be his next move? What was she expecting? And, most importantly, what would be the worst thing he could do right now?

Tentatively, he began to slip his hand under her sweater and to move it slowly up her abdomen toward her breast. She gently pulled the hand away with a smile and a giggle. Hunt didn't know if she'd done this because she didn't want him touching her, or because she didn't want him touching her while they were in such a public place. Bad move on his part. Somewhere in the back of his head it occurred to him that he might have had too much alcohol to think clearly about such things, but that voice was tiny and distant. He tried again a couple of minutes later with the same result.

Eventually, Hunt said, "Do you want to go someplace more private? I'm sure Moose would let us use his room, or we could go to mine, but it's on the other side of the campus."

She smiled at him and kissed his lips gently. "This is private enough for now." And then she kissed him long and hard. He didn't mind. In truth, this was far less complicated than going to a room. No expectations, no real chance that he might assume something that was not intended.

As it turned out, it would have been better if they'd gone to a room.

About fifteen minutes later, Joe Hackney discovered them on the steps, still in passionate embrace. Joe was Tricia's ex-boyfriend. Somehow, he'd failed to comprehend the "ex" part of the equation. Joe was accompanied by two friends. Hunt didn't know Joe, but was vaguely acquainted with one of the friends, Warren Bedotto. They'd had one class together freshman year, psychology. All three were drunk, Hackney, belligerently so.

"What the hell you doin' with my girl, creep?" he nearly shouted.

Hunt had barely noticed the three approaching and only then looked up. There were constantly people coming and going through the frat house doorway or walking down the sidewalk. Hunt hadn't given them a second thought until Hackney spoke.

Glancing up at this new complication, Hunt said, "Who are you and what are you talking about?"

"Oh God, Joe. Leave us alone," said Tricia as she pulled free of Hunt's embrace. This angered him. The girl was truly beautiful and she obviously wanted him. Who was this idiot, and didn't he know when to leave a guy alone?

Hackney was a wiry kid of about five ten and looked to be a couple of years older than Hunt. With the rolled shoulders of an accountant and Billy Idol hair ten years out of style, he somehow managed to appear simultaneously old and young. Hunt stood to face his newfound adversary. He'd been comfortably mellow, but the sudden surge of adrenaline made him want to smash the guys face in. "You're her boyfriend?" asked Hunt as he stepped forward, fist clenched.

"Yeah. I am. Who are you?"

Hunt ignored the question. "Tricia, is this guy your boyfriend?"

Tricia was up now, standing to the right rear of Hunt. "No. I mean, we dated a little. It was never a thing."

"Doesn't sound like you meet the boyfriend qualifications – *Joe*," said Hunt, using the name he'd heard Tricia use. He put his arm around her, probably a bit too presumptively. She pulled away.

"You're not my boyfriend either, Marc."

"Hey, I didn't mean anything by it," said Hunt. "I was just trying to lose this ugly jerk."

"Trish, we need to talk," said Hackney, now stepping forward.

Hunt gave him a sharp push at the shoulder. "Back off, Joe. She doesn't want to talk with you."

"Marc! Leave him alone." It was Tricia, obviously perturbed. This angered Hunt further. Things had been going so well.

"Listen, Joe. You're not wanted here."

Hunt stepped squarely between Tricia and Joe. Until now, Hackney's two friends had remained in the background. Sensing the mounting tension, they stepped forward to flank him on either side.

"I think it's you that should leave," said Hackney. "You're drunk."

Hunt never knew why he did it. He should have backed off, made a joke, and then tried to reconnect with Tricia another time. Obviously the magic of the evening had dissipated and things could only get worse from here. But, he wasn't thinking too clearly just then. A dangerous cocktail of hormones, adrenaline, and alcohol raced through his system and before he knew what he was doing, he'd launched himself at Hackney.

They landed on the leaf-covered lawn, Hunt atop Hackney, fists flaying wildly. Hackney's friends tried to pull him off, but Hunt was as a mad man. There was no skill, no technique; Hunt was fueled by irrational fury alone. Yet, nearly every blow hit true.

He was aware of blood – his or Hackney's he was unsure. There was an almost imperceptible crunch as he connected with the older student's face. He felt a jab to his gut, and a knee to the groin. Still, he persisted, no clear goal in mind, no rational thought invading his fury-filled brain, he simply pressed on.

They tumbled and rolled, Hackney getting in a few good shots, but Hunt's wild abandon gave him the upper hand. He was vaguely aware of other voices, cries of "Fight! Fight!" from all around. Hackney's friends continued to try to intervene and at some point Hunt discovered that Moose had joined the fray, taking on these two alone. The end result was a broken nose for Hackney, while Hunt was expelled from the school for under aged drinking and assault and battery. Moose received a suspension and ended up repeating the semester. Hunt would never return.

Chapter 21

The yellow slip of paper Thorpe had pulled from Gregory Milton's pocket contained a location and a time. The location was an inn located in a small outpost, not even a proper village, roughly fifteen miles southwest of Kutu. The time was this very day, eleven AM. Andrew Lindell's name was nowhere on the note, nor was there any overt indication that he was the person to be met. But, Thorpe had a theory. Well, a hunch at least.

Suppose Milton and Lindell had been in this thing together. Suppose they had planned to meet briefly at the cave. Lindell would move along to the next stop – this tiny community away from the investigation, yet near enough for same day travel between. Milton would remain behind for a day, attempting to misdirect the Huntingtons and any other prying eyes. But, something happened in there. Milton was somehow infected by whatever strange ailment had attacked the dozens of others in that chamber. Lindell panicked and fled. Thorpe couldn't blame the lad, really. It was a bizarre infliction and one with unsettling implications.

Thorpe knew he might not be quite solid on the details, but felt that the overall assumption – that Milton and Lindell had planned a meet – was sound. He knew this was entirely based on supposition, but Thorpe had built his career on less. He had a knack for connecting seemingly disconnected fragments and finding that they were all part of a greater whole.

As it turned out, he'd been correct.

Andrew Lindell was there for the meet. And while Milton failed to show, Thorpe and his two companions were there to keep him company.

Pacing back and forth in the small stuffy room, Thorpe gazed down upon the young man. Lindell could be no more than thirty years old, most likely younger, perhaps twenty-seven or twenty-eight. He had tousled brown hair, peach fuzz whiskers, and pudgy cheeks still clinging to the last vestiges of baby fat. He was not obese, but nor was he trim. He carried just enough extra cush to confirm that this man spent far more time in front of a computer screen than he had in any vigorous activity. It surprised Thorpe that he was the product of a military upbringing. Clearly young Lindell had not sought to follow in his father's footsteps.

Currently, Lindell sat in a wooden chair situated in the center of the room he'd rented at the inn. More of a shack, really. The entire outpost community consisted of only six buildings, none of which appeared to have the fortitude to withstand a hefty wind. Collins and Haas stood guard just inside the door, though there was no need, really. Thorpe could handle this baby faced egghead alone. In fact, he'd prefer to do so. Haas, in particular, had become a concern. The more Thorpe considered the events in the cave, the more he realized how little he cared for his current situation. Collins, for the most part, seemed to be just as advertised – strictly a support person, but Haas had a different set of marching orders. He'd collected tissue and blood samples from several of the comatose persons in the cave, placing each of these in plastic containers of the type used in hospitals and laboratories for keeping substances sterile.

The only logical explanation was that Haas had known about the bodies beforehand. Obviously, he had received this information from the client. So then, how had the client come to this knowledge? And what was his interest in dozens of comatose persons?

But, his interest wasn't in the persons themselves, was it?

No. The client sought to understand the cause of their state, maybe even to collect, through blood samples, the actual agent which caused the condition. Somehow, Thorpe doubted the man had humanitarian designs for this amazing find. Thorpe was not exactly a good will ambassador, but he in no way wanted to be involved in terrorist activity, and that, it seemed, might be exactly where this was headed. Wouldn't a substance, whether viral, bacterial, or some other unknown, that could place large numbers of people into deep coma be a frightful weapon?

And so, Thorpe turned toward the two guards and stepped in their direction, speaking to them in a lowered tone. "I'm going to interrogate the lad. He seems the sheepish type. Not hardened military. He's already nervous and twitchy. I believe our purposes would be best served should I interview him alone."

"I'll remain," said Haas.

"No. I think not," said Thorpe. "My dear man, you are a frightening sight. I tremble right now, just standing beside you." Thorpe let off a mock shiver, exaggerating his sarcasm. "I'm, shall we say, a gentler soul. He's more likely to open up if it's he and I alone."

"I need to report to the client."

"And you shall. Of course you shall. Report away. Have at it. But, do remember, I am the one tasked with locating the skull. Whatever additional assignment you might have is between you and our employer, but this he gave to me. Now, if the two of you would please retire to the opposite side of the door, I shall proceed."

Collins seemed to contemplate for a moment and then gave a subtle chuckle, whacked Haas playfully on the bicep, and said, "Come on, big guy. Johnny's probably got a point. You are an ugly S.O.B." She offered Thorpe an almost imperceptible nod and then turned to the door, opened it, and stepped outside. Haas held Thorpe's gaze for a moment before following his companion.

"Brilliant," muttered Thorpe as he closed the door behind them. "Bloody brilliant."

Next, he moved toward Lindell, in the process, snatching a ladder-backed wooden chair from beside a small fold-up card table. Placing the chair backward in front of Lindell, he straddled it, resting his elbows on the chair back, and his chin on his two balled fists. "Care for a spot of water?" he asked. "I've my canteen handy."

Lindell shook his head slowly, but remained silent.

"My name is Jonathan."

Still, Lindell did not speak.

Thorpe offered a smile and a nod. "Fair enough, I suppose." He paused for a moment, studying the man, just getting a feel for him before proceeding further. Finally, he said, "Well then, Andrew. It seems we have matters to discuss."

"Do we?" asked Lindell, his mouth creating somewhat of a puckered twist that reminded Thorpe of a goldfish pained with indigestion.

Thorpe grinned at the thought. "Ah yes, well we do, I suppose, need to speak. Now, I understand this is inconvenient, and well, I don't quite blame you for being perturbed, but the situation is what it is. That being, I have been tasked with retrieving the fossil known as the Amazon skull, and you are the last known person to possess said piece. As such, this conversation can be quite short and painless, if you were to simply share with me the skull's location."

"I don't have it."

Thorpe snapped his fingers enthusiastically. "Now, you see, that I'd already determined. We have, after all, inspected your vehicle as well as this entire hovel. Bit smutty here. Not exactly five star. Took us all of, what, two minutes to go over the entire place?"

"If you know it's not here, then what is there to talk about?" Lindell looked a bit dreamy, maybe not quite well. He was obviously trying to play it smooth, but Thorpe noticed the slight quiver in his hand.

"Listen, Andrew – do you mind that I call you Andrew? We know you were in possession of the skull. Seems there were plenty of witnesses to that. Oh, right! But, they're all dead! Care to comment on that particular situation?"

Lindell remained silent. His head cocked slightly to the left, eyes rheumy.

"Right. Didn't think so." Thorpe stared at the young man for another long moment and then said, "Andrew, are you alright? You look rather ill."

Again, no response.

"Well, it seems I'm having a bit of a one-sided conversation." Thorpe scooted his chair forward to where he was only inches from Lindell's face. "Listen," he said in a low tone. "You and I are adversaries, I know that full well. But, believe me when I tell you, I am not the worst of it. There's a man just beyond that door who would not hesitate to break you in two should he believe it would further his goal."

Lindell offered a wry grin. "Good cop, bad cop, huh?"

"No, no, no, no, no. There, you see, you're quite wrong. We are not cops, and this is no game. I, myself, am not entirely comfortable with the current situation, but I'm rather adept at maneuvering through such waters. You, my young man, are a scientist. I find it difficult to believe that you could handle Haas out there. Personally, I'd rather there be no need we find out."

Lindell stared at him for a time before speaking. Thorpe allowed him to do so. Silence, he knew, was now his ally. Most people are uncomfortable with prolonged quiet. They feel a need to fill the vacuum, to have something happening. Often, the worst thing an interrogator can do is to break a calm such as this. Let the subject stew. Allow his nerves to jitter and jump. Eventually, he'll say something, often offering just the information needed, or, at least, nearly.

"I don't have the skull."

Thorpe nodded, offering an encouraging grin. "Go on."

Lindell bit his lip, lowered his gaze to the floor.

"Andrew, seriously, I am your best option. You do want to work with me."

Lindell's lips twisted in that gastronomically challenged goldfish look. "This specimen is of great scientific value."

Thorpe nodded.

"It belongs with people who can study it."

"I understand all of that."

"You understand, but you don't care," Lindell nearly shouted. "I don't know who you are or who you're working for, but I'm sure that if you get hold of the skull it will be lost to science."

Thorpe shrugged. "None of that changes our current situation."

Lindell leveled his gaze and blinked. Again, Thorpe had the feeling that this man was not well. "By now, it's no longer in the region."

Well, that was curious. "And what exactly do you mean by that?"

"I had it shipped."

Thorpe chuckled. "Shipped? They have shipping out here in the middle of bleeding nowhere?"

"A postal carrier comes through Kutu twice monthly. Yesterday was one of those days."

"And where, pray tell, was it shipped?"

"To a place where one would need my retina scanned in order to gain access."

Thorpe narrowed his eyes, offering a wry grin. "Nice try, there. But, you and I both know they have no such capabilities in Kutu."

"In Kutu, of course not. But at the other end, where the package is to be received…" Lindell concluded the thought with a shrug.

"You're bleeding fooling me."

Lindell merely grinned.

Thorpe offered a broad smile of his own, reached forward and gave Lindell a hearty pat on the back. "Well played, lad. Well played."

Chapter 22

Chicago Illinois

Eldon Troxel sat in the back room of his ancient treasures retail establishment, "I'm History II." He'd only just recently opened the place after the original "I'm History" had burned to the ground some months before. He still wasn't satisfied with his selection. So many of the pieces lost in the blaze were quite rare. It would take some time to reestablish what he'd once had. Fortunately, the insurance money had come through and he mostly had the means to acquire the needed items. The difficulty was that these were not the kind of things one could just hop online and order from a supplier. Eldon stocked his store with ancient artifacts found at dig sites. Whenever there's a significant dig, say an archeologist in Israel explores a tell, uncovering an ancient city, there are hundreds of day-to-day items found: coins, pottery, idols, jewelry, sometimes swords or shields. Museums and universities don't have storage space for such a plethora of relatively common pieces. These institutions keep the major finds, the truly significant articles, and then warehouse or sell the remainder. Eldon's theory was that though these pieces might be rather common to the egghead university crowd, they would make very interesting collectables for the everyday Joe.

And so this was his business, selling ancient treasures at a very reasonable price, to the general public. He'd even come across several rather unique finds along the way. And it was the loss of these that he mourned. None of this, of course, matched the thrill of being out there at the dig site, uncovering the mysteries of the past, probing into the unknown. But, Eldon had exited the field rather abruptly, severing many of his closest ties. Returning to archeology proper seemed an unlikely option. Still, it seemed curious opportunities and even outright adventures followed him even in his current modest surroundings. Enigma's such as the one he now studied for his pal, Marc Huntington.

The images had not been spectacular. Though it was obvious that whoever took the shots had realized the problem and bettered the lighting after the first few shots. But, quality photography or not, this skull was an amazing find. Eldon had already begun his research and had found that the Amazon skull had a long and storied history. He'd not been familiar with the legend. But this was not surprising. His specialty had been the Middle East, and this fossil originated in South America.

Or not.

According to the lore surrounding the skull, it had journeyed from Egypt to South America somewhere around 200 BCE. That voyage alone would have been considered fanciful and purely apocryphal by most scholars. The civilized world didn't yet know of the Americas at that early point in history.

And yet, what of the skull?

It could be argued that this was not the same skull, that perhaps there had been similar legends held by primitive people of two different continents, and that at some point, once transoceanic travel had been normalized, that these similar, but different legends had been merged into one. The logical, scientific part of his brain would agree with these assessments. And truly, logic and verifiable fact had always been the cornerstone of his belief system. But recent events had opened Eldon up to possibilities he'd have previously dismissed out of hand. This skull, he thought, might fall into that rather controversial category.

Eldon clicked on his mouse, bringing up the next image and then rose to find another sweatshirt. He envied Hunt at this moment, down in the Amazon, probably slopping on suntan lotion while Eldon sat in this drafty backroom "enjoying" a Midwest winter. Slipping a red Chicago Blackhawks sweatshirt over his head, he returned to his seat, grabbed a swig of black syrupy coffee and studied the script on the interior of the skull.

"Well, that ain't right," he muttered before clicking to the next shot and then the next. He then backtracked, viewing the first again, before splitting the screen to view three shots simultaneously. Squinting, he studied and compared each to the other. "Yeah. Okay," he said, and then scanned through several more pictures, selecting two more.

He then zoomed in on each, scribbling notes furiously on a stained yellow legal pad as he did so.

Very strange. Very.

Rising, he moved across the small cluttered room to a bookshelf on the far wall; selecting a large dusty tome, he flipped through the pages while returning to his seat. Studying the images again, he clicked the mouse, zooming even closer and selecting specific regions of the skull.

Eldon grinned. He'd identified three distinctly different language groups on the interior. All very ancient, all from regions far distant from each other. And yet, it seemed, all were written by different persons. The angles, the swoops, the spacing between characters, the points of more and of less pressure, all indicated that the same person had not penned these words. Not surprising, he supposed. During the periods when these languages were coming into use, travel was quite difficult. People groups were largely isolated. It would have been quite unusual for one person to have been fluent in two, much less all three of these tongues. Even more unusual, would be for that one individual to possess writing skills in multiple languages. Written communication would have been in its infancy.

But, why would the skull be passed from region to region and new writing added at these three geographic locales? Would the person writing the second tongue, for instance, have the ability to read the first? Would the third scribe be able to interpret the writings of the previous two? By all logic, the answer would be no. And, that being the case, what prompted the second and third authors to add to the script?

The next thing was that each script appeared to have weathered differently. This indicated great periods of time between the writing of each. One was much less distinct than the other two, implying that it might have been the first. The one he'd come to consider to be the second of the three was dimmed as well, but the edges of the characters were more defined. This, he supposed, was consistent with the theory that the skull traveled from continent to continent before finally resting in the Amazon basin.

Each of these three scripts appeared to have been burned into the bone by some extremely hot, narrow, and sharp tool. There was no electricity back then, no means to keep an object at a consistently searing temperature. In order to accomplish this feat, each of the scribes would have had to have placed the instrument – either metal or stone – onto something such as a hot bed of coals, and then pulled it free to carve a character or two before returning it to the heat.

Tedious work. Very detailed. Very difficult. In principle, it was similar to wood burning. But even a hard wood is much softer than is bone. It would have taken not only heat, but strength to accomplish this feat. And skill. The writing was quite specific, decorative even. There was no evidence that the scribe struggled with his instrument or had difficulty penetrating the bone.

All of this in itself was fascinating, but there was another aspect that baffled Eldon. At first Eldon had thought that perhaps these images were of three separate, but similar skulls. The structure was all the same, the coloring, the dental size and placement.

But, the writing, the characters.

In some of the photographs it seemed the first script was the only one, that the other two did not exist; in other shots, the second, and in others the third. It was almost as if only one was present at a time. Each occupying the same space as the previous two. But then, upon closer scrutiny, he found that all three were present, and yes, they did overlap one another.

And yet each was clearly distinct.

Even now, as he reviewed the same shots, he found this to be true. It almost seemed as if each text faded in or out from one photograph to another. It could be the lighting, he supposed. Different camera angles. Different shades, bringing out different elements of the script. It was amazing. Almost as strange as the idea of the Cubbies winning a World Series.

Eldon poured over these for several hours, jotting notes, referencing resource material, translating each and then retranslating for accuracy. The similarity in content of the texts was amazing, and eliminated the idea that the second and third scribes were in the dark as to the meaning of the previous writers. And then, just as his eyes were becoming too blurry to focus, he caught sight of something that nearly caused his heart to stop beating. How could he have missed that?

A fourth ancient text.

And a very familiar one at that.

Chapter 23

Kutu Brazil

The Kutu jail was small, humid, and smelled of human excrement. The floor was of packed dirt, the walls uneven cinderblock, and the latrine was a scared and cracked wooden bucket. The bars, though, were firm enough. There were three that Hunt could jiggle just slightly, but it could take days before he could hope to dislodge one. Certainly, the place was used primarily to house village drunks and hotheaded youths. Hunt couldn't imagine that much noteworthy crime happened in such a small community. In his experience, communities of fewer than one hundred residents had very little crime. Everyone knew one another. Criminals in their midst could be easily identified. Usually, it was simply a case for social ostracism. Shun a person long enough and he'll usually come into compliance with social norms. In the rare instance where a person continued destructive behavior, the community tended to turn him out, forcing the lout from the village to make his own way in the outside world.

None of this, of course, had anything to do with the Huntington's predicament, but, thought Hunt, one's mind is prone to wander when incarcerated.

The gunshot had not connected with Hunt. Fortunately, it connected with no one. Hunt had, however, been rendered momentarily unconscious during the tumble. Massaging his temples with fingertips, he paced the confined space. "So, Cook was with the villagers."

"Correct," said Dana, who sat on the small yellowed cot in the corner of the cell. "He implicated us in each of the murders: the motel clerk, the deaths at the expedition site. He claimed to have witnessed it all."

"And then he conveniently disappeared."

"Correct."

"I don't get why Cook set us up. What's the gain?"

"He wants the skull," said Dana. "And he's terrified that it be made public. Since, we're seeking Andrew, who presumably has the skull, we're a threat."

"Yeah, makes sense. But, I'm worried for Andy. Cook has proven he's willing to kill in order to prevent the skull from going public. The only reason we're not still in that cavern starving to death is that Cook's not a skilled demolitions guy." Hunt turned, paced three steps, and then turned. "You spotted footsteps," he said at last. "We already knew there was an intruder in the cave. You think this is the same party?"

Dana nodded. "Most likely. But we know nothing of the newcomers. They might have an entirely different agenda. There may be no interest in Andrew or the skull."

Hunt glanced at Dana askew. "Do you believe that?"

"Well, I don't consider it likely, if that's what you mean. But we should leave it open as a possibility."

Hunt shook his head. "The real possibility is that Andy's in deep trouble. We can't afford to sit here like a couple of chimps in a zoo just waiting for the locals to decide we're innocent and set us free."

Dana rose, strolling toward the prison bars. "This cell is not well kept, the lock primitive. If I had any sort of lock picking apparatus, even makeshift, I could get us out of here in seconds."

Hunt nodded, staring at the empty room before him. The jail had but a single cell situated at the eastern wall of the police station. In addition to this, there was an old wooden desk, a couple of chairs, a beat up file cabinet and a desk-high tray containing fruit. "Seems the constable is the only official lawman in the village and he's nowhere to be seen."

"I believe he also owns the market," offered Dana. "I get the impression he fairly well runs the village."

"Well, he can go off playing little king all he wants. As far as I'm concerned, he's left us a window of opportunity. Brilliant minds like ours, we should come up with something."

"Dazzle me with you brilliance, dear."

"You've got your lock pick kit in your backpack."

"Which is across the room, well out of reach from our cozy little cell. I'm not dazzled."

Hunt gazed about the room again, taking in the scene, options tumbling through his brain. There had to be some opportunity, some hint of hope that he'd missed. The room was nearly empty, but not entirely so. He scanned the space, attempting to look beyond the obvious, to see each item for its potential rather than for its intended purpose. Still, it seemed there was nothing. Even if the key to the cell was sitting out there on the desk, he had no means to reach it.

Or did he?

Suddenly it was there. That one simple thought that could change the course of the day.

Doable? Yes.

Absurd? Absolutely.

"They didn't take my yo-yo," he said with some excitement.

Dana gave Hunt an exasperated look and rolled her eyes. "Here we go."

"No, no. I'm not being goofy. This is legit." Hunt reached into his pocket and retrieved his purple Duncan. Why the constable hadn't confiscated it, he couldn't say. Probably, the man saw it as harmless. A more accomplished lawman would have realized that you leave a prisoner with nothing. But this was a different, much smaller, less violent world these people lived in. The man had actually laughed at the yo-yo, and then casually allowed Hunt to shove it back into his pocket.

Hunt pumped the yo-yo a couple of times and then allowed it to remain fully extended – walking the dog style.

"Hunt, just what do you hope to accomplish?"

He didn't answer, but instead tossed the yo-yo out as far as he could. It bounced and skittered but missed his mark.

"That tray beside the desk?" asked Dana.

"Yep. If I can get the yo-yo to wrap around the leg. I should be able to pull it close."

"And this will help us how?"

"Take a look at what's on the tray," said Hunt as he retrieved the yo-yo, preparing for another attempt.

"Oranges, bananas. Is that a mango?"

Hunt chuckled. "Tasty, yes. A help, no. Look closer."

And then her eyes went wide and a grin wisped across her lips. "A fingernail file and tweezers."

"Bingo. Lock picking apparatus if ever I saw it."

"Well, maybe."

Hunt lobbed the Duncan again with a right to left sweep, gauging the distance and allowing for two bounces, which is what he'd observed on his previous attempts. The yo-yo bounced, once, twice, and the toy twirled around the tray leg twice and then settled. "Gotcha!" exclaimed Hunt.

"Please tell me you didn't learn this trick in Delta Force."

"Delta taught me to improvise, to use every tool available. So, yeah. I guess, in a way I did." Gently, ever so gently, he tugged on the string, careful not to pull too hard and undo the tenuous link. It took nearly a minute, but he did get the tray to within reach.

"I'm impressed," said Dana.

Hunt grinned. He was rather impressed himself. "Of course you are. Your turn now. Pick this lock before the constable or one of his buddies walks in."

"Hand me the fingernail file, dear. I'll show you how a master works."

Chapter 24

There was only one door to the police station and Hunt didn't feel comfortable strolling blithely out onto the street for all to see. Instead, he and Dana opted to climb through a back window and into a dirt-covered area that served as an alleyway. There were only two witnesses to the escape, an old gray and white mule whose only response was to offer a quick snort and a shake of the head, and a three foot lizard which scurried off without a sound. They'd "borrowed" two broad-rimmed hats from the station, and their plan was to avoid eye contact with locals, making their way through the village – preferably undetected. With luck, they'd come across an unattended vehicle, hotwire it, and be on their way.

But, on their way to where?

Presumably, Andy still had the skull. Also, presumably, Cook and perhaps one additional party were in pursuit, hoping to steal the skull from him, most likely with little regard for Andy's wellbeing. The question now became, where would Andy go? He'd obviously want to stay in hiding, but there was no gain in sneaking around the jungle or lying low in outlying villages. His goal, as Hunt understood it, was to get the fossil into the hands of the greater scientific community where it could be studied and authenticated.

Where might that be?

It was doubtful he could leave the country, not easily at least. Surely there was a warrant out on him. He'd be stopped at any international airport or border crossing. So, somewhere within Brazil. Some university or museum. Hunt wondered if Andy, or anyone else from the expedition, had such a connection. Probably so, he thought. In order for the Brazilian government to allow the team access to the site, they would likely want some local connection, some potential gain.

"I'm wondering if either Andy or anyone connected to the expedition has any connection to a university or museum in Brazil," he said, almost to himself.

Dana picked up on his line of reasoning. "You're thinking Andrew might attempt to take the skull to some institution to have it authenticated?"

Hunt nodded. "Makes better sense than anything else I've come up with."

The two rounded a corner, keeping heads low, and talking in hushed murmurs. There were only a handful of people visible, but Hunt knew that this was the type of place where everyone knew everyone. They couldn't remain in plain view long without being noticed. With luck, anyone that saw them would think they were simply tourists stopping by for supplies on the way into the jungle proper, but he couldn't count and that assumption.

There was a vibration in his pocket, followed by Hunt's ringtone, "Rock 'n Roll all Nite," by Kiss.

"Hunt! Silence your phone," shot Dana. "You'll draw attention."

Hunt nodded, pulling the phone from his pocket and slipping his Bluetooth onto his right ear. "It's Eldon. I'd better take the call." Hunt pushed the receive button, and then spoke in a soft furtive tone. "Hey, El. Perfect timing. Dana and I just broke out of jail. What you got for me?"

Eldon chuckled. "Jail! You've got some crazy stuff happening down there."

Dana offered Hunt a fierce you'd-better-not-get-us-caught look, but Hunt just smiled and shrugged, saying, "Go on."

"Well, the writing within the skull. Pretty unique stuff. It appears to spring from... let's say three entirely different language trees."

"You hesitated, El. There a problem?"

"Yeah, well, nothing for you to worry about right now. I need to do more research before I lay that one on ya."

Hunt glanced left and then right, head still lowered. It didn't seem they'd been spotted – yet. "Okay. I'll accept that for now. So, three different language trees. What's that mean to me?"

"Well, that ain't all that unusual in contemporary languages, but in ancient times, when contact between different cultures was limited, it..."

Hunt missed the rest of this sentence as shouts erupted from behind.

"Blimey, Hunt! We've been seen!" hollered Dana as they both broke into a full sprint.

They were toward the center of the village, but the place wasn't that big. Both instinctively ran in the direction of the closest intersection with the forest. Their best bet was to be outside of the village proper.

"Reader's Digest version, El. Suddenly, I'm being chased," said Hunt matter-of-factly as he raced past two startled children struggling to carry a full bucket of water from the nearby well. The little boy's mouth dropped open and the girl pointed, nearly dropping the bucket in the process.

"Yeah, yeah," said Eldon with a chuckle. "When aren't you bein' chased?"

"Hunt, will you please get off the blooming phone!"

"I'm multitasking, Hon. I'm multitasking."

Hunt glanced over his shoulder to find that the same man he had tackled and rolled into the stream with earlier was nearly upon him. The guy was swift, Olympic class swift. Too bad someone from a little semi-primitive village like this would never have a chance at an organized event such as the Olympics. He'd be a natural.

Stopping suddenly, Hunt turned, jabbed, and flipped, sending the young villager tumbling onto a table set out to sell vegetables. He was running again before the man had hit the ground. "Alright, El. The writing, what is it?"

"Before I get to the writing…"

"El, I really don't have time for this."

Something hit Hunt between the shoulder blades. A rock! Someone had thrown a rock at him. This was getting ridiculous. Glancing about, he realized that several additional villagers had joined the chase. He and Dana would need to do something quickly or they'd be right back in jail – or worse.

"Hunt, the background here is important," said Eldon, but Hunt barely heard him. Another man, middle aged, flabby, and swinging a jagged broom handle, came at him from his right side. Hunt felled him easily, then, twirling, struck another man in the solar plexus. Dana was slightly ahead of him now and seemed to be relatively in the clear. "Okay, El. I'm with you," said Hunt as he resumed his sprint, evading one man, and shouldering another onto the ground. Amazing. It seemed the entire village had joined the fun. Talk about community spirit.

"Yeah, yeah. I did some research. It looks like…"

"Dana! Hang a right! Toward the tree line. What was that, El?"

"The skull's unique. It's got a lotta myth surrounding it. Very ancient stuff. There are references to it in some of the earliest writings."

"The point, El. The point."

Hunt saw Dana take a hit from a young man, stumble a bit, and then fell him with a swift jab to the throat. "Dana! You alright?"

"I'm alright! I'm alright! Now hurry up!"

"The point," continued Eldon, "Is that the skull's supposed to have some mystic power."

"I don't buy into that stuff, El."

"It's supposed to grant immortality to the righteous and fiery death to the unjust. Supposedly, it originated in Egypt, but was eventually transported to a strange and lush land somewhere around the second millennium BCE."

Just then, Hunt heard two gun shots from behind. This thing had just escalated from nuisance to deadly.

"Hunt! They're shooting at us!"

"Yeah. In a public place. That's downright antisocial."

"Throughout history, seekers have been said to have traveled to a strange, dark land, presumably South America, in search of the sacred skull."

Another gunshot. It seemed whoever had the gun was shooting high – warning shots – but there was no telling when he'd lower his aim and take one of them down. "Eldon, you got the translation or what?" Hunt leapt over a low bush and angled left. He was less than two minutes from the edge of the forest now.

"Yeah, Hunt. Course I got the translation."

"Well, get to it, buddy. I've got bullets flying, dogs barking, and my wife glaring at me. This multitasking thing is not all its cut out to be."

But, Hunt didn't get to hear the translation. For it was then that he was finally stopped. It was a woman who did it. Heavyset, graying, with a leathered face and angry narrow eyes, she simply stepped directly out in front of him just as he was racing by. The move was so unexpected that Hunt didn't have time to evade her. Both went down in a tumble and it was only seconds before several men were pinning him to the ground.

Hunt managed to look up just long enough to see an all-terrain truck, of a kind often used by the military, sweep around from the left, skidding to a stop directly in front of Dana. Before she could react, two figures hopped out of the truck, the larger of the two grabbing her at her left bicep. There was a brief struggle, but they subdued her with practiced precision in less than a minute, hauling her into the vehicle which then sped away.

Chapter 25

The Lindell lad had been truculent, offering short clipped statements, bite-sized bits of information, or sometimes simply gazing ahead with that smarmy constipated goldfish look of his. But despite the annoying little weasel's unhelpfulness, information had emerged. One bit being the current location of the Amazon skull. Lindell had shipped it to a university in Sao Paulo with instructions that he alone would be allowed to retrieve it. And yes, of all things, the science department did utilize retina scans as a security measure.

Apparently, this particular institution was involved in top secret research and so precautions had been implemented. It was unclear what Lindell's connection was to the university, but it wasn't too grossly surprising that one existed. He had, after all, been involved in an expedition within the Brazilian borders, and intellectuals, like all professional groups, tended to have connections well beyond their own institutions. Thorpe had subverted retina scans before, and could do so again if necessary. But the simplest, most straightforward course of action would be to bring Lindell with him, gain access to the skull, and then flee, leaving the young scientist in some isolated place where he wouldn't be able to sound the alarm until well after they'd left the country.

The other piece of information gained was a bit more complicated. Lindell, it seemed, had allowed Gregory Milton to take several photographs of the skull's interior. Thorpe's client, upon hearing this, had insisted that the camera be retrieved, the photographs deleted, and the camera destroyed. A simple task if only the camera still resided in the cave with Milton. But, unknown to the Huntingtons, Lindell had still been in the cave, hiding behind a stalagmite formation, when they'd arrived in the cavern. Lindell saw Dana Huntington take the camera from the near-comatose Milton, view the photos, and then put the camera in the left outside pocket of her backpack. Thorpe had questioned Lindell on why – if he was truly in the cave at this time – he and his companions had not seen him exiting the cave soon thereafter, to which Lindell responded that there was an alternate cave opening roughly three quarters of a mile north of the entrance Thorpe had staked out.

But Lindell's comings and goings were no longer of concern. Dana had now become part of the equation.

Dana.

It really didn't seem so long ago that they were together. She was brilliant, beautiful, sly, witty, one of the few people he'd ever considered a near intellectual equal to himself. Her over-the-top cockney accent was perfectly dreadful, but her time at Cambridge followed by intense training with MI6 had taught her to hide it quite perfectly. In fact, she played a fine high-society socialite and had masterfully hidden her working class upbringing until well into their rather short marriage.

Never had he suspected that she was a MI6 plant assigned to get close to him in order to gain access to his many and varied connections. But even knowing this, Thorpe still believed that Dana had loved him. He knew it, could feel it almost tangibly. Thorpe was a student of humanity. And though he had not perceived her deception, he had clearly read the hurt in her eyes on that final day when all was exposed and she marched free of his life, presumably forever.

And he remembered the pain. The sense of loss. Even thoughts of suicide. Well, he was too clever for that. Or so he'd told himself. But then why had his thoughts scampered into that dark corner? Why had he contemplated different ways he might accomplish the deed? He couldn't sleep; his stomach was constantly upset, the loneliness stretched out before him into endless nights. If he hadn't kept himself occupied every waking hour he'd found himself weeping.

And he was a strong chap. An exceptional person. He couldn't imagine what such emotion might have done to a common sort.

But, here he was now. Not healed exactly, but functioning handily enough. He had risen above, moved on with his life. He was attractive, charming, witty, rich, and so never found himself at a loss for female companionship. Though, admittedly, it would be self deception to claim that any of this could replace what he'd lost. Humanity, he felt, would be so much better served if emotions came with a "delete all" function.

Women were complicated creatures. Unpredictable. Damn strange if a man was to be honest concerning the matter. It had been what? Four years now? She had remarried, started a new life, was living in a new country. Could he really expect her to hold any lingering affection for him? She was free of MI6, this, at least was a plus. There would be no conflict of interest from that corner. But, MI6 was merely a catalyst for the breakup. If Dana had truly loved him as he loved her, nothing could have pulled her away.

Pathetic!

He was better than this.

Thorpe gazed forward, sighed, and passed his palm across his face. He needed to focus on the problem at hand. That being, how to collect Milton's camera from Dana without endangering her. Haas, he knew, would not hesitate to use deadly force. To the best of Thorpe's knowledge, Dana and her husband were incarcerated in Kutu. He knew this because he and his two companions had witnessed the Huntington's capture. This meant that the camera could now be in the possession of that worthless "constable" – where had he come up with that title? – that seemed to run the tiny village like his own personal duchy.

Should this be the case, the job would be relatively simple. The constable and his untrained deputies would be no match for Thorpe and his crew. It would take them but moments to breach the primitive police station, subdue the opposition, secure the camera, and leave. Now, it was conceivable that Dana still held the camera. The local officials may not have had the wherewithal to confiscate the prisoner's possessions. This would add another level of complication to the situation, but nothing insurmountable.

Thorpe's primary concern was that Dana had most definitely viewed the photographs. This information had come to Thorpe during his private conversation with Lindell, and therefore Haas and Collins didn't know this – not technically at least – and Thorpe hoped he could slip by without putting Dana at further risk. The client didn't want witnesses after all.

But, witnesses to what?

The skull was supposed to be a bobble, a unique piece for the client's disgusting little gallery of the weird. Why all of the cloak and dagger? The writing within the skull was both ancient and foreign. As long as Dana had no access to the photographs, she'd never have opportunity to have the text translated. To Thorpe's understanding, modern alphabets weren't even used. There simply was no risk to the client. The whole thing was bizarre. What in God's name could be so important about this skull? Did the writing contain the location of some long lost treasure?

Rubbish!

If the client was thinking along those lines, he was a fool - a fool who had viewed far too many Hollywood extravaganzas.

Thorpe, Collins, and Haas were just entering Kutu on the village's one and only road. Collins was at the wheel, Thorpe in the front passenger seat, and Haas in the tight rear seat, seemingly meant more for children and supplies than for grown adults. As it was, Haas shared the space with whatever gear had not been loaded into the top carrier. The reason being, Thorpe had not wanted Lindell to have access to anything as he rode in the far back box compartment of the truck. And besides, it was rather amusing to see Haas so uncomfortable. And Thorpe knew it would always be Haas in this particular seat. The man always sat in the rear. Thorpe believed it was because Haas was a paranoid bugger who wanted to keep an ever-watchful eye on his companions.

It was late afternoon and few people were milling about. Most likely, the villagers were off preparing their evening meals. Two women beat rugs in front of a single-room dwelling, a young boy and girl carried a bucket toward the village well, a cluster of six men – one of which was the overfed constable – stood to the side of the road engaged in animated conversation. Thorpe and his companions rolled slowly up the way not wanting to draw attention.

The plan was to begin with a drive through, paying close attention to the police station. They'd just seen the constable, so knew he was away, but were still looking for activity, for any clues as to how many people might be within. They wanted to determine if there was any foot traffic in and out of the place, and generally get a feel for the environment. After this, they would play tourist, rent a room at the tiny dilapidated motel and then breach the station after dark.

But, wait…

What was that he saw?

"Tina, dear, slow down a bit. In fact, perhaps you should stop for a moment."

Grumbling that she was not his "dear," Collins complied, pulling to the side of the road and coming to rest beside a spindly tree with willow-like branches. "What is it you see?" she asked as Haas, silent as ever, scooted forward to peer out from between Thorpe and Collins.

"Is that?" began Thorpe, a grin creasing his face. "Yes. I do believe it is. There, there," he said pointing toward the police station. "You see them?"

"The two with the silly hats?"

"Yes. Yes. Ha! Dana, old girl. Brilliant! They've broken out of this backward jail. Ha!"

"She's former MI6. I'm assuming she's retrieved the camera," said Collins, her eyes focused on the two, her expression the emotionless mask of a professional soldier.

"Oh, most definitely. Dana's a clever sort. She wouldn't leave something like that behind."

"So, we drive up, jump out of the truck, grab her pack, and be on our way," said Haas.

"No, no, no. These are skilled operatives, trained in evasive maneuvers as well as hand-to-hand combat. Such a straightforward approach, they'd be onto us and disappear between buildings before we could initiate." Thorpe paused for a moment, scanning the scene before them. "The village is small. It'll take them less than ten minutes to reach the tree line. Most likely, though, they'll be looking to acquire transportation. That might slow them a bit. What we need is a distraction. Tina dear, would you back up, maybe five hundred meters or so?"

Tina complied, though her expression was one of concern. Surely she wondered what Thorpe had in mind.

"There, there," he said as they drew up alongside the chatting group of men. "Perfect. Hello! Hello, there!" he hollered. "You're constable of this fair village, am I correct?"

The constable nodded and moved forward. He was a heavyset man, with bushy black eyebrows and a walrus mustache to match. "Yes. What is it you need?" he asked in heavily accented English. His expression read, "Why are you bothering me, you stupid tourist?"

"Well," said Thorpe with a broad grin. "I don't presume to do your job or any such nonsense, but I do believe two prisoners have just escaped your prison. Thought you might like to know."

The man's eyes narrowed, and then turned in the direction to which Thorpe pointed. The constable shouted something – most likely a curse – in Portuguese, and the chase was on.

"Now, darlin', what in the hell do you plan on accomplishing by that?" asked Collins with a sly and devilish grin. The woman had spectacular lips.

"These two will evade capture, at least for a minute or two," offered Haas. "They'll likely become separated from each other. Then we swoop in and collect the backpack – right, Mate?" he added with a nod to Thorpe.

"Two of those men had guns," said Collins. "If they start shooting, the situation could escalate beyond our control. Our orders were to maintain a low profile."

"Firing shots in the middle of town?" scoffed Thorpe. "Please. They're not going to endanger bystanders."

Ninety seconds later the first shot was fired.

Thorpe and his companions trailed the ruckus in their truck. Thorpe was concerned now that guns were involved, but these were still clearly warning shots into the air. He honestly couldn't believe that anyone would risk shooting into the crowd.

"There we go," said Thorpe as he slipped a black ski mask over his face. "There we go. Dana's out ahead now. The husband is tied up in a skirmish." He paused, waiting, waiting… There! "Go! Now!"

A skilled driver, Collins floored the accelerator. The truck fishtailed on the dirt road and then the tires took hold. Sweeping around to the left of the mob, Collins took a sharp right to just in front of Dana, pulling to a stop amidst a flurry of dirt and dust.

Thorpe and Haas were out of the truck before Dana realized what was happening. But, instead of going for the backpack, Haas tackled the woman herself, grabbing her from behind and barking at Thorpe to help subdue her. Their window of opportunity was limited, not allowing Thorpe the convenience of debating tactics or countermanding the decision. Thorpe grabbed Dana's legs just as she was shifting in preparation to flip Haas onto the ground. This attack caused her to shift right, struggling not to lose her balance. Compensating now, she stumbled to the left, attempted to right herself, but by then both men had firm holds on her. Even so, Dana was an accomplished fighter and managed two solid kicks, one to each of the men, before she was subdued, and dragged into the back of the truck to be deposited beside Lindell. The whole incident took just over thirty seconds.

Chapter 26

Hunt was free of the mob in less than two minutes. He was a skilled fighter with literally thousands of hours of training and real life experience, where the villagers had none. Though Delta Force operatives regularly use deadly force, part of their code is that one did not endanger civilians unnecessarily. These men who fought with Hunt were civilians. They were innocents. And more so, these were people with the strength of character to launch themselves into a fray, to endanger themselves in order to do what they believed to be right. In their eyes, Hunt was an escaped felon, a dangerous man guilty of multiple murders.

And yet they didn't shy away from the task at hand.

Hunt respected them for this. He also committed himself to avoiding their serious injury. This caution probably cost him the needed time to reach the truck before it sped away with Dana captive inside.

He fought down emotion, pushed aside his fear for Dana, ignored that hollow stab within his gut. Emotion would not get her back. He knew this, and so fell back on his training, analyzing the situation, pouring through what little he already knew, seeking some clue, some pattern that might lead him to her. Who had taken her and why? There had to be a motive. There was always a motive. So what did he know? What was his starting point?

Point one: Dana didn't have the skull, which seemed to be at the heart of every recent happening. Point two: Hunt had to assume that whoever had taken Dana was that same third party that had left the female footprint at the cave – he had managed a quick look at the kidnappers, the two abductors were male and had worn ski masks, but the driver of the truck was unmasked and clearly a woman. Still, this told him nothing. Even the truck used had no license plate, no distinguishing markings. Unless he could get on their trail quickly, he might never find them.

And then what?

Dana had been taken. What did these people want with her? What were they willing to do to get what they desired? Hunt shook away the thoughts. No time for fruitless speculation. Stay on task. Make a plan. Take action.

It was now dark. Hunt had spent the previous hour quietly sneaking about the forest surrounding the village as the constable and his men searched for him.

He would not be found.

Hunt was far too skilled at this. He could have, of course, fled further into the jungle, but if he was to locate Dana, he needed transportation, and this meant remaining near to Kutu.

Shortly after dark, he ventured back toward the village. A handful of men still roamed the adjacent jungle in search of him, and that was all the better. Fewer people in town to discover him lurking. Hunt had a specific target in mind as he made his way through the shadows. During the course of the chase, he'd noticed a dirt bike leaning against a small hut just off the road. It would likely be a good vehicle for making swift time through the uneven jungle terrain.

He came upon the hut from the west. The shadows were long, the moon on-ly a quarter full. Yes, the bike was still there. A Yamaha WR450F. Decent horsepower for a dirt bike; and with an aluminum frame, heavy-duty shocks, knotted tires, it looked ideal for the terrain he'd be covering. Hunt looked right then left, and then, in a low crouch, made his way to the bike. Expertly, he went to the ignition wires. Delta Force operatives spend numerous hours training for just such a situation. "You're in hostile territory," Lucky Lindell would say. "You're cut off from your unit. Your job is to find transportation, start it up, and be on the move before anyone knew you were there."

Other intricate tasks, such as lock picking, had abandoned Hunt after his injuries. Not so hotwiring a vehicle. He couldn't explain how he'd maintained this skill and not the others. Maybe it simply didn't require the fine precision and intense focus, maybe it used a different part of the brain, but for whatever reason Hunt could still have most vehicles on the roll in just over thirty seconds.

The voice startled Hunt.

It was small, high. A child.

The boy was perhaps six, maybe seven years of age. Hunt believed it was the same child he'd seen earlier carrying the water bucket with his sister.

"Hey, kid. I'm sorry. I've got to borrow the bike."

The kid didn't understand him. English might as well have been Klingon. But, the child knew Hunt's intent none-the-less. Repeating the same word over and over, the boy raced to the bike and hopped onto the seat. *"Gatuno! Gatuno!"* he screamed, the translation probably meaning thief.

"No, no, kid please!" Hunt made a shooing motion, attempting to get the kid to hop down. And the boy's face went stark with momentary terror. He'd finally gotten a good look at Hunt's face. Hunt had always gotten along well with children. His younger brother Kenny had two of his own, and "Uncle Marc" had always been a favorite of theirs. That was until the explosion that had severely scared him. Now, most young children ran away in fear, and even his own niece and nephew had kept a safe distance for the first several months. This hurt Hunt more than he'd ever admit – even to himself – but he'd learned to deal with it. And with each surgery, he looked all the more human. Perhaps in another couple of years he'd be able to walk the streets without stares followed by averted glances.

This particular child was made from hearty stock. After his momentary shock at Hunt's visage, the boy crossed his arms defiantly and offered a resolute pout. Hunt couldn't help but grin. Gutsy little guy.

Now there was another voice, an adult female, most likely the boy's mother. She was calling for the boy.

"Mamae!," cried the boy. *"Mamae!"* Momma! Momma!

"Shhh! Shhh!" Hunt tried to quiet the lad. He was only moments from discovery.

Moving quickly, he lifted the boy, now kicking and screaming, from the bike. The mother, a squat heavyset woman of about thirty, emerged from around the corner of the shed and naturally assumed Hunt to be assaulting her child. She came at him, fists balled, and pounded on his back as he turned from her.

Hunt tried to put the boy down gently, but the kid was squirming and Hunt lost his grip at the last, sending the child tumbling to the ground, scraping his knee in the process. The woman screeched as if Hunt had just stabbed the kid.

The upside was that she raced to the boy, leaving Hunt to the bike. "Sorry. I'm so sorry," he said as he pulled two wires free. "I didn't do anything to him. Honest." She couldn't understand him, of course. But he hoped she could at least pick up on his tone.

More voices now, accompanied by running footsteps. The engine roared to life just as a tall lean man – the boy's father? – appeared from around the corner. Hunt mounted the bike in one fluid motion, and zipped past the man, missing him by only inches.

Alerted by the commotion, several people were on the road now; some were even daring enough to step out in front of the speeding bike in attempts to unseat the fugitive. But Hunt, an accomplished rider, was able to swerve and break, changing direction randomly. Only once, did he nearly spill, when a young woman of perhaps twenty-five darted at him from the right, hurling a rolling pin in his direction. The projectile bounced off of the front tire and spun erratically off to the left. Hunt didn't wait around to give anyone else a shot at him. He was outside of Kutu in under a minute, with luck, never to return. He'd definitely worn his welcome thin.

*****

Once safely clear of Kutu, Hunt pulled off the rough and uneven road to check his fuel level. Good. The tank was nearly full. For once something had gone his way. Dismounting the bike, he pulled his phone from his pocket, slipped his Bluetooth onto his ear, and dialed Lucky Lindell. The colonel answered after only one ring. "Hunt! Any news on Andy?"

"Sorry, Colonel. I don't have him yet. But, like I told you this morning, he has been seen alive within the last twenty-four."

There was a brief pause, and when the colonel spoke again, his voice lacked some of its previous vigor. "Well, keep me in the loop." Another pause. "Listen, I managed to secure a team to investigate that cave of yours. They should arrive by oh-eight-hundred."

Hunt strolled about ten yards southeast and then seated himself on the trunk of a fallen tree, retrieving his yo-yo from a pocket in the process. Three small lizards scurried away, startled by the intrusion. A large green and yellow snake dangled from a tree branch not fifteen feet forward. There was a light rain; barely more than a mist, and, like his reptilian companions, Hunt ignored it. "Sounds good, Colonel. You might want them in bio-hazard gear. I have no idea what kind of bug is responsible for that zombie slumber party, but it must be a kicker."

"Already on it, sergeant."

"Luck, one other thing. There's another player down here. I don't know who they are or how many. I know for certain that there are at least three of them, but there could be more."

"Do you know their objective?"

"That's a negative. But, they have Dana." Hunt went on to detail Dana's capture and related the discovery of the female footprint at the cave entrance and the unknown party spying on them in the chamber. "The fact that they were at the cave," he concluded, "suggests that they're interested in the skull."

"That's assuming this is the same group," warned Lindell. "That footprint could have been from someone else."

"Nah. Two things speak against that. One, heavy rainfall during the night washed away all but the most recent foot prints, and two, a woman was driving the truck when Dana was captured. I've got to assume it's the same group. It just doesn't make sense for there to be yet another party interested in this thing."

"What can I do for you?" asked Lindell.

"I'm going to give you Dana's cell phone number. I need you to access GPS and get a location on her."

There was a hesitation. "I don't mean to sound selfish, Hunt. But, what about Andy?"

Hunt squeezed the phone. Didn't the man understand? "I came down here to find Andy," he said. "That remains my objective. But we already know his cell phone's a bust and so right now my best bet in finding him is to locate that fossil. If my hunch is right and Dana's assailants are after the skull, I might learn something from them concerning Andy's whereabouts."

"Fair enough," sighed Lindell, but he was obviously disheartened.

"One more thing," said Hunt after a pause.

"Yes?"

"I need to know if either Andy or one of his colleagues has a connection down here with a local university or museum. If so, he might try to make his way to that place with the skull."

"You want me to find out if there's such an association."

"Right. I'm pretty disconnected down here."

"I'll get someone right on it. Now, give me your wife's phone number. I'll get going on that GPS."

*****

It was too dark to track the truck visually and it would take some time for Lucky Lindell to get back to him with the coordinates, so Hunt called Eldon Troxel to see if he'd uncovered anything else that might be helpful. "Hunt! What in blazes is going on down there? It sounded like downtown Iraq descended on you," Eldon nearly bellowed.

Hunt allowed a weak chuckle and flicked his yo-yo. "It seems the locals didn't care for our prison break. The whole village turned out to recapture us."

"Well, that's just anti-American. Don't they know that respectable people just sit back and pretend they didn't see anything?"

Another flick of the wrist. The yo-yo dropped and then returned. "Listen, El. I don't have much time here. What do you have for me?"

"Okay, right. I've got a translation for the writing carved on the skull's interior. I think I'm pretty close, but these were not known dialects. They sprang from at least three language trees, though they're much earlier incarnations of the tongues than anything I've seen before."

"Okay, buddy. Hit me with it."

"Well, it starts off, 'O chosen be brave, for you shall awaken anew to a glorious dawning.' Chosen might also be translated righteous. Seems that one could go either way."

Hunt twirled his yo-yo. "Go on."

"'Flee o harbinger of evil. For you will soon know the searing pain of the dead man's fire.'"

"That's what it says on the inside of the skull? Dead man's fire?"

"Kinda creepy, huh?"

"Nah. In a way it makes sense. Before that it said, 'the chosen will awaken anew.' The people in the cave seem to be in some sort of hibernation. Before Greg Milton succumbed, he indicated that some agent on the inside of the skull was the cause. I'm guessing that's the reference."

"I'm following."

"There have also been several people that appear to have literally burned to death from the inside out. Spontaneous combustion. You know, like Spinal Tap's drummers."

"And they had contact with the skull?"

Hunt paused for a moment. "I'm going to say yes on that, but that's unconfirmed."

"Interesting. Listen, Hunt. There have been cases where ancient curses were traced back to viral infections. A contaminant was initially spread by some witch doctor. As the symptoms appeared, the tribe members naturally thought they'd been cursed, but really it was just a contagion. At that point in history, the witch doc himself wouldn't have heard of a virus. He just took advantage of the symptoms."

Hunt flicked his wrist, sending the purple Duncan into a break away, a trick in which the yo-yo appears to defy gravity. "So, you think there might be a viral agent on the interior of the skull?"

"That's one theory."

"But, we have two entirely different symptoms. Some people slip into a coma and others incinerate."

Eldon paused for a moment before responding. "That is strange," he said finally. "Could be there are two different agents. Or, maybe the same agent hits different people in dissimilar ways. The burning, though. Very weird. Never heard of a virus that could do that."

Another flick of the wrist, sending the Duncan into two consecutive round-the-world loops and then an over-the-waterfall, before snapping back into Hunt's palm. "No argument there, El. This whole thing is nuts."

"Yeah, well, listen. There's more to the translation. There are instructions for waking the chosen to a new age. Specific ingredients, herbs and whatnot as well as incantations."

Hunt nodded. "That could be the cure for the comatose. Tell you what. How about you email me that complete translation? I've got a Pentagon connection that might be able to pull the Center for Disease Control in on this thing. Maybe they can use your info to cook up a cure for our sleeping beauties."

"Not a problem. But it's all speculation. I can't vouch for the content and even my translation is still in first draft mode. I need to study this thing further to do ya right."

"Well, speculation and first draft still beats anything we've got going."

There was another pause on the line, this one stretching into multiple seconds.

"El? You still there?"

"I got one more thing to throw at ya – an alternate theory."

"I'm game," said Hunt as he stared forward at the hanging snake. The thing seemed to have taken an interest in him.

"This one's going to sound kinda far-fetched," warned Eldon. "I don't want you ta think I've gone one-flew-over on ya."

"El, we're friends. I trust your judgment. What are you thinking?"

Eldon sighed. Obviously he was uncomfortable with this alternate theory.

"Spill it, El. I don't have all day."

"Alright. Just… Well, okay. Some things happened a few months back. Kinda changed my perspective on things. Seems there might be a connection to your skull."

"Well, now I'm totally confused."

"There's a fourth language tree on the skull. One I haven't mentioned up until now. Hunt, crazy as this may seem, you might be dealing with real live curses here."

"You're talking magic?"

"Magic, I dunno anything about. But, supernatural, yeah. Maybe."

"I don't buy into that stuff, El. You're a scientist. I didn't think you did either."

"Yeah, well, I never did. But, things happened. Stuff you'd never believe if I told you. Just be careful. You got that? This thing could get really weird on you."

There was a beep on Hunt's phone. It was Lucky Lindell calling through. "Listen, El. I've got another call. Gotta take it."

"Just be careful, Hunt. I don't want…"

And Hunt cut him off mid sentence. "Lucky? You there?"

"I'm here."

"You got those coordinates for me?" Hunt didn't have time for small talk. If Lucky had a lead on Dana's whereabouts, he needed to be on the move.

"I've got them, soldier."

"Alright, Luck. Hit me with them."

Chapter 27

The Amazon Rainforest, Brazil

Dana stared into the shadowed face of Andrew Lindell. The young man was a bit puffy in his appearance, not seriously overweight, but flabby and not toned. His eyes were narrow and dark, his hair a muddy brown, tossed and in need of a cut. He sat, arms tied behind his back, shivering as if the temperature ranged somewhere under zero rather than near 80 degrees. He seemed listless and uninterested in his current circumstance.

The truck bounced, nearly sending Dana to the floor. The road was dreadful, and the truck's suspension worse. Dana was certain she'd have whiplash by day's end. Though, if that was the worst of it, she couldn't really complain. Who knew what this crew had in mind for her. And Hunt! Likely, he'd escaped the villagers. He was a skilled combatant and they were civilians. Still, all it would take was a stray bullet and...

No. She couldn't dwell on that now. Not while she was held captive. The most productive use of her time was to deal with the situation at hand. Once she was free, she could concern herself with her missing husband.

"Andrew," she said, hoping to open actual dialogue with the lad. Thus far he'd responded with mostly grunts and gasps. At first, Dana thought their captors had drugged him, but that didn't seem quite right. This was something else entirely. "Are you unwell? What is the matter with you?" she asked.

Another bounce and then a kind of waddle from side-to-side. Had the truck left the road? Unlikely. There was no room for a vehicle this size to traverse untouched forest land.

Lindell lulled his head in Dana's direction, staring at her as if seeing her for the first time - this, by Dana's calculation, after they'd spent the past three or better hours together. Though, she couldn't be certain of the time passage. They were locked in the rear of a moving truck with only minimal moonlight sneaking in through the tiny window to the front cab. "What did you say?" asked Lindell who seemed to be coming out of his stupor.

Ah, a full sentence. Progress, it seemed. "Yes. I asked if you're ill."

Lindell offered a wry grin. "No. Not ill. Well... not in a traditional sense, I suppose." He paused, studying her as if only now seeing her for the first time. "You're Marc Huntington's wife."

Interesting. How would he know that?

Obviously noting the puzzlement on her face, he added, "I saw you in the cave."

"You were there?"

A slow nod. "Hiding."

"That was you. The one scrambling out after Hunt cleared the way? I'd thought that bloke was part of this lot that captured us."

Lindell seemed to drift off for a moment, his eyes becoming glassy, his mouth drooping just a bit on the left. Finally, he nodded in agreement.

"Andrew, what is the matter? You look perfectly horrible."

A shake of the head. Several blinks of the eyes. "I could only guess. But, my assumption is that it's not good."

Dana attempted to steady herself as the vehicle took a steep dip and turn. "Marc and I came down here to find you. To bring you home."

"So, was getting captured a part of your rescue plan?" It seemed he was trying to be funny, not hurtful. Mostly, he just seemed ill.

"No plan goes exactly as designed," admitted Dana.

Another bounce, this one literally lifting Dana from her seat.

"My father sent you, I'm sure. He would need to protect his little boy."

Ah! Some bitterness there. Seems the father son relationship might be a tad strained. "Actually, it was Hunt that contacted your father with the offer to come to your aid."

Lindell nodded, pondering this. "Marc's a good guy. I knew him when I was younger." He paused for a moment, screwing his face as if concentrating, and then added, "I wish I had my board."

"Your board?"

"Backgammon. It helps me to clear my thoughts."

Dana nodded. Bound in the back of a truck, likely on the road to execution and the man wants to play board games! "I assume our captors are after the skull," she said.

"Of course."

"You didn't tell them where it is, I hope."

Lindell looked down and away. Of course he had. He wasn't a trained operative. Most likely he couldn't withstand even a mild interrogation. The young man just didn't seem to be of that make up.

"Alright," said Dana. "Where is it, and how long before we get to it?"

"I was able to ship it before my capture. It's in Sao Paulo. On this terrain, I have no idea how long it will take."

Dana thought about this. It would be unlikely that they'd remain in this truck for the entire journey. Sao Paulo was multiple hundreds of kilometers away. More likely, they'd charter a plane. "Andrew, this is very important. Do they need you in order to gain access to the skull, or can they get to it on their own?"

Lindell was listing again, but pulled himself back in focus to answer the question. "They need me. There's a retina scan."

"Good. Brilliant, even. That gives them a reason to keep you alive until they have the skull in hand. By then, we'd have better found a means of escape."

Dana gazed about the place for what had to be the fortieth time. She saw nothing to use as a weapon, nothing she could even use to cut her bindings. Even though the light was minimal, she'd been able to determine that the space was nearly empty. Just two cold metal benches and a couple pairs of hiking boots. This crew either traveled very light, or they'd moved everything out of the truck before taking Lindell captive.

She might be able to do something with the shoelaces, she supposed, perhaps a makeshift garrote. Or, even the boots themselves. They would be far from a lethal weapon, but they had some weight, and a hearty smack across the face would definitely startle a captor and perhaps buy her a few seconds. But, she could do none of that while her hands were bound behind her back. She'd attempted to free herself, but the binds were tight, the knot secure. If anything, her efforts had made things worse.

Dana noticed a change. The truck was decreasing in speed, coming to a stop. She heard no signs of civilization, no planes taking off or landing, no other traffic. They hadn't reached an airstrip, she was fairly certain. More likely, they had pulled over with the purpose of executing her. In her mind she couldn't determine what use she might be to these people. They'd taken her backpack. For whatever reason, that seemed to be the objective. But, beyond that, why was she being kept alive?

They were now at a full stop.

She heard the passenger side door open and then close followed by similar sounds from the driver's side. Footsteps moved toward the back of the truck from both sides. There was the sound of a key inserted into a padlock. Dana rose slowly and moved quietly toward the door, muscles tensed, her entire form coiled to pounce. Though bound, she had to give it at least a good go, surprise the blokes, perhaps give Andrew a chance to escape – though he seemed in no condition for the exertion.

The door opened.

In the less than one second before she attacked, Dana identified three shadowy figures in the dim moonlight: two with guns: a female with an AK47, a male with a Sig Sauer semi-automatic pistol, and one male, the closest, apparently unarmed.

Dana launched herself, colliding squarely with the lead man at mid chest.

Both tumbled to the grassy ground with a sudden jar.

Before Dana could head butt the bloke and roll into the legs of the next, the man laughed a too-familiar laugh.

Jonathan?

Oh, bloody hell!

*****

They sat across from one another, Jonathan on a lopsided tree stump, Dana on a flat-topped stone about the size of a large beach ball. Her hands were still bound, and Thorpe's two companions flanked her from a distance allowing the two only marginal privacy. Lindell had been allowed to empty his bladder and was once again seated in the truck, which was only about ten meters from the female guard. It was unlikely he'd go anywhere.

Minimal moonlight made it through the trees, but still Dana could see the so-familiar features: Jonathan's broad easy grin, his piercing milk chocolate eyes, narrow, almost sculpted chin, black hair spilling over his intelligent brow.

"Well, this explains the ski masks," she said. "It wasn't that you were afraid of being recognized by the villagers. You didn't want Hunt to recognize you as you kidnapped me."

Jonathan's smile broadened.

Why did he have to be so bleeding gorgeous?

"Well, loose ends and what not," he said with a boyish shrug. "Actually, the mask was meant as a favor to your man. My companions are not, shall we say, fond of witnesses."

"And yet you've revealed yourself to me. Am I expendable then?"

Jonathan looked pained. "Dana," he said in a near whisper, obviously hoping his companions couldn't hear his words. "I revealed myself to you because I love you."

"Oh, bleeding…"

"Dana. Listen." His voice was a near hiss. "The plan was to take your backpack, not to abduct you. My… companion, Haas, made a last minute decision to take you as well. I've just revealed myself to you because I want you to believe me when I tell you that you must find a way to escape." At this, he glanced toward the large man holding the Sig Sauer.

"Why did you need my backpack?" asked Dana.

"Milton's camera. The photos of the skull's interior."

This made sense. Someone in search of the skull might not want photos of its most peculiar trait floating about. "And your man Haas took me because I've seen the photographs. He obviously means to eliminate the witness. So, why not capture Hunt as well?"

"Well, there, you see, the decision to take you was rather spontaneous, at least, as near as I can tell. We had been after the backpack alone. Haas has been quite close-lipped concerning the decision. I've no notion as to his plan."

"Tell me about Haas."

Jonathan nodded and chanced another glance in the larger man's direction. "Peculiar man. I trust neither him nor his motives."

"Have you no control over your own man? You are in charge I presume. I can't imagine your ego allowing you to play second string to that lumbering plonker."

Jonathan hesitated. "Officially, I'm the expedition leader, true. But, some things have come to light since arriving - some hidden agendas. I am not entirely in control of the situation." Jonathan paused, again glancing at the hulking man. "I'm going to strike you, Dana. I apologize, but I must make it seem as if we are at odds."

"We are at odds."

Jonathan slapped her harshly across the face, shouting, "Tell me what you know about the photographs!"

Despite the forewarning, Dana realized what he was doing only at the last second and so was only able to deflect a fraction of the strike. Surely it left a red handprint on her left cheek. "I'm not telling you anything!" she shot back.

"Good. Good," whispered Jonathan. "He'll think you're being uncooperative."

"I am being bleeding uncooperative!"

Another strike. Not so hard this time, nor as unexpected. "Tell me what you know about the skull."

"We're here for Andrew Lindell!" shouted Dana, this, for the benefit of the two guards. "We could care less about the bleeding skull except that it might lead us to the lad."

"Perfect," said Jonathan. "Now, bring the volume down, but act like we're still arguing."

Dana acquiesced by spitting in Jonathan's face.

"Brilliant. Perfectly brilliant," muttered Jonathan as he wiped the spittle onto his sleeve. "I will assist you in any way within my means. But Haas is largely beyond my control. Use that clever mind of yours and plan an escape for within the next two hours."

Dana cocked her head. "Why within the next two hours?"

167

"We'll be reaching an airstrip by then. If we make a stop before then, I must assume it will be for the purpose of your execution. That being the case, I will open the door and step to my right, your left. I suggest you bolt right immediately and into the brush. You'll only have a second or two, but I will delay him, trust me on that. He will not have opportunity to give chase, at least not immediately."

"There's a woman with you as well. What of her?"

Jonathan hesitated for a moment. "She, I believe to be neutral. Her assignment was to aid me. I'm not under the impression that she has a part in Haas's agenda. Fact is, I have hopes of enlisting her as an ally. I've noticed her expressions when Haas oversteps his role. She is displeased."

"She's attracted to you. I'm sure you've noticed."

"Tina? No. She'd just as soon kill me as anything."

Dana shrugged. "Just because she'd be willing to eliminate you doesn't mean she wouldn't like to bed you first. She is an attractive young woman, after all. And there aren't many options out here in the jungle."

Thorpe shook his head. "No. Nonsense. I mean, yes, she's attractive and all, but, she and I. No. Not an option from either of our perspectives." He paused, seeming to think of something, and then rose. "If we haven't stopped before the airstrip, you can assume that I have convinced that Neanderthal that your marvelous computer skills could be utilized in bypassing security and getting us to within reach of the skull." Jonathan then pulled Dana's cell phone from a pocket and tossed it onto the ground.

"And you did that why?" asked Dana.

"Well, we wouldn't want your husband tracking us by GPS now would we? He might just muddle everything."

"You're a beast. You do know that," said Dana as she slid her right foot about in the dirt in quick broad sweeps.

"Of course, of the two of us I'm the beast," said Jonathan grabbing Dana under the right arm and pulling her harshly to her feet. "Up you go. We've wasted enough time here."

Haas moved forward as if to intercept the two. Jonathan met him face to face. "I'm not done with her yet. You'll have to wait."

"Wait? What would I be waiting for?" asked Haas in a rather strong Australian accent.

Jonathan seemed momentarily taken aback, his brow furrowing, and jaw shifting slightly left.

"Ah!" chuckled the Aussie with a craggy grin. "You thought I meant to eliminate her. Why, you have misread the situation haven't you, mate?"

It was unusual to see Jonathan so off guard. If the situation wasn't so dire, Dana would have thoroughly enjoyed the experience. "Well, I, um..." stammered Thorpe. "Excuse me?"

Haas smiled. His face was ruddy, sun damaged, and spotted with uneven blond stubble, his eyes cool, dark, humorless. "Our dear lady is a hostage," he said.

Jonathan nodded. "A hostage. But that seems rather backward. You see, she could be used to detour the husband from complicating matters, I suppose. But the very fact that we have her, gives him all the more reason to interfere. His objective, let us not forget, is Lindell, not the skull."

Haas could have smiled but chose against it. Obviously, this was a dangerous one. Dana wondered how Jonathan had managed to get caught up with this lot. "Once again," said the Aussie. "You've misread the situation."

"Well, would you care to enlighten me?" asked Jonathan with a bit of a snit.

"I'm holding her hostage for you, mate. You see, I know of your former relationship with the woman. I can see in your eyes that she still has a hold on you. The way I see it, you're not going to do anything other than exactly what I say unless you want to see your girlfriend take two rounds in the forehead."

Oh, this was a bloody troublesome bloke!

Chapter 28

Hunt cut the Yamaha's engine nearly three quarters of a mile from the coordinates given to him by Lucky Lindell. Sound was tricky in the rainforest. The constant rustling of foliage, the chirps and chatters of wildlife, it seemed an endless cacophony of noise and thus a perfect foil that might even cover the sound of an approaching motorcycle. But winds were fickle here, changing direction on a whim, or ceasing altogether. The wildlife as well, might become spooked and go strangely silent. Hunt couldn't risk that he might be detected.

It took nearly fifteen minutes to make the coordinate on foot, but well before this he sensed that something was not right. For one thing, why was Dana's phone stationary? There was no obvious reason for them to remain in a particular wooded area and Hunt's mind raced through the possible explanation for such an extended layover. The first – and most unsettling - was that Dana had been executed and the body tossed into the brush. Hunt did his best to push this horrific thought from his mind. It was unproductive and could only diminish his focus. Though, despite his best efforts, ghastly images of Dana's bullet-ridden form continued to claw their way back into his thoughts, to shout and fuss, clamoring for attention.

No.

Unproductive.

Stop.

Think of the other possibilities. Focus. Rely on your training.

They might have bedded down for the night, he supposed; they could be planning to continue forward at daybreak. This certainly would be a logical course of action. The going was very tough – even in broad daylight – and nighttime travel was extremely hazardous. Case in point, Hunt had spilled the bike twice during the night. There were just too many unseen obstacles. Fortunately, neither he nor the bike had been seriously damaged in either fall.

But there was no indication of a campsite: no voices, no footsteps, no flashlight beams, not even a campfire, nothing to indicate human inhabitation.

Upon making the clearing, Hunt was able to locate the tire tracks and identify five separate sets of footprints: three male, two female. One of the females was definitely Dana. Even in the minimal moonlight, he recognized her boot tread. By the looks of it, she had apparently leapt out of the back of the truck and scuffled with one of the men before rising and retreating with the same man to perhaps fifteen yards from where the vehicle sat. Good girl, he thought. At least she put up a fight.

Upon further inspection, he determined that she and one of the males had returned to the back of the truck while the remaining three had retreated to the cab.

Relief spilled over Hunt like a hot wave. She was alive. Whatever the purpose in abducting Dana, the intent had not been to kill – at least not yet. Not until she'd fulfilled whatever purpose they desired.

Hunt paced back and forth, examining the site again, studying nuances, seeking that which he might have missed on the first walkthrough.

Interesting.

Was this third male a part of the team, left in back to guard, or perhaps, interrogate Dana, or was this another captive? Hunt singled out the man's tracks. It was difficult in some areas because the ground alternated from dirt to foliage and back again. But, it was fairly clear that this man had exited the rear of the truck and was escorted by the female to about fifty feet distant. The man continued slightly further, but obviously remained within sight of the woman, and was then returned to the rear of the truck where he remained until departure.

A bathroom break. Nothing more.

Another captive.

Cook possibly?

But it was just as likely that Cook was involved with this team, perhaps hiring them to track down Andy and the skull.

No. That made no sense. As slimy as Cook was, he was a scientist. He wouldn't know how to find a team for this type of operation. Cook was a lone rogue, frightened and out of his element, nothing more.

So, yes, Cook could be the second captive, but not part of the operation.

Who else might be the captive?

Another member of the paleontological expedition, he supposed. Another survivor. It was entirely possible that someone else had survived without Hunt's knowledge.

Or, perhaps, a villager, someone who knew the local lore and legend concerning the skull. Depending on the team's objective, such a person might be of value.

Or maybe Andy.

Yes. Andy.

That would make sense. If they'd found Andy they would most likely have the skull.

But then, why take Dana?

This had plagued Hunt since her capture. She was here in search of Andy. She was not part of the expedition. She had no connection to the skull whatsoever. What was the gain in abducting her?

Hunt moved about the place where Dana had sat, presumably talking with one of the men. Not surprisingly, he found Dana's cell phone on the ground perhaps seven feet distant. He knew it was here. Lucky's GPS had told him as much. There was no effort made to conceal it. The phone sat in the open, still turned on, a silent slap in Hunt's face. He was meant to find it. Hunt scooped it up, immediately checking it for messages and texts in hopes that Dana had somehow been able to leave him a clue.

There was nothing.

Hunt retraced Dana's steps, scanning the ground for something, anything that she might have left as a clue. In truth, the clue was rather large and obvious. In broad sweeping strokes, on the right side of where Dana had been seated, the words, "Sao Pau" had been drawn in the dirt. She obviously hadn't had the opportunity to complete the message, but the meaning was clear. Sao Pau - Sao Paulo. They were headed to Sao Paulo.

Hunt was cautiously optimistic. Sao Paulo was the seventh largest city in the world. Saying that someone was in Sao Paulo was like saying they were in New York or Chicago. There were millions of people in the metropolitan area. Someone could hide there for years and never be found.

Hunt pulled his phone free of his pocket and punched in a recently-added speed dial number. The phone was answered almost immediately. "Lucky, this is Marc Huntington. The party holding Dana is headed to Sao Paulo. I have reason to believe that Andy may also be a captive of this same group. Did you learn if anyone on the expedition has connections to a Brazilian research institution, particularly in Sao Paulo?"

Chapter 29

Sao Paulo, Brazil

The plane ride had been horrible: a cramped single engine Cessna, aged and battered, excessive turbulence, and worst of all, Jonathan Thorpe. Dana simply didn't know how to manage her emotions where he was concerned. Here he was, charming as ever, apparently caught up in something beyond his control, attempting to help her to escape, while simultaneously plotting his next theft. She'd been a fool to have ever let him creep into her heart to begin with. He'd been an assignment, nothing more.

But, he had been more.

Jonathan Thorpe was a complex person, much more so than what his profession might suggest – a simple thief. Jonathan viewed the world through a peculiar lens. To him, it was an exciting place, full of possibility and challenge. He felt stifled by what he considered to be the laws and regulations of small-minded persons. True, there had to be a certain level of order to a society, Jonathan was not an anarchist, but he felt that those of superior intellect and insight should be given a certain latitude concerning societal restraints.

It all sounded terribly egocentric – and it was – but this mindset was only one element of the man. He enjoyed life – reveled in it. Rarely did a smile not illuminate his face. He took great pleasure in people, loved mingling and joking, learning about others and their goals and desires. He might consider himself superior, but he was a master at encouraging and edifying the people within his sphere of influence. He would always uncover someone's special gift, compliment it, support it, and in this way, gain access to not only their hearts, but to their trust as well. This he often did without malice or ulterior motive; yet, frequently these same relationships gave him opportunity to practice his craft. Strange as it might seem, Jonathan often loved and respected those from whom he thieved.

His criminal enterprise, felt Dana, was really an extension of his verve for life. The son of a wealthy investment banker, Jonathan wanted more out of his days than debits and credits. He enjoyed the finer things, the upper crust lifestyle, but also knew it to be as monotonous as a dull throbbing ache. His thievery really grew out of adolescent pranks designed to unsettle his father's stuffed-shirt friends. But, intelligent and enterprising as he was, he soon found that he was quite good at it all. And even more importantly, escaping with a near-priceless piece of art gave him an adrenaline rush like none other. In this respect, Jonathan was like a little boy. He played a game: a deadly game, an illegal game, but a game none-the-less.

But, where did this leave Dana?

This close proximity to Jonathan stirred her emotions, brought back the old feelings, but she couldn't allow herself to act on these. Not even for a moment. She loved Hunt. She always would. He was honest, loyal, faithful to the bone. God, she made him sound like a Saint Bernard! But, Hunt was a good man. He had issues, yes. But, who didn't? And considering what he'd been through, he was amazingly good natured and well balanced. A bit daft at times, true. But, he loved her.

Loved her fully and completely.

So, why the nettling emotions? Why the doubts? Why the stirring whenever she met Jonathan's gaze?

Silliness. She was being a schoolgirl, nothing more, and she would not allow herself to dwell on this a moment longer – if for no other reason, the bloke had kidnapped her! Was she really so shallow as to allow this man to weasel his way into her life again?

No.

Never…

…Most likely not.

They were at a small airfield now, having just disembarked the chartered plane. Dana and Lindell were no longer bound. Too many questions would be asked should they appear as such in public. Likewise, they'd chosen to fly into a small airport on the outskirts of Sao Paulo instead of directly into the metropolis. Much less opportunity for the captives to make an escape into a crowd or draw the attention of a nosy security guard. This airfield had no security to speak of. And only a half dozen people were visible at any one time. No crowds.

Dana walked beside Jonathan as the party made their way across the tarmac and to the small building with a hand painted sign reading, *de aluguer de automoveis*. Rental Cars. Haas trailed only perhaps five meters behind, and Andrew Lindell and Tina Collins followed an equal distance behind Haas. "What are you caught up in this time?" whispered Dana.

"That," said Jonathan, glancing behind him to ascertain the Aussie's proximity, "is something I'm still attempting to determine."

"Who hired you?"

A chuckle and a shake of the head. "Now, you know I never divulge a client."

"Don't be a bore, Jonathan. You brought me into this. Give me something to work with."

Jonathan glanced back again. Haas was no nearer than he had been. "The client is anonymous," said Jonathan. "I don't know his name, nor much else about him."

"That's unusual. You usually do quite the thorough vetting."

Jonathan nodded. "I do. And I did. This man is a ghost, it seems. He's a yank, I know that much. But, I've met him at properties in Switzerland, Hong Kong, and Virginia. All with very high security and often with dubious allies present."

"And still you aligned yourself with him?"

An embarrassed shrug. "He pays rather well. And the work he gives me, quite challenging. I must admit, I've enjoyed the ride."

"And what does he want with the Amazon skull?"

At first, it seemed Jonathan contemplated how much to divulge, if anything at all, but then, after a pause and a sigh, he said, "At the onset, I believed it was simply to be another piece for his rather peculiar antiquities collection. Now, I'm not sure that it's so benign."

"Meaning what exactly?"

"Well, my dear, you've been to the cave as well as to the expedition site. You saw the comatose bodies, witnessed the peculiar blaze."

"And you believe the skull is responsible for both of those scenarios?"

"Let's just say I haven't found a way to discount the possibility."

"So, you think your client wants the skull so that he can duplicate these events? You're saying he believes the bloody old bone to be a weapon?"

Jonathan chuckled and shrugged. "Well, it sounds rather silly when you put it that way."

"Jonathan, it is silly."

Jonathan gazed at her, his expression unreadable. "Normally, I'd be inclined to agree with you. But, this man Haas, he's onto something and not letting go. That leads me to believe the skull is more than a trinket."

"Then, why continue? Why not just walk away?"

Jonathan offered his winning smile. "Well, that wouldn't be any fun, now would it?"

"No. It wouldn't be any fun at all, mate," said Haas from behind.

Dana wondered how much he'd heard and if their conversation had endangered Jonathan.

*****

Sao Paulo Brazil has some of the most aggressive drivers on the planet. Speed limit signs are given about as much attention as a two pack a day smoker gives the surgeon general's warning. A red stop light is regarded as a signal to drop the speed by about ten miles per hour and to toot the horn twice on the way through. Even sidewalks aren't entirely off limits and wise pedestrians keep an eye out for ever impatient motorists.

Dana wondered how anyone ever grew old in such a place.

Gratefully turning off of the primary thoroughfares, Tina Collins maneuvered the rented SUV slowly down a narrow lane and through the maze of university buildings. According to Lindell, the skull was in Building H.

Dana scanned the scene. She and the lad were running short on time. Dana's use as a hostage and Lindell's as a means to gain access to the skull were near an end. Haas was a killer. She'd seen his type, knew the look, the mannerisms, the eager glint as the time drew near. If she was to make a move, it would need to be soon.

Jonathan was in danger as well, though she wasn't sure that he fully comprehended the threat. He was a master at breaking and entering, deft at stealth and subterfuge. If, for whatever reason, Lindell's retina scan failed to be sufficient, Haas would look to Jonathan to gain access to the skull. But, once he had outlived his usefulness... Well, Dana couldn't worry about Jonathan just now. Lingering feelings for the man aside, he'd allied himself with this lot; he was a professional; he'd bloody well have to tend to his own safety.

The woman, Tina was her name, drove; Jonathan sat in the front passenger seat; Haas, Dana, and Lindell occupied the rear, left to right respectively. Dana hadn't had an opportunity to share her plan – if she could even call it a plan – with Lindell, but hoped he'd be clever enough to follow her lead. This concerned her some. Lindell continued to appear listless, and, seated beside him as she was, Dana could feel his body heat on her right arm. The lad had a bugger of a fever.

Dana continued to scan the scene, looking for a likely opportunity, waiting for the proper moment. It was summer in Brazil, and thus fewer students strolled the walkways than during the primary school year.

A boy and a girl sat cross-legged under a tree, textbooks open on the ground, laptop computers resting on their legs. They chuckled nervously, grinning, averting eye contact. Each was romantically interested in the other, deduced Dana, yet neither had spoken openly of it. Likely, they'd be dating within the week.

A balding man, two decades older than the students, and so most likely a professor, cut across the grassy lawn on his way from one building to another. He carried a laptop case over his left shoulder and a stack of manila files under his right arm.

A group of six students stood to the side of the lane laughing and talking.

A young woman of perhaps twenty walked a Labrador retriever to Dana's left.

Two young men played Frisbee ahead and to the right.

Tina Collins slowed in order to allow three giggling female students to cross before her. The lane was narrowing and within a minute they would be directly between two red bricked buildings. The structure on the right was at the top of a gentle rise which angled sharply off to the rear left of the structure. It wasn't ideal, the cover not spectacular, but this might be Dana's best option. This was Building F. H could not be far distant.

She nudged Lindell gently with her right elbow. No response. She nudged again, this time harder. A grunt, a lulled head in her direction. Silently, Dana angled her head and shifted her eyes, indicating the door handle. Lindell stared stupidly, not comprehending her meaning. Dana repeated the gesture. Surely Lindell had to understand the need for escape.

He closed his eyes, allowed his head to lull.

No. Apparently he did not.

Now, they were nearly to the top of the rise. Dana could see buildings G and H just down the slope on the left side. If she was to make a move, it would need to be now.

Without warning, Dana simultaneously slammed her left fist into Haas's groin while reaching across Lindell, catching the door handle with a quick twist, and tossing the door open with her right. Throwing herself powerfully against Lindell, her hope was that the force of her thrust would carry them both out of the slow moving vehicle and onto the ground before their captors could react. They would have only seconds to get to their feet and race toward the building, but at least it gave them a chance. Dana hoped against all logic that Haas wouldn't be so foolhardy as to open fire in public, but she couldn't count on it. They would need to move fast, plain and simple.

The ploy nearly worked.

The startled Lindell tumbled through the now open door with Dana pressed closely against him. Lindell was free of the vehicle, but at the last moment Dana fell still. Haas had her by the left ankle, his grip nearly vice-like.

Hanging halfway out of the door as the SUV came to an abrupt halt, Dana just about hit her head against the pavement; but she managed to angle up at the last, lifting herself with a quickly tightened abdomen. Dana twisted, rolling right, then abruptly left, slamming the heal of her free foot into Haas's jaw.

He released the ankle.

Dana slid onto the ground, landing on her right shoulder. Rolling rather ungracefully, she rose to her feet, and slammed the door in Haas's face as he scrambled across the seat to catch her.

Jonathan and Collins were exiting the vehicle as well, Jonathan only two meters from her. She hit him mid chest with a roundhouse kick and then turned, running toward Building F. There were shouts and screams from just ahead as students ran toward the scene of the commotion.

Where was Lindell? He couldn't be far. Not in his condition.

Dana was three quarters up the rise, almost to the building now, nearly to the safety of the door. Maybe Lindell had already made the building. It was possible, she supposed, that he'd had a sudden burst of adrenaline and raced inside while she'd scraped with Haas.

She was reaching for the handle now, clasping it. She pulled. Just another couple of seconds.

And then the bullet struck her.

Chapter 30

Unlike Thorpe's team, Hunt took a commercial airliner into Sao Paulo. He'd had to endure a short jump from the same airstrip the others had used three hours earlier in order to meet the Boeing 727 that would take him the rest of the way, but the speed of the jet versus the single engine plane, as well as the fact that Hunt's craft had sufficient fuel to traverse the entire distance uninterrupted, allowed him to reach his destination slightly before the others.

The campus was large, spread out, and, as far as Hunt could determine, followed no logical layout. Hunt was good with languages. In addition to English he could handle basic conversations in Arabic, Farsi, Hindi, and Spanish. Portuguese shared its roots with Spanish, but they were not interchangeable tongues, and so Hunt found himself driving slowly through the university calling, "English? Anyone speak English?"

Fortunately, English was a required language for most students, and so it wasn't too long before a Frisbee throwing young man was able to point him in the direction of Building H, the science building. Hunt had no actual knowledge as to where the skull would be held, but the science building seemed a logical starting point. He wasn't exactly sure how to proceed once attaining the building, but supposed he'd ask around until he learned where a significant fossil might be stored, and then inquire concerning sightings of either Dana or Andy – preferably both.

Something else was troubling him as well. Just after arriving in Sao Paulo, he'd received another call from Lucky Lindell. A team from the CDC (Center for Disease Control) had been sent to the cave in order to examine and rescue the numerous comatose victims contained within. The problem had been that they'd discovered an empty chamber. Not one human form present. Hunt had questioned Lucky, initially assuming that they'd located the wrong cave. But, Lucky had assured him that they were at the proper coordinates, that the stone slabs on which the bodies had lain were still there, that there were signs of heavy foot traffic in and out, but that the slumbering inhabitants were gone. Though, there were some interesting articles left behind: a bronze helmet of

Asian origin, a metal shield of the type used in iron age Europe, an Egyptian headdress that was guessed to date back to a period long before Christ.

The whole thing was strange beyond belief and so after disconnecting with Lucky, Hunt set his mind on more mundane matters: Who would have both the resources and the motive to slip in and relocate these people? Another question was why? Lucky Lindell was in contact with the Brazilian government. They claimed no involvement in the relocation of these people. So, assuming the government was not connected, what purpose could there possibly be in stealing several dozen comatose persons?

There were a few students milling about Building H, but the hallways were not well populated. Hunt did walk past two lecture halls where classes were being held, and so assumed that most students that were on campus at ten AM in the middle of the summer were in class. As well, there was a conference at the far end of the building. As with the classes, this was already in session, nearly all of the participants seated within a large convention room. There just wouldn't be a lot of hanging around just now.

Hunt strolled down a long hallway in search of some sort of office. If possible, he wanted to avoid barging into a classroom to ask his questions. He didn't think this approach would find people very helpful, and also, not knowing who Dana's captors might be and what their capabilities were, he wanted to keep a relatively low profile. His best option was to learn the location of the skull, determine if Andy, Dana, or anyone else had come inquiring about it, and then determine a course of action.

He was worried about Dana.

She was skilled at hand-to-hand combat, but apparently so were her captors. The two men had neutralized her and deposited her into the truck in under a minute. That was not an easy feat where Dana was concerned.

But now that they had her, what had they done? Were they hoping that she could lead them to the skull? Was there some other, as yet unknown, reason she might be held? And if Dana was unable to provide whatever information they sought, would they leave her alive – a potential witness – or eliminate her?

Hunt rounded a corner and noticed a familiar figure just ahead: early forties, pale, rather slight of build, a thin nutmeg mustache. The man had just exited an office door and then paused, seeming to ponder which direction to move. Hunt slipped into a recessed doorway. He did not want to be seen by Daniel Cook.

Hunt could hear Cook's footsteps now, hard rubber soles on vinyl tile. Cook was moving closer. Perfect. Hunt wanted to question the man. But he couldn't very well interrogate him in the middle of a hallway. Despite the sparse foot traffic, there were classes in session, and there was always the possibility of a random student strolling unknowingly into the area at an awkward moment.

If he remembered correctly, there was an empty classroom just two doors to his left. With luck, the door would be unlocked.

Hunt waited... waited. Now!

Cook didn't have a chance to scream or to fight back as Hunt clasped a hand over his jaw, pulling sharply upward so the man could not speak, while keeping his fingers clear of the mouth as to avoid a potential bite. His other arm crossed over Cook's right shoulder and to just under and behind the man's left armpit. Hunt swept a leg from left to right, causing Cook to lose his footing. In less than three seconds, Hunt was in complete control of the situation.

Swiftly, he dragged the struggling man into the vacant classroom and whispered. "We're going to have a conversation, Cook. I'm a skilled operative with extensive martial arts training. I could kill you before you blink twice. Do you understand?"

Cook nodded and whimpered.

Hunt was in full combat mode now. No joking about, no banter. Hunt's face was an emotionless mask, his form taut, his muscles coiled for action. He had no time to play games with this sniveling little man. "I'm going to release you so we can talk like two civilized human beings," said Hunt. "But I will remain between you and the doorway. You've already shot at me and dynamited us into a cave. I am willing to kill you if necessary. Is that clear?"

Another nod.

"Good. Now, when I let go, I want you to sit on the nearest stool, that one right in front of us. Turn so you're facing away from the door. You'll have your back to me. That's how I want it."

Cook nodded again and Hunt released him, but remained within three feet as Cook nervously seated himself on the tall stool and then turned away as Hunt had instructed. Cook shivered involuntarily, though the place was far from cool.

The room wasn't a classroom, but a laboratory, the college campus variety: four rows of long tables, Bunsen burners, Petri dishes, the smell of formalde-hyde, posters depicting equations and formulas. Hunt glanced around, but found nothing with which to bind the man. He'd just need to make do.

Cook started babbling almost immediately. "Mr. Huntington, the cave, I'm so sorry for that. I suppose I'd best explain."

Hunt came up beside him, bent, and whispered into his right ear. "What's to explain? You tried to kill us. Right now I'm wondering if you can give me a reason not to return the favor."

Cook shuddered. The man really was a coward to the core. A dangerous coward, true. But a coward none-the-less.

"Now," continued Hunt. "Do you know the whereabouts of the skull?"

Cook shook his head. "No... No, I came here because Andrew..." he trailed off.

"Yes?" prodded Hunt.

"Andrew would likely bring the skull here for testing. We have connections with the university, you see. I need to secure the skull."

"And Andy? Where is Andy?"

"I... I don't know. I haven't seen him since the cave. I..."

"And my wife? Have you seen my wife?"

At this, Cook almost turned to face Hunt, but then stopped himself with a jerking shudder. "Do you mean she's not with you?"

"That's right. She's not with me. Any idea who would kidnap her?"

Cook shook his head. "No. None at all. I wasn't aware. I'm sorry." The re-sponse seemed genuine. Hunt accepted it.

"There's another party involved. Someone else seeking the skull. Are they connected with you in any way?"

"No. No. Absolutely not." A pause. "When last I was at the cave, I saw a vehicle perhaps five hundred meters from the cave entrance. A truck. It looked military in design, obviously meant for off-road excursions." Cook's brogue was becoming more pronounced, most likely due to his escalating fear. All the better. The more fearful the man, the more likely he'd blather something of use.

"And you have no idea who these people might be or what their connection is to the skull or to the expedition?"

Another shake of the head. "No. None. In truth, I didn't know without question that they were involved. I have no knowledge where they are concerned."

Hunt nodded. Cook was telling the truth. He was certain of that. The man was simply too frightened to lie. "Alright," said Hunt after a moment. "You feel like telling me why you're willing to kill just to put your hands on that skull?"

"Killing? I... haven't killed anyone, I..."

"Nah, nah, nah. Let's keep it honest. You tried to kill Dana and me back in the cave."

"Yes... I'm terribly sorry, but..."

"And then there's the expedition. The fire. A lot of people died there."

Cook's eyes went wide. He shook his head vehemently. Forgetting himself, he turned to face Hunt. For the moment, Hunt allowed him to remain as such. "My team? You think I'm the one who burned our base camp? You think I killed my own colleagues?"

Hunt shrugged. "Either you or Greg Milton. My bet's on you."

Cook's mouth dropped open, but no sound escaped.

Hunt stepped forward and bent as to place them eye-to-eye. "I need you to tell me what happened at the excavation site. Those were your people, Cook. Yours! You betrayed them."

Cook shrank back, nearly toppling off of the stool. "Um... I'm not sure what you want me to say."

"Why don't we begin with why you faked your own death? Whose body did they find incinerated in your tent?"

Cook hesitated for a moment, averting Hunt's gaze.

"Cook, we can do this easy or hard. But, I don't have time to be patient and I'm looking for you to give some answers."

Cook nodded, still avoiding eye contact. "The body was Bradley Lyons. A young man. An intern. He assisted Andrew."

"Okay, and why was Lyons in your tent?"

"I had gone out. Just taking a walk. Contemplating the ramifications of the find. Apparently, Bradley crept into my tent intending to make off with the skull."

"Why would Lyons want the skull?"

"He worked closely with Andrew. I'm sure he wanted to return the skull to him, since…" Here he hesitated for a moment, apparently searching for a clear explanation. "Well, I suppose it was because I'd dismissed the find."

"Yeah, about that," said Hunt. "You discounted Andy's find because he thought it was too old. Is that really what started this mess?" It seemed incredulous to Hunt that such a minor intellectual squabble could lead to the deaths of so many.

Cook tightened his lips. There was something here. Something he didn't want to say.

"Spill it, Cook."

The frightened PHD nodded, gazing at his twitching hands which lay folded in his lap. "That is what I wanted Andrew to believe," he said at last. "That he was dating the skull incorrectly. And, in truth, the contour of the skull was not what we expected to find at this specific dig."

"Go on."

"But, the skull is unique - beyond the paleontological aspects."

"I assume you're referring to the legends surrounding this particular skull – a bunch of hoodoo mumbo jumbo."

"Um, well… Yes. There are legends about the skull. It's well, extraordinary."

And there was a strange timbre to Cook's tone, a nervous excitement. And at last, at least one of the pieces fell into place. "The expedition was a front," said Hunt. "Sure, there were other finds. You could justify the expense. But your real goal was to find the Amazon skull. You came out here specifically to find that particular fossil."

Cook looked away and to the ground, but Hunt continued to press.

"You put this entire expedition together because you knew the lore; you knew where the skull was rumored to have been buried. And when that mudslide uncovered human bones, you recognized the opportunity."

Again, Cook hesitated. "I... did not know the lore. Not initially. I'm a scientist, Mr. Huntington. I have no use for silly superstitions."

Hunt contemplated Cook for a moment, studying him. "Okay, you didn't know the lore. Who did?"

Cook turned away from Hunt, offering a nervous profile. Hunt stepped forward, grabbed Cook by the left bicep, and roughly turned him so that they were face-to-face. "Who conceived this expedition? Whose idea was it?" And then, following his line of reasoning to the next logical step, he added, "Who's funding it?"

"An anonymous donor." Cook nearly squeaked the words.

As strange as it seemed, this made sense. For whatever reason, this unknown person desired the skull. He'd evidently learned of the mudslide that had uncovered ancient human bones and that it was in the vicinity where this sacred totem was supposedly buried. The man was obviously well funded, whether personally or through associations, and so offered to finance the expedition - but with the caveat that Cook, the expedition leader, secretly search for the prized fossil. At the onset, Cook believed none of the legend, but jumped at the chance to head an expedition. Who cared if some fool wanted to fund a treasure hunt, Cook could still do real science on the man's dime.

But then things went awry. The skull was found, Cook tried to downplay it to Andy Lindell because, in order to give it to the donor, he'd agreed to exclude it from the expedition's official finds. Most likely, Cook hadn't even believed there was such a thing as the Amazon skull. So what possible risk could there have been in agreeing to hand it over? But then one thing led to another and the skull went missing. Cook was most likely threatened by his anonymous employer and set out to recover the skull – based on his presence here at the university; it was a task that he still sought to accomplish. Meanwhile, this donor, this mystery man desiring the skull, sent a second team – this one not scientific, but military – to locate the missing prize.

Was it possible that Cook had been unaware of this second team, that even now he hadn't made the connection? Yes. It was likely even. Otherwise, Cook would not have taken things into his own hands. He wouldn't have tried to seal Hunt and Dana into the cave, he wouldn't have taken pot shots at them, he wouldn't be in this room at this moment. No, Cook would have left these things for those better suited for the task. As well, the more Hunt thought about it, the more likely it seemed that this group – the anonymous donor's back-up team – was involved in the disappearance of the comatose victims. That being the case, if he had known of their intent, Cook would not have tried to seal the cave.

Hunt leaned in toward Cook again, narrowing his eyes, studying the man. "Okay, I'm getting a handle on this thing, but I still have some questions."

Cook nodded wearily.

"You didn't believe in the Amazon skull. It was just a legend some rich fool told you about when he handed you a wad of cash and sent you to the Amazon."

Again, Cook nodded.

"But, when Andy found the skull, you recognized it for what it was, probably due to the writing on the interior. When the fossil went missing, you were threatened by your benefactor. That's when the killing began."

Cook shook his head vehemently. "No! That is not how it happened. Well, the initial bit, yes. But, not the killing."

"Then, explain to me what happened."

"My interest in the skull, initially, was as you say, motivated by the anonymous donor. I never believed in his hoodoo, as you call it. But, once I saw the specimen, held it in my hand, saw the strange and wonderful writing on the interior of the cranium, do you realize how difficult that must have been to…"

"I don't care how amazing the skull is. The killings – who? How?"

"Well, the killing was…" He paused, nearly swallowing his lower lip behind his upper teeth. "It was the skull itself. Initially, at least."

Hunt had to restrain himself from decking the guy. "The skull? You want me to believe that an inanimate object is our murderer? Why not just blame Professor Plum and his candlestick and be done with it?"

Cook flinched at the harsh tone. "The skull has… Well, there's apparently an agent within."

Hunt nodded. "I've been told there might be some sort of virus."

"Assumedly so, yes. Though I cannot verify the composition of the substance."

"Go on."

"Apparently, when young Lyons touched the stuff, it, well, I suppose it infected him – quite rapidly. I saw the body. His blood literally boiled. His skin popped. Blood spurted everywhere. It looked as if the poor lad had cooked from the inside out."

Cook was visibly disturbed by the memory, but Hunt pressed on. "And the rest of the team, those killed four days later when the base camp was set ablaze?"

"That occurred shortly after Andrew returned with the skull. I suppose he needed access to some of our equipment, maybe he wanted to reconnect with the expedition. I don't know. But by this time, rumors had taken hold. Some people believed that Andrew had killed me. Lyons was missing, but they, I believe, assumed he had run off with Andrew. In any event, the crowd encircled Andrew. They meant to restrain him, to take him to the authorities. But, you see, the skull had changed."

"Changed? How so?"

"The viral agent within, I'm not a biologist, but I suppose exposure to oxygen and sunlight after millennia buried beneath the earth activated it in some way. The quantity of the stuff had grown. What had been a thin coating of mucus now filled the skull to near overflowing."

"You're saying the virus – or whatever it is – multiplied."

Cook nodded. "Just as infections produce puss, so did this agent."

"I'm still not seeing how this led to the killings."

"Andrew was unarmed," said Cook. "His former colleagues were surrounding him, accusing him of killing me. Andrew had no gun, no weapon, so he simply splashed the mucus onto those attempting to subdue him. Almost immediately, some fell to the ground as if dead, others began to boil from within. Clothing burst into flame as their bodies sizzled. Flaming scientists raced about the camp, some coming in contact with flammable substances. Soon there were small fires everywhere, people running about in panic. Within minutes, the entire site was ablaze, and once again, Andrew made off with the skull."

Hunt leveled his gaze at Cook. "That's far-fetched, Cook. You wanna try again?"

For once, Cook actually acted as if he might possess a spine. "Believe me or no, Mr. Huntington. But, if you locate Andrew Lindell, and if he still has that infectious skull, beware. I have no idea as to how much of that vile substance has been produced, but I do know it to be quite lethal. There's no telling how readily that contagion will spread."

Hunt shook his head. "I've never heard of a virus that made people spontaneously combust."

"And four decades ago no one had heard of a virus called HIV. Viruses change, Mr. Huntington. They mutate into new and peculiar strains. Many viruses cause high fever. It seems this one takes that to the extreme."

Hunt still didn't buy it, but he was getting the idea that Cook did. The whole thing seemed so uncanny. He had a hard time getting his head around it. "One more thing," he said after a pause. "You just described this scene as if you were a witness. What did you do, hide in the bushes and watch it all happen? Didn't you try to help anyone, to maybe prevent some of this?"

"I... After encountering you and your wife in the rainforest... After I'd fired those warning shots... I returned. Andrew was already present. There was nothing more to be done." Cook dropped his gaze and turned away. The man had been armed, and yet was too cowardly to assist his own companions. Hunt was about to press Cook further, but then he heard something from outside and a ways up the rise.

Was that a gun shot?

Chapter 31

Thorpe fell back through the open door and onto the passenger seat. What was Dana thinking? She'd felled him with a solid roundhouse kick. Did she actually think he'd been about to attack her? Bloody woman! He'd never figure her out. This was all Haas's fault. The Aussie's entire plan had been ill-conceived. It was one thing to bring the listless and docile Lindell onto the campus, but Dana was a skilled operative. Bringing her as a hostage into a public situation was bound to fail. Now, Thorpe only hoped he could intervene before one of these military types decided to open fire.

God, he hoped they weren't that stupid.

As quick as he could right himself, Thorpe was again up and out of the seat. Dana was sprinting across the yard, Haas was scrambling out of the backseat where Dana had slammed the door in his face as he'd grasped for her, and Collins was rounding the front of the SUV in pursuit of Dana.

Collins was the most immediate threat.

Thorpe tackled her from behind, catching her entirely off guard.

They hit the ground hard, Collins scraping her chin on the asphalt. But, the woman was quick. Almost immediately, her left elbow snapped back connecting with Thorpe's solar plexus. Thorpe had only a moment to react, and angled just enough so that the blow glanced instead of landing squarely. Still, the hit set Thorpe off balance and Collins was able to twist beneath him, freeing an arm.

She gave him a swift chop that landed on the curve of his left shoulder. She'd aimed for the neck, but Thorpe twisted at the last, while offering a jab of his own.

A flip.

A jab.

A twist and a chop.

Thorpe had the upper hand again, but wouldn't maintain the position for long. Collins, a trained military operative, was the more skilled fighter; Thorpe just had body mass, desperation, and classroom-learned jiu-jitsu on his side. He needed to finish this quickly.

Out of the corner of his eye, he saw movement.

Haas.

The Aussie had finally managed to exit the vehicle, and was aiming a gun in Dana's direction.

Slamming his fist into Collins' jaw, Thorpe launched himself at the man catching him by the ankle just as Haas squeezed the trigger of his Sig Sauer P556 SWAT semi-automatic pistol, a big nasty bugger with a military-grade barrel and a 30 round magazine.

Haas responded with an off-balanced kick, connecting with Thorpe mid chest. Thorpe managed to intercept the thrust, minimizing the impact. Still, the gun had discharged, the sharp tone of the gun burst ringing in Thorpe's ears.

Dana!

Snapping his arms in a quick clockwise motion, one on either side of the Aussie's left leg and just below the knee, Thorpe brought Haas to the ground, the weapon tumbling from his grasp, the back of his head striking the asphalt with a loud *thunk*!

Thorpe and Collins simultaneously dove for the Sig Sauer.

Haas was still conscious, groggy it seemed, but still in the fight.

Now, the three of them clawed and scraped for the weapon. Haas blinked rapidly, shaking his head as if trying to focus. It seemed the whack to the cranium had juggled his marbles. Still though, he was a threat.

Thorpe pulled down and right, attempting to jerk the Sig Sauer free. Instead, he found the barrel of the Sig staring him in the face. Angling left, he jerked down and away. Collins chose the same moment to give a fierce two-handed tug.

The weapon discharged a short burst, the recoil pulling the semi-automatic free of Thorpe's grasp.

Thorpe was aware of students racing for cover, screaming. One young man stumbled to the ground, a sudden font of blood erupting from just below his kneecap.

Thorpe elbowed Haas in the chin, and, with a quick jerk, somehow pulled the Sig Sauer free, immediately slamming its butt into Collins' forehead. The woman tumbled backward, stunned, possibly near unconscious, as Thorpe swung the gun around right to left like a big league baseball player, smacking Haas across the left side of his face and sending him tumbling.

Maintaining his hold on the weapon, Thorpe scrambled to his feet amidst screams and shouts.

There was a group of four students huddled about the boy who'd taken the shot to the knee. He'd survive, thought Thorpe. Besides, the lad wasn't his concern.

Dana. He needed to reach Dana.

She was face down on the steps leading to the nearest building. Thorpe had pulled Haas off balance just as he'd fired the round. How had his aim remained true?

It took less than a minute for Thorpe to reach her, and even as he drew near, he could see it.

Blood.

There was blood on the concrete.

Blood in her tumbled black hair.

"Dana," he cried. "Dana!" as he fell to his knees, nearly dropping the offending weapon beside him.

Immediately, he pressed two fingers against her neck. Was there a pulse? Please let there be a pulse.

He couldn't find one and so moved his fingers a few inches forward. Nothing.

Wait.

Yes. Yes, there it was. Good. Good.

Glancing over his shoulder, he saw Tina Collins sit upright, shake her head, and then stare in his direction. She rose.

Thorpe had no time to examine Dana's injuries or to worry about damaging her further by moving her. In one desperate motion, he scooped her up, settling her across the back of his neck and shoulders like a sack of flour, while almost simultaneously, snatching the gun. Thorpe was fit, not weak by any means, but he was not a special operations soldier such as Hunt. Dana's weight nearly sent him tumbling backward. Still, he managed to find his equilibrium and step cautiously forward. Leaning the Sig Sauer against the building, he managed to pull the door open, retrieve the weapon, and step inside.

There was a long narrow hallway lined with classroom doors and intersected at the end by another hallway and a staircase. Thorpe hurried forward, unable to run with Dana slumped over his shoulders, but moving as quickly as possible with a kind of uneven waddle.

Twice, he stumbled, tried to right himself, but to no avail. Dana's dead weight was too great and she slid off to his left. Thorpe was barely able to slow her decent and minimize the fall as she slid gracelessly to the cool tile floor.

The door opened behind them. It was Collins.

Thorpe fired a short burst, the sound of the rounds reverberating about the narrow way.

Not waiting to see the result of the shots, Thorpe hefted Dana, wrapping his right arm about her just under the arm pits, and began to drag her toward the end of the hallway.

The door was now closed behind them. There was no sign of Collins. Presumably, she'd ducked Thorpe's off balanced shots, and was waiting cautiously outside of the door, contemplating her next move.

They made it to the end of the hallway. The building seemed deserted, at least on this level. If there were any classes in session, they were elsewhere, perhaps on another floor. Needing to find someplace out of sight where he could hole up for a few minutes and determine Dana's condition, Thorpe decided to turn left at the T.

There was an office toward the end of the corridor. It was locked from the inside. Perfect. Leaning Dana against the wall, Thorpe picked the lock in less than thirty seconds. Quickly, he pulled her inside, and then closed the door behind them, locking it as he did. Thorpe left the lights off as he didn't want to draw attention. Quickly, he slid Dana to behind the large oak desk at the opposite wall. A glass block window offered enough light to see, and if they remained on the floor behind the massive hardwood desk, they would not be immediately visible should Collins and Haas come calling. Thorpe had the Sig Sauer. If that door opened, he was firing.

*****

Three minutes later, Dana let off her first moan. By this time, Thorpe had determined that her injury was not life threatening. She'd been grazed above her right ear. At first it seemed she'd lost a good deal of blood, but upon further inspection Thorpe realized that he'd panicked a bit. There was blood in her hair, yes, but nothing truly substantial.

Another minute and she was fairly well conscious. "Hunt?" she asked in a breathy growl.

"No, no, dear. It's your other man." They were seated on the floor against the wall behind the desk. Thorpe had positioned Dana so as her head would lean between his left shoulder and neck, her body, pressed firmly against his. The Sig Sauer lay on the floor to his right. The room was stuffy, no air conditioning, and Thorpe wiped a dribble of sweat from the end of his nose before it could drop into Dana's blood-matted hair.

"Jonathan?" she asked as her eyes fluttered open, her mouth twisting as if she'd tasted something sour.

"Yes, dear. It's me," he said with a smile and a gentle pat to her shoulder. He'd really missed being close to her.

"Bleeding Jonathan Thorpe?" Her voice notched up a degree in volume.

"Well, yes. I suppose you could put it that way, but..."

She smacked him across the face. Hard!

"What in bleeding Sunday was that about?" he gasped.

"What was... What! Blimey, Jonathan. You need to ask?"

"Well, I..."

"You kidnapped me."

"Not entirely. Well, yes, technically, I suppose. But, I was..."

"You tied me up, locked me away with that lunatic Haas."

"But..."

"You bloody well got me shot!"

"Shh. Shh. Now you're getting rather loud. Quiet down, dear, unless you want to be shot again."

"And now you threaten me!"

"Shhhh. Please. No. I'm not threatening you. We're hiding from Haas and Collins. If it's all the same with you, I'd prefer they didn't barge into this room, guns blazing. Frankly, I think they'd have the upper hand."

Dana's eyes narrowed. She was a smart girl. She'd figure it out. Pulling away from him, she tapped her head injury lightly with the tips of her fingers and then examined them for blood. "The bullet wound, just a graze, I take it?"

"Not much more than a scratch. You'll be fine."

"You'd bleeding well better hope I'll be fine. You and your dodgy crew, opening fire on a university campus. Looney, that."

Thorpe shrugged. He couldn't exactly disagree.

Scanning the small office from behind the oversized desk, Dana noted the family pictures adorning the walls, the four university degrees, the tiny round end table, and the wooden chair beside it. Still, though, she remained on the floor and hidden from the thick wooden door. "By the looks of it, we're in a faculty member's office. What precisely is our situation?"

Thorpe explained the scenario as he saw it, spending most of the time expounding in great detail on his heroic efforts to maintain her safety.

"Bloody mess," said Dana. "And Andrew Lindell? He's not been seen?"

"To be honest, dear, I was far too preoccupied trying to prevent Haas from shooting your beautiful head off to worry about the lad. Though, I can't say what might have happened while we've been holed away like frightened mice. In truth, I'd have thought Haas and Collins would have come gunning for us by now."

Dana contemplated this for a moment and then shook her head. "No. We're not the priority. They're here for the skull. A semi-automatic weapon has been discharged, and from what you've told me, at least one student was shot. Both campus security and local police will be traipsing all about the campus in no time. Most likely, they already are. Haas and Collins will need to make their move straight away; otherwise they might miss their window of opportunity to secure the skull."

Dana rose to her feet surprisingly quickly for someone who had just been shot. In truth, she appeared rather vigorous. "Where are you going?" asked Thorpe, now rising.

Dana made her way toward the door. "Building H. Science department. I need to find Lindell before he gets his bleeding head shot off." She paused, glanced back at him as he rose to follow, and said, "Jonathan, please put that gun down."

Thorpe stared at the weapon in his hand and then back toward Dana. "It might come in handy if we encounter my former companions."

Dana shook her head as if dealing with a frustrating school boy. "The campus will be on high alert. Shots have been fired. You're holding the very weapon that injured a student. Don't you think that might draw attention?"

Thorpe grinned and placed the Sig Sauer atop the paper strewn desk. He, of course, would have come to this same conclusion had he given it but a moment's thought, but Dana would never believe this, so he simply followed her silently through the door.

"You're welcome," he said, stepping into the hallway and following her to the right.

"For what?"

"For saving your life, of course. You were going to thank me, I assume."

Chapter 32

Andy Lindell tumbled onto the asphalt, his left shoulder blade connecting first, and then somehow he'd rolled onto the grassy lawn. The vehicle had been moving at less than ten miles per hour, and the fall barely knocked the air from his lungs. He hadn't quite understood what the Huntington woman was trying to accomplish until he fell free of the door, but then immediately knew that he had a very brief opportunity for escape.

Andy wasn't athletic by nature, but much could be said for adrenaline. He'd scrambled to his feet, and, crouching low, crossed behind the now-breaking SUV and raced down the gentle slope on the opposite side of the vehicle from which he'd been thrown. His hope had been that all attention would be directed to the passenger side, where Dana Huntington still dangled as she fought the brute Haas.

His theory had apparently worked as he'd slipped first behind a large and craggy redwood tree, and then to beside the nearest building where he quickly circled around the back, turned right, and continued toward the nearby science building. He'd visited the campus only two months before, and knew the layout fairly well. Aside from the threat of immediate danger, his biggest concern was whether or not Dr. Eduardo Matos was present. It was to him that Andrew had shipped the skull, and he needed to know where the man had hidden the thing.

Despite the grave situation, a little twist of a smile slipped across Andy's lips as he moved toward Building H. No. There was no retina scan involved. The campus did have such security for some of its classified work – he'd learned this on a previous trip – but, Andy had no authority to authorize or even request such measures. Though, he suspected the ruse had likely saved his life.

A sudden stab of pain in his gut.

He'd had these periodically over the past three days: severe, debilitating pains, short lived, but increasing in frequency. Along with the listlessness and the high fever – most likely verging on 103 or better – he was convinced that a competent doctor would hospitalize him. And truly, that was where he belonged. It was evident that something was seriously wrong. But, first the skull. He had to reclaim the skull.

But, why?

He was nearly obsessed with the thing. He recognized this, but couldn't seem to dislodge the strange mentality. What was it about this find that drove him so? Why had the skull become such an all-consuming passion?

The easy answer was that it belonged to science, that such an amazing find should not be marginalized or hidden away in some private collection. And initially this had been his thinking. From a logical standpoint, it still was his position. But now, after having held the skull, after cradling it, carrying it, hiding it, even using its amazing characteristic as a weapon...

Had he really done that? Had he been capable of such a thing? It all seemed a blur, vague images, distorted and out of sync with reality. But, it had happened. All of those people had died. His friends, colleagues.

Sarah had died.

Sarah Mitchell. He'd... well, not loved her. They were too early into the relationship for love. But, they were in a relationship: new, fragile, exciting. And he'd killed her. He'd tossed that vile stuff onto her and onto everyone else he'd known and respected. How could he have done that? What kind of a person was he to be capable of such a thing? He'd been threatened, yes. But, until that point, he'd been innocent of any crime. He could have let them take him to the authorities. It would have all worked itself out. How had things become so crazy?

Again, it came to the skull.

There was something about the skull. Something indefinable. Something special.

Andy blinked. His head was swimming again. It was hard to concentrate. Vague shadowy images flitted at the corners of his vision. Another stab to his stomach, this one nearly causing him to stumble.

Andy paused, steadying himself with a palm against the red brick building. He breathed deep. Slow, deliberate breaths. A young couple strolled past, staring at him. The girl muttered something to the boy, most likely urging him to help this man. The young man made to move in Andy's direction, but Andy waved him off. No need for further complications. No need for anyone else to be involved. The kid shrugged, said something to his girlfriend, and they moved on. Andy breathed deeply – again, again.

He needed to find that skull. It seemed irrational, and perhaps it was, but the need was nearly physical. And maybe not just nearly. Andy couldn't escape the fact that his symptoms had appeared soon after he'd had close contact with the piece. No, he hadn't boiled from the inside or slipped into coma like so many of the others, but wasn't he displaying mild symptoms of each? His listlessness, his trouble concentrating. Frequently, he'd found it difficult to remain conscious at all. And his fever. No, not near as severe as what he'd witnessed, but still it continued to climb, and if it wasn't abated, wouldn't this prove equally fatal? Maybe not quite so dramatic as what he'd seen at the camp, but fatal none-the-less.

This was all tied to the skull. He needed to find it, to keep it safe, have it examined, analyzed before it was too late. Perhaps there was a cure. Maybe, some way of synthesizing the mucus from within the thing. No. That could take months, even years. He didn't have that kind of time. Still, everything hinged on the skull. It might be crazy, but it was true.

Another stab of pain, and this time Andy fell to his knees. Blinking, panting, he rose on unsteady legs. There was no time for this. He had to get to the skull before those thugs located it. He just didn't have time to be deathly ill just now.

There was a gunshot in the distance. Back from the direction he'd come.

Andy took a step. And then another. Deep breaths. He was moving now. Quickly. He must move quickly. Building H was no more than thirty yards distant. Eduardo Matos' office was thankfully on the first floor, only midway down the nearest hallway. Andy was almost there.

From behind him: screams, panic.

The side door to Building H was unlocked. Andy stumbled in, glanced right to left, and then moved forward. Eduardo's door would be the seventh on the left.

No. This was a different hallway. Andy paused, again steadying himself against a wall. He needed to orient himself. He'd entered through the southern side of the building. That meant that he should move forward to the interesting hallway, turn right, and then Matos' door would be on the right. How many doors down, he couldn't remember, not coming from this direction. But, not many, three to five at most.

Andy took at tentative step, and then another. His vision swam before him. He shivered uncontrollably. The fever had spiked. He could only guess that it now exceeded one hundred five degrees. At the very least, he needed something to combat the fever – aspirin even. Tylenol. Anything.

A little further. Just a little further. He rounded the corner. Good. There were name plates on the office doors.

Another few steps. A stumble. Another stab to the gut, doubling him over. He nearly fell.

Yet, he continued. One office, two, three. There it was, just on the right. Dr. Eduardo Matos.

Andy fumbled with the handle, his sweaty palm and jittery fingers having difficulty with the grip. The door opened on the third attempt. He fell through, onto the tiled floor.

Chapter 33

Dana was fortunate that the gunshot wound wasn't worse. Even another inch to the left and she'd likely have been dead, her gray matter splattered across the front of the building. As it was, she'd gotten away with a mild headache and a bit of a burning sensation where the bullet had nicked her. Lucky girl, she supposed.

She and Jonathan had slipped silently through a service door at the backside of the building. There was a gravel alleyway containing rubbish bins and an old and dysfunctional-looking bicycle. Just beyond this was a continuation of the lawn leading to a narrow and winding road some 500 meters distant. As expected, squad cars littered the narrow roadway toward the front of the building where the altercation had occurred. Jonathan's rental truck was still there – and was at the center of much of the commotion – but Dana saw no sign of either Haas or Collins. Knowing that it would be a beacon to every law enforcement agent within fifty kilometers, they'd probably abandoned the vehicle.

Jonathan had donned a slightly oversized wool suit jacket he'd found in the office where they'd hidden. It was not of the quality he normally desired, nor was it a particularly fantastic fit, but it gave him a different appearance than that which any witnesses to the altercation might give. The real difficulty came with the pants. Jonathan still wore the coarse baggy black pants with the numerous large pockets that he'd worn in the Amazon. These in no way matched the suit jacket, but, at least for the time being, there was nothing he could do about it.

For her part, Dana had found a red and black striped soccer jersey in an adjacent office along with a black baseball-style cap. Despite the bullet wound, she'd slid the jersey over her muddied shirt, pulled her blood-matted hair back into a pony tail, and slipped the cap onto her head. At first glance, she looked like a college student, though she was more than a decade older than most, and her Asian/European features were a bit out of place. Still, she'd pass a cursory glance.

There was far too much commotion for the pair to walk directly toward Building H. This would have taken them through the heart of the investigation.

So they decided to stroll further east toward the rear roadway and to then follow this around northwest to their destination. With luck, Building H would not be crawling with police officers. Likely, it would not, as presumably no one had knowledge that this was the gunman's intended destination. She had to assume that Haas and Collins were bright enough to use some stealth as they approached the place, not making their destination obvious to onlookers.

Of course, in the event of a campus shooting, every building would be locked down. But gaining entry was not an issue for two skilled lock picks such as Dana and Jonathan. The concern was heightened security. Dana hoped that the majority of the security personnel had been dispatched to the area they'd just left behind. Standard lockdown procedure would dictate that students and faculty lock themselves in classrooms and offices, barricade doors, shut blinds, and stay clear of windows. They'd be told not to leave the building or to sound the fire alarm. With luck, all of this would work in Dana's favor. That was, as long as she could locate Andrew Lindell and get him clear of the place before either Haas and Collins or the police found her. She'd done nothing wrong, and would be happy to give the authorities a complete statement – after she'd located the lad and assured that he was no longer in harm's way.

For that, she needed the ability to move unrestricted by well-meaning authorities.

Dana was so preoccupied with the situation that at first she didn't realize that Jonathan was talking. "I'm sorry. Did you say something?" she asked almost absently.

Jonathan sighed and gave her his puppy dog look. Apparently, he was put out that she hadn't hung on his every word. Well, Jonathan could get stuffed. If it wasn't for him they wouldn't be in this mess.

"I said," he repeated. "You and I, we need to talk."

"Not much to talk about," quipped Dana. "I'm here for Lindell. You're here for the skull. At whatever point our searches deviate, we part ways. Simple, that."

"I'm talking about us, Dana. We need to talk about us."

Dana angled her head at him. Could he really be so daft as to bring this up now? "Jonathan, you kidnapped me."

Jonathan grabbed her by the bicep, stopping her in her tracks. "I understand that. But, after this is over I don't know when – or if – I'll see you again."

"I'm fine with that."

"Are you?"

Dana hesitated. Was she really fine with that? She was furious with Jonathan, true. She was married to Hunt – madly in love with Hunt – but was she truly willing to allow Jonathan to walk forever from her life?

"See! See," he said with some excitement. "You hesitated."

"It means nothing, Jonathan."

Jonathan shrugged. "Maybe so, maybe not. But, I'll take what little options are left me."

"Really, we don't have time for this now."

"I'll be quick and we can walk while we talk. Besides, it'll look more natural to onlookers if we're having a conversation." He paused, but only momentarily. "You still feel something. Maybe not much, but at least a twinge. I know you well enough. I can see it."

Dana didn't respond.

"All I'm asking is for you to acknowledge this and allow yourself the opportunity to explore it, to see if there's something real between us. I am your husband, after all."

"You are not!" shot Dana. "Jonathan, you're acting like a school boy. We had something, yes. But, much of it was false. And whatever truth we had, it is now a part of the past. And once and for all, we were never legally married. I was living under an assumed name, an alias created by MI6. None of my documentation was authentic – including our marriage certificate. Now, will you please let it rest?"

Dana quickened her pace, outdistancing Jonathan, who had the common sense to trail behind. This was good. She didn't want him to see the lone tear trickling down her left cheek and onto the jersey.

*****

Building H was four stories tall, sandstone in color, and looked to have been constructed sometime in the mid twentieth century. It was both inviting and austere, warm yet classic. Everything about it spoke of higher learning. A more university-like structure would be difficult to imagine. They made the rear entrance in less than five minutes. As expected, the door was now locked. Quickly, Dana pulled her pick kit from her pocket, and opened the door. The hallway was empty. No sign of life. Though, Dana suspected that there were frightened students and faculty huddled in classrooms throughout the building. She also guessed that both Lindell and the two grunts were not far distant.

"Did Lindell reveal anything concerning the skull's whereabouts?" whispered Dana. "Likely he's made a beeline to the thing."

"He said he'd need to pass a retina scan in order to retrieve it."

Dana narrowed her gaze. Lindell had told her the same rot. "Jonathan, I do believe you've become gullible in your old age."

"Old age! Now, now, now. I'm simply preoccupied by matters of the heart, dearest. I am a sentimentalist at the core."

"Remember who you're speaking with," said Dana. "We both know you're a scoundrel at the core. Did Lindell mention a department, possibly a contact person?"

Jonathan shrugged. "No. Nothing. The plan was that he'd direct us once we'd arrived."

"Brilliant plan, that," muttered Dana. "I suppose we'll conduct a systematic search of the building. They will be on lockdown, though. To divert suspicion we'll need a cover story."

"Well, that should be simple enough. We're colleagues of Dr. Lindell's from the dig site. We'd arranged to meet him here. Would you please direct us? Thank you."

Dana nodded. Simple, plausible, and effective. Jonathan did excel at the art of scam.

But, there would be no need for subtlety or deception. For it was then that they heard the first screams.

Chapter 34

At the first sound of gunfire, Hunt had bolted from the laboratory where he and Cook had had their discussion, and run toward the nearest window facing the sound. He was done with Cook. The spineless weasel could fend for himself.

Hunt's view of the scene was partially blocked by two trees and obstructed further by an adjacent building. He could hear the shouts and screams of frightened students, see frenetic movement as these same students fled in every direction, but he could discern no details. As well, there was commotion from down the hall where he'd earlier seen a lecture in progress. Either the sound of the shot had been heard in the classroom, or someone had already notified these students of the happening. In an age of constant text messaging, this was likely the case. He just hoped that the professor had the wherewithal to quell the panic and keep the students in the relative safety of the lecture hall.

Hunt's first impulse was to rush to the scene of the shots, to insert himself into the situation, but he forced himself to hang tight. Shots fired on a college campus. There could be dozens of students endangered, campus security would be swarming, the culprit or culprits fleeing discovery. Everything would be in flux for at least the next minute or two. By the time Hunt could make his way to the scene, the perpetrator might be in hiding and Hunt – an outsider on campus, and a foreigner to boot - might appear as a prime suspect. He couldn't afford to waste time answering questions just now. He needed to determine what was happening and if Dana and/or Andy were involved.

No, it was better to seek a clearer vantage, to get a view of the situation, and then make an informed decision. His course of action determined, Hunt bound up a nearby flight of stairs, not stopping till he came to the uppermost floor. Here, he would view the scene from above. While in the stairwell, Hunt thought he'd heard a second shot, but he couldn't be certain. The pounding of his own footfall echoed about him, and the walls were thick plaster, nearly soundproof.

Gazing through an upper window, Hunt now had a clear view and saw that a blue SUV was at the center of the commotion. He wondered if this vehicle had carried Dana and her captors. There was a man on the ground, just getting to his feet beside the SUV, large, blond, brutish. It seemed he might fit the body type of one of Dana's abductors. A woman was running off to Hunt's left toward the building closest the vehicle; a man with a body slung over his shoulders was just entering the building. There had been a woman driver that night. This was adding up. But where was Dana? And what of Andy Lindell? Hunt forced himself to remain calm. The body. He could only pray that the body was not Dana or Andy.

He steadied his breath. Combat mode. No emotional distractions. Observe. Analyze. Plan. Execute. If Hunt was to aid those he cared about, he would need to remain focused and on tack.

Students were running in every direction and it looked as if one had been shot. One unidentified body and one injured student. That would account for both gunshot bursts. The student was obviously an innocent bystander, the other, yet to be determined.

The woman made the door of the three story red brick building, hesitated briefly, flattening herself against the face of the structure, and then cautiously pulling the door back to peek inside. There was a burst of automatic weapon fire from within. She backed away, retreating toward the vehicle as the wooden door splintered beside her.

Sirens could already be heard in the distance.

The large blond haired man was now reaching into the truck, under the front seat, pulling out a weapon, and then waving the gun about. Hunt couldn't quite make out the weapon, an AK perhaps? The former gun burst had sounded like a Sig Sauer. At the sight of the weapon in this man's hand, what few students remained scattered and dove behind trees and benches. When, less than a minute later, the woman rejoined the man, they broke into a steady jog, making their way toward Building H. Everything had happened so quickly that authorities were yet to make it to the scene. These two lunatics were unobstructed.

Still gazing through the window, Hunt tried to put the pieces together. He only had moments before the duo entered this building. Hunt was unarmed, but he was resourceful. When Dana had been captured, he'd seen three individuals: the two males that had taken her and the female driver. He knew from footprints in the jungle that there was another male in the back of the truck. Assuming this was the same party, and, also assuming that there were indeed only three perpetrators, the scene he had just witnessed made no sense. For if this was the same team, likely the blond man had fired at one of his compatriots, the one entering the building with the body. Was this, in fact, the other abductor, or was that man elsewhere, injured or dead? If so, who was the man at the door? Not Andy Lindell. In no way did Hunt believe Andy capable of slinging a body over his shoulders.

Too many questions. The two perpetrators were nearly to the building. Hunt's only logical option was to intercept them, disarm and incapacitate them, and then interrogate them.

Still calculating, Hunt moved to the stairwell, prepared to join the fray.

*****

Once again, on the ground floor, Hunt proceeded cautiously. Certainly, the two perpetrators were in the building by now, likely seeking the skull. Slipping quietly around the first corner, Hunt held close to the wall, attempting to remain unseen, though, in truth, there was nothing to obscure a view. If someone turned his way, he would be almost immediately obvious.

In under a minute, he came across an open door leading into an office. Peeking in, he saw a middle aged man, short, balding, likely a professor, struggling to his feet as he gasped for air. Glancing in both directions, Hunt entered the office, first marching past the man and opening a closet door to confirm that they were indeed alone in the small room. "English?" asked Hunt as he then helped the man to a chair.

The man nodded, croaking out a weak, "Yes. English."

"What happened to you?" asked Hunt as he returned to the doorway, scanning the corridor for intruders.

The man swallowed. "Attacked." And then, after a pause. "Who are you?" The man's English was accented but precise, his voice still raspy from his ordeal.

Hunt glanced back at the man. "I'm an American. Not an enemy, if that's what you're asking. Who attacked you?"

The little man eyed Hunt suspiciously. "An American attacked me. A colleague."

Hunt's heart leapt. "An American colleague – Andy Lindell?"

The man's face registered shock. Obviously, Hunt had been correct.

"I'm here in search of Andy," said Hunt. "He's in a lot of trouble. His life might be in danger. I need your help. Quickly, what happened? Where did he go?"

The man hesitated, seemingly unsure of how to respond.

"Please, sir. There are armed gunmen on campus. At least two people have already been shot. They're after a fossil, a skull. The same one Andy Lindell came for. If I don't act now, there might be a lot more bloodshed." Hunt wasn't certain that the gunmen were after the skull, but it was a reasonable assumption. He just didn't have time for subtleties and conjecture at this point.

The man nodded, seemingly deciding to trust Hunt. "Dr. Lindell came to my office. He is ill, feverish, delirious even."

"Go on," prompted Hunt. He really couldn't waste much time.

"Dr. Lindell stumbled into my office, mumbling about the skull. He had shipped it to me and it was here in a box on the floor. When he learned of its close proximity, Dr. Lindell became agitated. He was feverish. I do not believe he was in his right mind."

"So, he took the skull. Where did he go?"

"I tried to stop him. He was so ill. I wanted to call a physician."

"I'm sorry, sir. I need to know, where is Dr, Lindell now?"

"When I tried to call a physician, he grabbed me, started to strangle me. So, what else could I do? I gave him the skull. He has it. I don't know where he went. He is not in his right mind."

Once again, Hunt scanned the corridor from the doorway. None of this sounded like Andy, this irrational behavior, the violence. "Did he turn right or left out of this room?" asked Hunt.

"Left, but sir. You must know."

"Yes?"

"The skull. There is a substance within. Something infectious."

Hunt nodded and moved through the door and to the left.

It was then that he heard the screams.

Chapter 35

Hunt raced toward the sound of the escalating screams. Rounding a corner, he nearly collided with two figures. "Dana!" he gasped in relieved shock. And then, "Thorpe! Why are you with Thorpe?" In no known universe would he be glad to see this man with his wife.

"I'm not with him," she said.

"Well, technically you are," quipped Thorpe.

"He's like a bleeding puppy dog," said Dana a bit nervously. "Traipsing about at my heels. A nuisance, really."

Hunt didn't like Dana's agitation. She seemed nervous at the sight of him. He wanted to get to the bottom of this, but there was so little time. Still, Dana and Thorpe together. His gut felt about as hollow as an abandoned railway tunnel. Why was she with him? What was he even doing on this continent, much less here on this campus?

And then it hit him. Of course. It all made sense.

"You're here for the skull," he said.

"Well, yes. I…"

"And you kidnapped Dana."

"Technically, yes, but again…"

Thorpe never finished the sentence. Hunt's fist was in the way. The thief hit the ground hard and lay there stunned as the two Huntingtons made their way up the corridor. Hunt didn't much care for the look of concern on Dana's face as she glanced back at the dazed Thorpe.

"Andy Lindell's here. He has the skull," said Hunt, forcing himself to remain focused on the task at hand.

Dana nodded. "He arrived with us. Jonathan and his crew held him captive." After a moment, she added, "He's not well and needs immediate medical attention."

"You said Thorpe's crew? You mean the man and woman? The ones who opened fire?"

"Yes."

"I didn't think open aggression was Thorpe's style."

"It's not. Those two were forced upon him by a client. They're now working independent of Jonathan. Be wary. The bloke's already shot me once."

Hunt stopped, turning to face Dana who did likewise. "Shot?"

"Nothing serious. A graze. I'm fine."

Hunt pictured the scene in his mind: the man struggling to slip through a doorway while lugging a body over his shoulders. "That was you – and Thorpe. You were shot. He carried you into that other building for safety."

Dana cocked her head. "You saw that, did you?"

"From a window in this building. I didn't see you get shot, only him carrying you through the door."

There was another eruption of screams. Hunt and Dana raced forward.

Moments later, Dana pointed up and to the right. "Hunt, ahead, leaning against the wall."

Hunt saw. There was a man down. As they approached it became clear that it was no gunshot wound that had felled him. The poor guy's skin was bubbling and popping. Clear liquid oozed from blistering sores, and blood crept from cracked skin. He could actually hear the fluids sizzle. "My God, it's Cook," gasped Hunt as he drew near.

Hunt knelt to beside him. "Cook, can you hear me? What happened?" How could this be? He'd left the man only ten minutes before.

Cook lulled his festering face toward Hunt, but said nothing.

"Cook, talk to me."

"Lindell. Skull," gasped the dying man. It seemed a supreme effort which he followed with a hollow gurgle. Despite what Cook had done, Hunt felt compassion for the man. No one should die like this. It was horrible at so many levels. Hunt could read the sheer misery in the blood-filled eyes, read the pain on the agonized face. What could he do for this man? How could he offer some small hint of comfort?

Dana was at Hunt's side. "What's happened to him?"

"From what he described to me just a few minutes ago, it looks like he's encountered the viral agent in the skull. I just can't believe it could work this fast."

It seemed to Hunt that Dana may have shuddered. "Hunt, not so near; don't touch him. If this thing's viral, he could be highly contagious."

Hunt scrutinized Cook for several moments. "Viral seems to be the going theory, but looking at him, I'm wondering if radiation could be a factor."

"I wouldn't rule it out," allowed Dana. "But, how would radiation at that level be found in a fossil?"

"Right now I'm just asking questions, hon. We'll have to look to some egg-heads for the answers."

At that moment, Cook arched his back, a strange liquid hiss erupting from somewhere deep within his form. Nearly all of his exposed skin bubbled to a breaking point and popped in a flurry of ooze. Ten seconds later, he slumped dead on the floor.

"We really should vacate the building," said Thorpe, still rubbing his newly-bruised jaw as he stepped to behind Hunt. "If that is a contagion, this could become a quarantine zone."

Hunt stared at Cook's disfigured form, still wrestling with the reality of this brutal death. "Do what you want, Thorpe. Andy's in here. He's in trouble. I find him first."

"Jonathan may be right," said Dana. "This could be highly contagious."

Hunt stood abruptly, facing Dana. "Then run off with your boyfriend and get out of the way. Me, I've come all this way for Andy. I'm not leaving without him."

Dana faced him squarely. "Don't be a jealous oaf. Jonathan has nothing to do with this."

Hunt was about to respond with something petty and damaging, but was saved from his own mouth by a sudden burst of gunfire followed by hysterical screams, both from further up the way. There simply was no time for personal issues. Without a word, he turned and raced toward the sound of the commotion.

*****

The large rectangular meeting room was being used for some sort of convention or conference. For the most part, these were not students, but adults, most in their forties or fifties. There were lengthy tables along the long walls featuring continental breakfast makings: coffee, tea, croissants, fruits. The guests – perhaps three dozen in total – were in frightened clusters, mostly silent now. Clearly, they'd been instructed to stay put and remain quiet. One gray-haired man was on the floor, attended by two women. There was no blood. It seemed he might have fainted, or perhaps suffered a heart attack. Several people cried; there was spilled drink and discarded food on the carpeted floor. One table had been knocked over in the commotion. The two thugs were at the opposite side of the room, the large blond man holding an AK47. There were bullet holes in the ceiling where he'd fired warning shots.

And then there was Andy Lindell.

No one went near to him. Not even the thugs.

His face was crimson with fever, his skin beginning to bubble and blister as had Cook's. Sweat poured over his face and his clothing was drenched with perspiration. His eyes were wide, glassy, and a rich pink, nearly red. He twitched and shuddered, seeming to just barely maintain control of his own bodily functions.

And cradled in his arms: the skull. It almost seemed the way one might hold an infant.

To Hunt, it looked like any other skull, darker to be sure, it was clearly a fossil, but size and configuration seemed normal to his layman's eye. Hunt was always surprised at how small the human skull appeared. It was amazing how much mass was added by musculature, skin, and even hair. Andy held this one upside-down, and so it acted like a cup, keeping the thick yellow/green sub-stance which filled the thing from spilling over as he paced back and forth like a caged tiger, muttering to himself, and drooling as he hugged his prize. Even Thorpe's thugs seemed frightened at the sight.

"He looks horribly infected," said Dana as she stepped to beside Hunt. "I don't know if there's anything that can be done."

They were pressed against the wall, just outside of the meeting room, gazing through the tall vertical window adjacent the wooden door. "That's Andy, Dana."

"I know who it is."

"I've got to at least try."

"Hunt, his skin is nearly melting from his frame. You'll be infected."

In truth, Hunt felt the situation nearly as hopeless as did Dana. Even if he got Andy safely from the room, the medical issues seemed insurmountable. Hunt had tracked the young man halfway across the country. He'd done all that he could do. Surely Lucky Lindell would understand that this was something beyond Hunt's ability to control. And what of personal risk? He'd seen Cook. Seen what that infection, or virus, whatever it was, could do in just a few minutes. It was foolhardy to purposely have any physical contact with Andy. Any idiot could see that. Face grim, he turned, staring at Dana for only a moment. "I promised Lucky I'd bring his boy back. That's what I've got to do."

There were sounds from further down the corridor: hushed voices, running footsteps, most likely a SWAT team. "There's no more time for arguing," said Hunt as he pushed open the door and walked into the conference area before Dana could stop him.

*****

Thorpe did not remain with the Huntingtons, but, after taking a quick peek through the doorway window to assess the situation, continued past them. Haas and Collins were just within a door on the opposite side of the large room. He was certain that if he followed the corridor around, turning right twice, he'd wind up outside of this door.

And then what?

He'd obviously alienated himself from his former companions. Haas might very well shoot him on sight. Thanks to Dana, he was unarmed. True, the Sig Sauer would have been conspicuous, and might have caused them unwelcome attention, but it would be handy about now.

Thorpe heard the sounds of racing footfall in the distance. Some sort of strike force, he was certain. He couldn't allow himself to be captured by these. While Marc and Dana Huntington were in the country legally, and their mission even sanctioned – however unofficially – by a high-ranking Pentagon official, Thorpe was here with bogus credentials. The false passport and visa looked quite passable, and would likely pass routine inspection, but if it was suspected that he was connected to Haas and Collins, a closer look would be his undoing. The legend constructed for this enterprise had not been designed to sustain intense scrutiny.

Haas had really fouled this up. The entire operation could have been conducted without ever once drawing a weapon. This was why the client had hired Thorpe in the first place, or so he was told. Thorpe was discrete and professional. In most cases he could be in and out of a building, having acquired the desired piece, without anyone taking notice till the item was found missing the following morning. Gunfire and grandstanding drew unwanted attention. If only Haas had stayed with the plan, if only he'd simply stolen Dana's backpack instead of kidnapping her, they wouldn't be in this position.

Thorpe had a decision to make. Fleeing the building would not be an option at this point. Surely by now, the place was surrounded by police officers, and he would be detained for questioning. He could, he supposed, slip into the room and simply join the crowd of hostages. It would be simple to feign membership in the group. With luck, he'd draw no attention. He could simply let everything play out to its conclusion and then walk away as an innocent bystander. Likely, he'd face much less specific questioning as a hostage than as a suspicious stranger sneaking from the building in the middle of a crisis.

But, what of the skull?

His mission was to claim the prized fossil. Despite Haas' mismanagement of the situation, that directive had not changed. And truly, Thorpe desired to please this client. He was being paid quite handsomely to retrieve this old bone, and future, equally lucrative, opportunities hinged on this performance. Whatever happened, he must put himself in a position to acquire that relic.

It was then that Marc Huntington charged into the room with about as much finesse as a misfired nuclear missile. A perfect distraction. Quickly, Thorpe cracked the door, slipping in, and joining the terrified crowd.

Tina Collins made eye contact. Haas did not. He'd aimed his weapon at Hunt.

Chapter 36

The blond male turned toward Hunt, aiming his AK47 toward him. But he didn't fire – not yet. He was probably still determining if Hunt was a threat. A smart man would weigh his options before acting. Opening fire in a room full of hostages would bring things to an entirely different level.

Feigning indifference, Hunt ignored the man, turning instead to Andy. Those slime balls could take the skull. He didn't care. All he wanted was to get Andy safely out of this room and to a hospital before it was too late. He couldn't believe what had happened to the kid. Physically, Andy wasn't quite as bad as Cook, but if this thing accelerated as fast as Hunt thought it did, he could be dead within another ten minutes. What could Hunt do? He wasn't a doctor. And even if he was, there might not be anything that could be done. There was no time to analyze the contagion or experiment with antidotes.

"Hunt, be careful. Please."

It was Dana. She'd followed him in through the door. Not surprising, he supposed, she wasn't prone to letting him walk into danger alone.

"Dana," he said, digging into his pocket and withdrawing her cell phone which he'd kept since finding it in the clearing. "Call a hospital. Get an ambulance for Andy." He handed the phone to her.

"You!" barked the blond brute. "Huntington! Put that phone on the floor." He was Australian, by the accent. Interesting.

"She's calling an ambulance for Andy Lindell!" hollered Hunt. "I don't care about you or the skull. I just want to help him."

Not waiting for a reply, Hunt stepped toward Andy. The thug might very well shoot, but Hunt didn't think so. The man was clearly volatile, but Hunt doubted he was stupid. He had to know that a SWAT team was even now congregating beyond the doorway. The man's best shot at getting out of here alive was to refrain from opening fire on his hostages. Move slowly. Don't give the authorities a reason to engage. Bide some time.

"Drop the phone!" hollered the brute as he trained his gun on Dana. A frightened mummer skittered through the crowd. One woman offered a little shriek followed by jabbering Portuguese.

"Better do as he says," advised Hunt. "I don't think he's dumb enough to open fire with a SWAT team thirty seconds away, but no need to provoke him." Hunt said this as much for the Aussie to hear as to Dana. The power of suggestion could be a powerful thing.

Dana complied, first holding the phone up for the brute to see and then placing it on the ground.

Turning again to Andy, Hunt said, "Hey, kid. Remember me?"

Andy turned, his lips drooping on the left side, some sort of substance dribbling from his mouth and onto his shirt. It seemed he was trying to focus, but his eyes were red with blood, his pupils wide and black.

"It's me," said Hunt. "Marc Huntington."

"Uncle Marc?"

Hunt attempted a weak smile. "Yeah. Uncle Marc." The title reminded him of how close he and Lucky had been. Bittersweet memories.

Hunt squinted at a sharp shot of pain to his temples. He really didn't need this now. Breathe. Steady. Just breathe. Separate from the migraine. He refocused his eyes on Andy. The guy looked like something out of a drive-in horror flick. What could cause such radical symptoms?

There was the sound of a bullhorn from the corridor, short bursts of Portuguese, most likely a hostage negotiator initiating contact with the Australian. Hunt had a feeling the Aussie didn't speak Portuguese and hoped the negotiator knew English. This thing could go either way and Hunt hoped the guy on the other end of the bullhorn had his act together.

"Get the skull from him," shouted the Aussie, obviously speaking to Hunt and ignoring the bullhorn. "Give me the skull and I'll let you and your lady live."

Hunt ignored him. "Andy, you're ill. I've got to get you to a doctor."

Andy shook his head like a two year-old refusing to give up a stolen cookie. "Uncle Marc, they don't understand."

Another bark from the bullhorn. The sound of armed men at each of the four doorways. This thing was escalating.

"Huntington! The skull!" ordered the Australian.

"They don't understand the importance," stammered Andy. "The importance of the... importance."

Hunt was getting closer to him now, within ten feet. But he needed to move carefully. He couldn't risk spooking Andy just now.

"Hunt, not too close," warned Dana. "Don't come in contact with that bleeding rot."

He nodded. "I've got it under control, hon."

Another command from the bullhorn, this one in accented English. "You are surrounded. Relinquish your weapons!"

"Uncle Marc, they want to take it away from me. They don't understand." Andy was completely unhinged.

There was a flurry of commotion behind and to the right. Hunt whirled to see the Australian grab a young woman from the crowd and poke the barrel of the AK47 straight up under her chin. If Hunt had been armed, he'd have been able to take the man's head off before he ever had a chance to touch the trigger. But, Hunt wasn't armed.

*****

"Do not come in here!" hollered Haas. "I will kill this woman if you try to gain entrance!"

"Understood," said the distorted bullhorn voice. "I just wish to talk with you."

Haas was being smart, remaining in constant motion, crouching behind his hostage, and crossing back and forth behind other innocents. It would be very difficult for a sniper to get a clear shot off. "Well, I don't want to talk with you," shouted Haas. "Now, move away from the windows. I can see movement out there. If you don't withdraw, I will kill this hostage and then take another. Do you understand?"

There was a short pause, and then, "If you kill a hostage we will open fire on you."

"Listen mate, I pull the trigger in three seconds. One. Two…"

The bullhorn crackled almost instantly. "Alright. We are moving away from the windows. Hold your fire."

Haas scanned the crowd, looked toward the four doors to the room, each with a vertical window to the left of the door frame. "You, you, you, and you," he said, indicating four hostages, three women and a man, each rather hefty in form. "I want each of you to stand in front of one of the windows." At first the four stood staring dumbly at him. "Move!" barked Haas, and the terrified hostages did as instructed. At first, they nearly stumbled over one another as they determined which window would belong to each. Bloody brilliant, thought Dana. The hostages acted both as visual blocks as well as shields. The strike force would have difficulty seeing past these people who obscured the windows, and couldn't dare shoot because hostages were squarely between them and their target. Clever.

Dana understood that Haas was reactionary, definitely brutal. But during her captivity, he'd seemed to have a plan. The man was calculating, intelligent. Now, this whole situation had spiraled out of control and likely innocent people would die before it all played out.

She supposed at some level it was her fault. If she hadn't escaped, Haas never would have opened fire on campus, a SWAT team wouldn't be at the doorways, weapons drawn, and these people wouldn't be endangered.

Bollocks!

She needed to rectify this situation.

"Haas!" she shouted, stepping forward, arms held high. "I'd make a better hostage. Former British Secret Service. A whole load of political ramifications should they allow me to get capped. Let the woman go. I won't fight you."

Haas grinned. He probably relished the thought of reclaiming the escapee that had caused him such grief. "Nothing porky," he warned.

"I won't pull anything."

*****

Thorpe inched forward in the crowd, attempting to gain a closer proximity to the unfolding scene without drawing attention. What was Dana thinking? What type of foolhardy heroic rubbish was this? Haas was behaving irrationally; he had been ever since they'd arrived on campus. Was she trying to get herself killed?

"Dana!" cried Huntington from his spot some twenty meters distant. "Stop!"

"I'll be fine, dear. No worries."

As Dana drew near to Haas, he tossed the other woman aside, causing her to stumble onto the carpeted floor with a high-pitched whimper. Immediately, he extended his weapon, pressing the end of the barrel to Dana's forehead. "You've caused me a load of trouble, missy."

For once, Dana had no response. Thorpe assumed it was because she knew just how volatile Haas truly could be.

The bullhorn barked again from somewhere in the hallway. Andrew Lindell was babbling something crazy about the blooming skull. And, Marc Huntington seemed nearly paralyzed as he tried to determine how to aid Dana, while not abandoning Lindell. Thorpe actually felt for the guy. He was experiencing similar feelings himself.

Thorpe was now about as close to Haas as he could manage without being noticed. Situated somewhere between Haas and Marc Huntington, he kept an eye on both parties. He glanced to Collins. The woman was separated from her partner by about ten meters. Her expression was stony, unreadable. She was very aware of Thorpe's position and even made occasional eye contact. As yet, it didn't appear she'd informed Haas of Thorpe's presence. Perhaps, she didn't consider him a factor yet. Certainly, she underestimated him. What Thorpe needed now was a distraction. He considered removing a shoe and hurling it at Haas, but decided against it. That might cause him to pull the trigger.

"On your knees," said Haas.

Dana complied.

"Huntington!" he hollered. "Bring me that skull, or the little lady dies."

*****

Hunt stared at the scene through migraine lightning bolts. Dana on her knees, the Aussie's gun to her head. He really had no choice in the matter. "Andy," he said. "I need you to do something for me."

Andy shook his head, not in refusal, but as if trying to clear his mind.

"Andy, I need you to walk over to that table and set the skull down." Hunt pointed to where he wanted Andy to place the skull.

"No, Uncle Marc," he nearly stuttered. "No, no, no. I know what you're doing. You want to take her away from me."

He'd lost all sense of reality. How was Hunt supposed to reason with him? "Andy, that skull is killing you. I don't know if it's a virus or radiation or what, but you've got to get away from that thing."

"Liar!"

"No. Not lying," said Hunt as he attempted a sincere grin. "Yes, I need to borrow the skull so that Dana doesn't get shot. But, what I said is true. That thing is killing you. Try to think, Andy. Look at your arms. They're all blistered. Your face is the same way. Probably your whole body."

Andy's face became a mask of rage. He lifted the skull above his head, screeching the high pitched howl of the insane as he charged forward.

*****

Haas looked away, momentarily distracted by Andrew's outburst. Dana didn't hesitate. In one swift move, she snatched the gun barrel from the Aussie's grip, pressing it onto the floor as she rolled into his shins, sending him tumbling to the carpet. Before Haas could right himself, Tina Collins stepped forward. Pulling a Beretta px4 handgun from a side pocket, she calmly fired two rounds into the back of his head.

*****

The bullhorn barked at the sound of gunfire, but it would be nearly a minute before the decision to storm the room would be made. And when they did, Tina

Collins slowly placed the gun on the floor and then raised her hands in cooperation. Of course, by then, the tragedy had already occurred.

*****

Thorpe was positioned between Huntington and Haas, but nearer Huntington. His first instinct was to aid Dana, but even before he could move, Collins stepped forward, discharging her handgun at Haas. What in bleeding hell! Lindell screeched again, nearly ear-splitting. Thorpe turned at the sound. The lunatic was racing into the crowd with that infectious muck.

*****

At first, Hunt thought Andy was charging him, but he veered right toward the hostages. Hunt couldn't let him splash that corrosive slime onto anyone. He remembered the horribly charred and disfigured bodies at the dig site and couldn't allow a repeat of the scene.

There was a long rectangular table perhaps five feet distant loaded with croissants, beverages, and finger foods. It bore a plastic tablecloth. Hunt tore the red plastic sheet from the table with one swift jerk, sending food and beverages tumbling to the floor.

"Huntington, here!" It was Thorpe's voice. Hunt didn't have time for him now, and turned to race toward Andy, who was now pacing back and forth in front of the cowering hostages, the muck sloshing onto the floor.

"Not now, Thorpe!"

Without responding, Thorpe grabbed the trailing end of the plastic and moved forward with Hunt. "It'll work better if we do it together," said the Brit as they came at Andy from behind just as he raised the skull to toss the goop onto the crowd.

Hunt hit him from the right, Thorpe, the left, each wrapping him — and most importantly, the skull — in the plastic as they wrestled him to the floor.

Andy shuddered and struggled, thrashing about, screaming an agonized squeal. Still the two men held firm. That substance was simply too dangerous to risk it being flung about.

"Andy! Stop!" ordered Hunt. "Stop it, Andy. You need to calm down. You need to stop."

But, still he fought, and screamed, and cursed. And suddenly, less than a minute into the battle, his body gave a sudden violent jerk and then fell limp.

It was over.

Hunt had failed Andy, failed Lucky. "I'm sorry, Andy," he finally managed through a retching sob. "I'm so very sorry."

EPILOGUE

Dana opened the door and strolled into Hunt's hospital room. Hunt wanted to be glad to see her, and at some level he was, but he was still too numb to allow any true happiness to seep in. "No mask and gown," he observed.

"I've just spoken with the doctor. You've checked out. No sign of contamination."

"Yea-rah for me. What about Thorpe?"

Dana hesitated for a moment. "He was never admitted."

Now, why would that be? "He helped me to wrestle Andy to the floor. He had the same risk of exposure."

"Tina Collins flashed CIA credentials. She claimed Thorpe as an associate and the two disappeared before the authorities had much of a chance to bring matters under control. It was a rather chaotic scene."

"She wasn't CIA," offered Hunt.

Dana shrugged. "I find it doubtful, but not beyond reason. She'd had plenty of opportunity to stop Haas before then, but sometimes operatives will allow events to unfold, even lethal events, for the sake of keeping a cover intact. Truthfully, dear, I don't know."

"And the skull?"

"Gone."

"Thorpe?"

"Most likely. Jonathan almost always gets what he desires."

Hunt eyed Dana askance. "I'm sure he does."

"Though the skull itself is gone," said Dana, ignoring the implication. "There was a rather significant amount of that horrid goop left behind. It will be analyzed along with Dr. Milton's photographs of the skull's interior. Add to that Eldon Troxel's translation, someone should be able to determine the makeup of the substance."

Hunt nodded and stared ahead, avoiding eye contact. "I killed him, Dana. I killed Lucky's boy."

Dana placed a hand on Hunt's shoulder. He didn't desire human contact just then, but didn't try to shrug her off. "No, Hunt. Andrew was already dead. And quite mad. No matter what you would have done, he still would have died within a matter of minutes. He was trying to toss that mucus onto the crowd when you and Jonathan tackled him with that plastic sheet. Quick thinking, that."

"The entire skull full of that puss spilled onto Andy in the process."

Dana lowered her face to within a foot of Hunt's, staring at him eye-to-eye. "He was already badly infected. His skin was bubbling, almost melting from his bones. There was nothing you could have done."

She didn't get it. This was just like Iraq. Someone he was responsible for didn't come out alive.

Dana stood upright and slid her smart phone from her pocket, pressing several buttons before handing it to Hunt.

"What's this?" he asked.

"Information sent to me by Jonathan."

"And I want to read this why?"

"Because it concerns you. Apparently, he's been doing a bit of research on you. Scrutinizing the competition and all that. I think you'll find that bit rather interesting."

Hunt scanned the screen, skeptical at first, and then intrigued. Where had Thorpe found this information? It had to be classified. And was it accurate? Could this really be true? "That little girl?" he asked at last. "The one they say I shot."

"She wasn't a hostage, Hunt. She only pretended to be. She was the one who detonated the explosive – apparently, just as you shot her. You had no choice."

"She was just a little girl."

"She was a suicide bomber. If you hadn't stopped her when you did, if she'd been allowed to detonate in a more public place, dozens more may have died."

Hunt stared at the screen, his brow furrowed. "Why would Thorpe send information that could absolve me?"

Dana offered a sly grin. "All things considered – and I doubt he'd acknowledge this – I think you rather impressed the man. You two have more similarities than either of you will ever admit."

Hunt shook his head. This didn't add up. If only he had his memory to guide him through the truth and the lies, if he had some means of sifting through the conflicting accounts. "If this report is true, then why the disciplinary action? Why boot me from Delta? Why the claims that I was drunk, that I acted against orders?"

Dana shook her head. "I've read through all that Jonathan sent. There are holes in the official account. It seems you had had a couple of drinks that night. You'd been on alert, and then told to stand down on two separate occasions. From what I can ascertain, the mission was officially cancelled, and then new intel came through. Your unit was called back into duty."

"So, I might have been drunk."

"This information indicates a couple of beers. I doubt that constitutes drunk. The official report makes it sound like you'd been on an all night bender. I've always found that unlikely."

"Then, why the discrepancy? Why the testimony against me?"

"Well, dear, I think that's just what we need to find out."

*****

Tina Collins stood beside the client as they gazed across the large wood-paneled room. There were seven rows of stretchers, each baring a comatose body connected to heart monitors, I.V.'s, and other equipment. The client smiled broadly as he kissed Collins gently on the cheek and thanked her for her efforts. It had been a shame about Haas, but the man had overstretched his authority and become reckless. He'd accomplished his mission, finding these incredible human specimens and arraigning for them to be airlifted out of the country. If only he'd then followed the client's instructions and allowed Thorpe to take the lead on the skull, things would have unfolded much differently.

But, he'd become bullheaded, jealous, he didn't like the idea of the client testing new talent. As such, he endangered their mission, threatened exposure to the client at this most delicate time. The behavior could not be tolerated. Fortunately, Collins had been there to take control of the situation. The client was happy. He had his bodies. He had his skull. And with it, an amazing new weapon. Everything could move forward as planned.

THE END

VISIT

SPEAKING VOLUMES ON-LINE

National Best-Selling

&

Award Winning Authors

www.speakingvolumes.us